BRACKEN POINT

Bracken Point

David Pickup

RABY

First published in 2002
by Raby Books
The Coach House
Eggleston Hall
Eggleston
Barnard Castle
County Durham
DL12 0AG

ISBN 1-84410-000-6

Printed and bound by Bookcraft Ltd

To my wife Patricia,
for her patience and encouragement

I am grateful to Sasha Hermons for her assistance in typing the successive manuscripts; and to David Andrews for his critical guidance and assiduous proof-reading.

CHAPTER ONE

Looking south the house commanded a view of the landward intrusion of Roaringwater Bay, while northwards he could faintly discern intimations of the town despite its half-reluctant effort to ignore its relationship with the tides. Shaggy grass, laced with brambles and wild fuchsia, ran from the building's rear down to an encounter with a fringe of rocks at the water's edge. To its front an overgrown drive curved some twenty yards to the road where, reinforced by a dense thorn hedge, an ugly barrier of metal rods, chained heavily together, discouraged exploration.

Nevertheless he had hauled himself over the crude palisade and, driven by curiosity, moved tentatively towards the house. Evidence of its abandonment lay all about him. Sure, he told himself, the west of Ireland was characterised by ruined cottages rotting away mournfully in the shadow of Euro-funded replacements, breeze-block supplanting stone, the remnants being allowed to adopt their own pace at which to subside back into the bony landscape. But this particular dwelling, he judged, had been built within the last twenty years, its angle of roof, its russet brickwork, its generous (albeit rust-assaulted) windows announcing a confidence in the efficacy of central heating not shared by its vernacular predecessors confronting Atlantic gales.

In the last half-hour, following the country road out of Ballydehob, he had passed several houses of similar vintage, each overlooking the estuary, vying with their neighbours in the degree of bright come-hitherness that might be achieved by pastel exteriors and manicured presentability of lawns and shrubbery. Moreover, although his house – for he had already begun to experience a tingle of appropriation – could scarcely be described as remote, being little more than a mile from the town, it enjoyed the required measure of seclusion afforded by a gentle folding of the headland which closed off any view from proximate properties. Why, then, its signal neglect?

His puzzlement had intensified as he reached the east-facing rear of the house where he found further signs of desertion: a small dinghy half-submerged by shrouding undergrowth and – more intriguingly – a three-year-old Dodge van, begrimed, oxidising, festooned by weeds, its tyres subsiding into the gravel. He moved shamelessly to the nearest window, still curtained, and stared into the shadowed interior: two nondescript armchairs, a table, a television set in the corner, a blue and white striped rug, no ornamentation. Circling to the kitchen he observed the same pattern: basic functional facilities offering no clues as to the personality of their users. It was as though the owners had simply walked away, leaving behind nothing to guide an inquisitive interloper like himself towards an appreciation of what kind of life had been chiselled out behind those anonymous walls. Even a rack of metal shelving along the rear of the third ground-floor room, facing south to the sea, was unadorned by a single artefact, naked and strangely desolate.

He lingered by a small jetty at the water's edge, staring about him, the afternoon sun gifting the unthreatening waves with a silver coating. Even were he to seat himself on a nearby elevated outcrop of rock, he judged that the landing area would be beyond the vision of anyone – as inquisitive as himself – that might be straining to examine the place from the road. Perhaps this place would meet his brother's requirements? After a few moments' thought he took his mobile 'phone from his jacket pocket and spoke rapidly, question-ingly, for some three minutes before retracing his steps to the breached gate, attempting as he did so to rationalise an involvement towards which he appeared to be moving.

Why, after nearly a decade of what he thought of as liberation, was he allowing his family's interests to intrude into his life again? It had not been difficult to resist the pressure of Colin's early messages; nor had his sister's unexpected visit in May, during which she had urged him to return to Ontario, dented his resolve to remain a free agent. But something had weakened, was still weakening, and it hurt.

He had to admit to himself that it had, finally, proved to be easier than anticipated to leave London. Although uncertain as to whether he was moving away from or towards some better rooted sense of identity, he had persuaded himself that the simple act of migration might serve to sharpen his perspective. On waking from sleep one

June morning he had known with absolute certainty that one phase of his life had ended. It was only now, weeks later, that the emotional price was beginning to be exacted. His final bout of growing pains, perhaps?

His then editor, Jennings, had reacted to his announcement of imminent departure with feigned indifference. 'Well, I've grown accustomed to fellows like you – gilded gypsies – buggering off when it suits. Never rely on chaps of independent means. What's it to be: a book? Politics?'

'Nothing in mind at present.'

Jennings had shifted his well-polished shoes, perched on the edge of his conference table, sunlight glinting off his gold-rimmed half-moon spectacles.

'I suppose Harris could provide a couple of fillers until I sort out something more permanent. It would please Central Office. That is, if you are determined to move on more or less immediately.'

'It would be for the best. Not keen on extended valedictions.'

He wondered if Jennings ever harboured doubts about the intrinsic value of journalism. Probably not, so firmly attached was he to the seductive interplay of fact and perception, to the making and unmaking of reputations, to the access it provided to those in authority, to easy public recognition. It was unlikely that Jennings had entertained, however fleetingly, the notion that his calling, in essence, might be no more than another form of harlotry. Doubtless from time to time Jennings had been given occasion to reflect upon the motives of his proprietors, but it was equally certain that whatever troublesome conclusions might have emerged from such reflexion would have been speedily, metaphorically, spiked. The great game must continue. Ministers must be stroked, or prodded; continental drifts – political, economic, philosophical – must be defined, impugned, occasionally invented; cultural trends required recognition and the endowment of commercial substance; icons must be held before an admiring populace; reputations must be established prior to being torn down; all, of course, in the public interest.

Jennings had changed tack. 'What about Phyllis? What does she make of all this?'

'You know very well that she's a tough-minded girl. Not her style to be devastated when a man lives down to her expectations.'

Was that only a month ago? He lengthened his stride as the wind freshened, now drawing near the town. Would Jennings have already offered consolation to Phyllis? Have discovered that she had not taken the news at all calmly? He had invited her to come with him to Ireland but she had chosen to see it as an act of condescension, declining brusquely. Only then had he been fully seized of her assumption that their relationship was destined to become less elastic, that he had seriously disappointed her.

Aware that he was clenching his jaw, he sought to switch his mind to other – less self-flagellating – matters as he turned left into the main street which climbed steeply from a recently-engineered bridge marking the point at which the river flowed into the bay, and where the road westwards from Cork met that running south from Bantry.

There had been no particular reason for his having fetched up at Ballydehob other than that its location, when viewed on his road map, had seemed promising in relation to Joseph Marotti's specifications. The reality was drab and depressing. Inducements to linger, having reported the house's merits, were lacking, except for his tired disinclination to return over the mountains into Kerry that evening. The town's only residential hotel, to which he had committed himself for the night, was distinctly uninspiring. He had been given absolute choice of all its five rooms, there being no other guests. Indeed, his request for accommodation had been met with ill-disguised alarm. The landlady, a woman of lumpish proportions, had fussed around with fresh linen, explaining confusedly that apart from a few regular commercial travellers, who arrived on predetermined days, demands for her rooms were rare.

'Even in summer?' he had ventured.

'Ah well, 'tis off the beaten track we are. Most visitors head further west, to the good beaches, you know. Still, you're most welcome. Would you be after a nice cup of tea now?' Which he had consumed in his room – the largest on offer – furnished just about adequately with, he judged, an ill-matching collection of second-hand cupboards, rugs, mirror, drawers and bed. He had not unpacked but had decided to embark on his exploratory walk with no great sense of optimism. Perhaps his expectations had been lowered sufficiently to ensure that anything slightly abnormal encountered in such a backwater – for example, an abandoned house – would trigger disproportionate interest.

Approaching the inn, he underwent blatant gender appraisal by a few schoolgirls exchanging shrill exchanges whilst waiting for a local bus, a gaggle of Gaelic Emma Bovaries, hot for it, wild imaginings swelling in pubescent breasts, frustrated he judged, by the thin cultural gruel of church and State-controlled television. Did they, like so many of their forebears, still look westwards for salvation to America, that meretricious Mecca; or were they once more succumbing to the blandishments of Catholic Europe whose charms had held a steady appeal for the Irish over the centuries? Two days earlier he had visited Bantry House with its flamboyant gardens shamelessly plagiarising the Tuscan baroque of Villa Garzoni; and its museum, equally shameless in its attempt to celebrate the bathos of Wolfe Tone's participation in the last serious attempt by the French to invade Britain, an enterprise which had foundered in December 1796 off Bantry Bay. Five days out from Brest, under command of General Lazare Hoche, the 33 year-old Dublin barrister, clad in the accoutrements of a French adjutant-general, had paced the decks of the warship named, with perilous presumption, the *Indomptable.* The expeditionary fleet had sat in clear view of observers on the snow-covered hills, waiting the propitious moment to disembark its 12,000 fighting men. The time never came. Instead an awesome gale struck, reaching the height of its fury on Christmas Eve. The god of storms had again been recruited to serve the English flag. The fleet was ordered by Hoche to cut its cables and run before the tempest. The *Indomptable* alone declined at first to do so but eventually, bowing to the inevitable, limped away as the New Year dawned. Tone had a genius for anticlimax: two years later – a prisoner of the English – he was to cut his throat in order to escape hanging but, failing to locate his jugular, was obliged to linger for another week before his severed windpipe finally took pity on his inadequate anatomising. Thus, the visitor thought, are Irish heroes established. Its towns are littered with monuments to under-achievement: Emmet, Casement and various fallen Republican *condotierri.*

He recalled the ballad celebrating the crushing of the brave Connaught Rangers by 'Cromwell's khaki hordes' when, according to legend, they had risen against the Crown in 1920. The reality, however, was that a handful of bored and inebriated malcontents had staged a protest over the conditions in their garrison, had been easily disciplined by a few regimental bandsmen and had shortly petitioned the Home Secretary to be allowed to combat the IRA during the Irish Civil War. And what of Sean Ruiseal whose garlanded statue he had seen in Dublin, a Sinn Fein eminence who had died in 1940 aboard a Nazi U-boat off the Kerry coast on his return from having successfully negotiated with Von Ribbentrop a deal aimed at destabilising Ulster? He had died, however, not by a glorious bullet but from a perforated ulcer. The monument, regrettably, failed to depict Ruiseal in his true travail of martyrdom astride a German naval-issue bucket spattered with faeces and blood.

Was there, he pondered, a profound melancholy at the core of Ireland's psyche, an ineradicable wistfulness for what might have been, heightened by an unadmitted fear of the reality that would have to be faced should aspirations become concrete. He had been struck, as which traveller to its shores could not, by the burden of history on this land, its people haunted by a past which sustained them but rarely impelled them forward, by a dense nostalgia captured in the harping plagency of songs floating in the temperate air from the windows of innumerable alehouses.

He decided not to return immediately to his hotel but crossed the road to Casey's Bar, having noticed a sign in its window announcing that its proprietor, Maurice Colclough, doubled enterprisingly as an estate agent. The interior was snug and warm. He asked the professionally hospitable brunette behind the bar for a large whiskey and settled into a seat from which he discreetly surveyed the only two other occupants: one a be-jeaned youngster intently watching silent coverage of horse-racing on the corner television; the other a much older fellow seated just inside the bar's entrance. The latter's rheumy eyes glimmered above his jar of stout.

'Is it on holiday you are?' The barmaid, probably bored, called across to the new face.

'Partly.' Always he clung to ambiguity. 'But I'm the sort that's usually doing more than one thing at a time.'

The old fellow spoke up. 'One bloody thing is more than most buggers in this town can usually manage, like keeping my glass full.'

'Oh, you can be a right shite, Brendan.' She flicked back her thick brown hair, an arm action that drew attention to her full figure. 'Since the ceasefire up north we've had a lot more of the English through here.'

'Passing through, to be sure, like hot curry.' Brendan was determined to make himself heard. 'Two hours for the entire tour. Not much to keep a body hanging around these parts.'

She persisted, 'Things can change, you miserable old sod. If the troubles don't come back ... which God forbid they should ... there's no reason why the town shouldn't prosper. Plenty of incomers have settled along the coast. That's what Maurice says, at any rate.'

'Aye, well, he says a lot.' Brendan rose, somewhat unsteadily, and moved to the bar to demand replenishment.

'Actually ...' the visitor drew out his vowels provocatively, reclaiming her attention, imposing himself – 'I was wondering if Mr Colclough is around.'

'You know him, so?'

'No, but the notice outside says that he deals in property.'

'So he does.' Her gaze sharpened. 'But he's out and about this afternoon. Not due back from Toormore until around eight this evening, at the earliest.'

He considered his options: perhaps first dinner? Then call in again? Probably worth the effort. He said, 'I'd appreciate a word with him. I'm moving on tomorrow. As our friend over there points out, there's not much to detain me, is there?' He sipped his whiskey thoughtfully. 'Perhaps you could advise me where I might find a decent meal tonight? I don't fancy anything on offer across in the hotel.'

This prompted a lively debate. Even the horse-fancier essayed an opinion. All agreed he would have to look outside Ballydehob, the town's only tolerable restaurant having closed down six months previously, an event which simultaneously reinforced Brendan's prejudices whilst providing for the woman – now identified as Annie – evidence that things could only improve. Consensus finally pointed him towards a choice of two eating houses in Schull, some six miles distant. Annie showed him the road on a map pinned on the wall.

He studied it briefly. 'Toormore, I see, lies not far beyond Schull. Could you possibly contact Mr Colclough by 'phone? I was thinking it might be possible to meet halfway, so to speak.'

'So it's keen you are.'

Lentement, lentement. 'Only an idea.'

She again examined his alert, thin features: dominant prow of a nose, restless green eyes across which there seemed to lie a film of darkness, a sensual mouth which had yet to smile, a face used to being appeased; not smug but self-centred; closing in upon itself. She said, 'If he calls in I'll tell him you'll be at Emilio's ... probably. But he doesn't always telephone, and he may have other plans. He's a busy man. The only thing you can be sure of is that he'll be here close to ten.' She turned away to attend to Brendan's half-settled Guinness. It was only after he had left the bar that Annie realised she had neglected to ask for his name. No sweat. She could always nip across to Maeve Rafferty's if Maurice needed it.

Before leaving for Schull he spoke again to Joseph Marotti in New York, using the hotel's pay-phone located in the lobby where, had she been inclined, the landlady could have overheard his conversation. As it happened, he could hear her moving around in the rear kitchen preparing her own dinner. She had been relieved to learn that he would not be making demands on her culinary skills. 'To be sure, Emilio's will do fine. I can tell you're used to eating in good restaurants. Something about the cut of you.' She had smiled, folding her arms across her ample bosom. 'No need to hurry back. The door will be open till midnight.'

'How kind.'

He had brought his book from the room and read quietly in the old-fashioned snug until he was confident that she was otherwise occupied. He had decided that his having made an international call might impress the locals; a few more would be registered before departure; but he did not wish the content of this particular conversation to be noised abroad.

Marotti's harsh accent vibrated over the wires. He had not known a time when Marotti had not been in his life, and, although he did not doubt his value to the company, he could not bring himself to like the man, perhaps because Marotti had been closer to his father than any of the latter's offspring, having been successively his childhood friend, student colleague, respected adviser and, bizarrely, father-in-law. He could not avoid the conclusion that Marotti, an instinctive predator, had deprived him of the affection that ought to have been his, had left him emotionally starved, outcast, lacking the psychic tendrils essential for forming warm and durable attachments.

'I've discovered the local property man. Hoping to make contact later this evening. How far should I go?'

'Not too far. We need to be sure the place is right. Not that I'm doubting your judgement, James, but–hell–I'd like an expert to sniff around. It sounds real promising.'

'So, I try to establish ownership?'

'Right. And check out as much neighbourly data as you can without getting too pushy. Hey, James, you've come up with the goods. The best prospect yet.'

'OK. I'll be in touch in a couple of days. In person. I plan to fly out on Thursday.'

'See you, soon. Hey, and don't be giving the guy the idea that price is no object. This isn't an addition to your art collection, OK?'

'Whatever you say.'

An hour later, as he unlocked his rented Mercedes, he observed Annie across the road, taking the evening air at Casey's doorway. He waved. She nodded in response, smiling, arms folded across her generous breasts.

He drove with unnecessary aggression up the hill westwards, towards the crimson-streaked horizon, through broken pastures fringed by blackthorn. He knew the land to be wondrously beautiful but could not warm to it.

The meal at Emilio's proved to be excellent: sea bass with almonds followed by a Dickensian portion of apple pie. He had brought his book for company: Teilhard de Chardin, the wayward Jesuit to whose thoughts he had been redirected by recent controversies pertaining to genetics which he had been following in various academic journals. His brother – pragmatic, relatively unschooled, dismissive of intellect – had always scorned his penchant for philosophical speculation. 'Free will? Or bred in the bones? In a hundred years time who'll know the difference? Screw it!' But the lean, dark man stirring his espresso in a restaurant in West Cork could not shrug off the disturbing possibility that he might have arrived in that particular place at that precise hour not wholly by chance. He found himself, as often of late, thinking of his father, that dour and resentful product of inherited wealth derived originally from timber, nickel, copper, iron – the unforgiving fruits of the earth – a man who had never been other than a distant, unloving shadow, more mysterious, albeit more proximate, than his mother who had died too young to leave any lasting impression upon him. Where else but from them – from him – came the insistent messages of his blood that he had to stand apart; to withhold all trust; never to doubt that corruption lay at the universe's root, the comprehensive grasp of which a few – an unscrupulous few – unhesitatingly used to their material advantage; a sense that nothing, finally, really mattered at all? Except expanding their domination over others. Could he excuse – on the grounds that we are what we are, whether we like it or not – his enjoyment of deception and ambiguity, sometimes verging upon manipulativeness; his profound cynicism; his combination of sensuality and absence of passion, his irremediable sense of a hollowness deep at the heart of things? His eyes re-engaged with the Jesuit: 'Even in the supremely intellectual act of science (at any rate as long as it remains purely speculative and abstract) the impact of our souls operates only obliquely and indirectly. Contact remains superficial, involving the danger of yet another servitude. Love alone is capable of uniting living beings in such a way as to complete and fulfil them, for it alone takes them and joins them by what is deepest in themselves.'

Had his parents loved? His brother believed they had not. If he was right, did this imply that he was merely the product of an act of servitude; incomplete and unfulfilled? That could explain a great deal.

He was in the process of ordering a consoling whiskey when he became aware of the presence at his elbow of a short, sharply-dressed man aged around fifty with the unsettling smile of a hyena and whose brown eyes had an irritating habit of focusing somewhere over the listener's shoulder.

'Sorry to intrude, but may I introduce myself? I'm Maurice Colclough. Would you by any chance be the English gentleman that was enquiring after me in Casey's earlier this evening? In Bally-dehob?' His voice was light, free-floating, ingratiating.

'Ah, so Annie was good enough to pass on my enquiry.'

Colclough promptly slid into a vacant chair. 'I just happened, as luck would have it, to 'phone in ten minutes ago, and she told me that she'd recommended Emilio's and that you were driving a red Mercedes. Added to which, you're the only person in this place I don't recognise.' As if in proof he waved expansively towards the nearest group of diners who made cheerful response. 'Although West Cork is fast becoming a veritable honeypot for incomers,' he added. 'English, French, Germans, you name it.'

'It was kind of you to search me out. I answer to the name of James Tull, and I'm not actually English as it happens.' He did not elaborate. 'Would you care to join me in a glass of Chablis? The bottle I've just emptied was not quite sufficiently chilled, but very drinkable.' He summoned the waiter with a barely perceptible gesture, observing Colclough's vague unease as he began to register Tull's innate exercise of authority. The latter allowed the silence between them to prompt Colclough into offering the next remark.

'Really? Not English? Well, come to that I'm only half Irish myself. My father hailed from Pembroke. Used to work on the ferries.' He grinned nervously. 'We foreigners need to stick together, don't you agree?'

'It might prove helpful, Mr Colclough.' Tull poured out the newly-delivered wine. 'I understand that you're the local estate agent?'

'A sideline to running the bar. One of several.' Colclough fingered his right nostril. 'So I take it, Mr Tull, that you're looking for a property around here? You've come to the right man.' He glistened with anticipation.

'Actually, I think I may have found the house I'm after. Or, rather, one that would suit me tolerably well. A place just outside Bally-dehob has caught my eye.'

'That's unusual. Most buyers look further west, or out towards Waterford in the other direction. Not much of a centre, Ballydehob.'

Tull said evenly, 'I'm not aiming for centrality. I find fringes more interesting. This Chablis is still not as chilled as it should be, don't you agree? If you know the chef perhaps you might have a word in his ear. As I was saying, the house I've come across seems to be available. Certainly it's not currently occupied. You must know it. It stands about a mile and a half down the road towards Rossbrin, fronting the bay.'

Colclough stirred with what his potential client identified as unease but which was sought to be passed off as disappointment. 'Ah, I know the place. Yes, indeed! What a pity!' He fluttered his hands in a gesture of frustration. 'The house is fast becoming an eyesore, to be sure, and would certainly benefit from having a caring owner. But I don't think it's on the market. The people who used to live there have moved away, that's true; but as far as I know they've shown no interest in selling.'

'Might they be persuaded?'

'I'm not sure where I'd find them. They've been gone for over a year.' He grimaced. 'I fear you may have laid out unnecessarily on this extra bottle.'

Tull shrugged but persisted. 'Does nobody around here know of their present whereabouts? Were they local people?'

'Well now, that's a debatable point.' Colclough fell into a reflective silence, his dun-coloured eyes ranging around the restaurant for inspiration, a faint mist of perspiration rising above his lips. 'I could make some inquiries, but they were an unsociable couple. Didn't really know them well myself.'

'There must be some way of finding out where they live.' Tull was now becoming intrigued. The house was acquiring a further layer of mystery. 'For instance, I assume they worked nearby. Or were they perhaps elderly?'

'No, not retired or anything such. Just reclusive.' Colclough squared his shoulders. 'Look now, I do recall that there was a woman – an antique dealer – over in Glenmore who sold them bits and pieces of furniture and suchlike from time to time. She used to drop into Casey's on the way back home for a quick gin and to pass the time of day. It's just possible that she'd know where they've shifted to. I could have a word with her, if you're really interested, that is. I wouldn't want to be wasting my time.'

'I'll make it worth your while.'

Colclough's smile returned. 'I'll do what I can. But even if I trace them, they may not want to sell.'

'I can be very persuasive, Mr Colclough. Although, of course, I would want the place properly surveyed before I could contemplate making an offer. All its hidden vices must be fully exposed, as well as its obvious virtues.'

'Mr Tull, you must realise that all this will take time. Annie tells me you're moving on tomorrow.'

'True, but I've noted Casey's telephone number. If I don't contact you again within a week, one of my associates will certainly do so.' He gestured to the waiter that he was ready to settle his bill. 'It really was most considerate of you to seek me out here tonight, and I'm sure your efforts will eventually be rewarded. Let me leave my business card with you. And you must help me to empty this bottle.'

Much later, couched in his customary corner of Casey's, Colclough savoured his third whiskey and stared morosely at the gilt-edged card embossed in cobalt blue. Onaping Enterprises. A London address. Tull's name in neat manuscript on the reverse. Smug bastard! He eyed Annie vigorously scouring the bar top, her heavy breasts bobbing in rhythmic accompaniment to her determined assault on the day's accumulation of grime and spilt beer. As she paused to straighten her back he observed, with a faint onset of lust, the delicate skein of reddish-black hair along her nether arms, the moistness above her full upper lip. He said, 'Don't wear yourself out. Keep some of that spark for later.'

'It's a wee bold fellow you are,' she protested; but they both acknowledged that her lingering so casually after closing time denoted the absence of her lorry-driving husband. Nevertheless, for form's sake, she added, 'You take a lot for granted.'

'Well now, if it's variety you're after you could try your luck with the not-quite English fella across the way.' She noted the irritated edge to his voice. 'He's a self-important prick, to be sure. It might be best for me to forget all about him. Let someone else have his business. Too much trouble all round. Except that it sounds like easy money.'

'What's it about, then?'

'Bracken Point.'

'Bloody hell. Forgetting would be a fine thing.'

He rubbed his chin. 'But maybe not altogether wise. I'll have to pass the word on. Just in case.'

She commiserated. ''Tis right you are. Take advice.' She remembered the slight unease which had stirred in her when she noticed the darkness behind Tull's green eyes, the otherness.

'Let's sleep on it.'

But the satisfaction he managed to extract from her generous body, before falling into a shallow slumber, was scanter than usual. He rose unaccustomedly early to telephone the man he knew would be busy parcelling out the newspapers in his corner shop in Bandon. After receiving instructions he breakfasted before, at 9.15 precisely, ringing the London number of Onaping Enterprises. A woman advised him that Mr Tull was not immediately available but if he would be so good as to leave his name? Ah, Mr Colclough … she had been told by Mr Tull to expect his call. Did he have any fresh information she might pass on to Mr Tull about the property in question? As she was speaking, Colclough, from his first floor window, was observing the said individual emerge from the Ballydehob Arms to stow two suitcases into the boot of his Mercedes. No, he replied, but would be glad if Mr Tull could kindly contact him directly whenever convenient. Snotty bitch! He watched Tull drive away, then stepped into the damp street, drawing his raincoat around him, and headed towards the hotel.

The dumpy proprietress, Maeve Rafferty, was happy enough to be diverted away from disposing of the remains of Tull's breakfast into a description of the impressive length of time her departed guest had spent on the telephone. 'Cost him a fair piece, more than the price of his breakfast. London, Toronto, New York, God knows where.'

'And what would he be talking about, I wonder?'

'Ah, that I couldn't be saying, Maurice. Sounded like business, but nothing I could make sense of. There was something about buying a property but I couldn't say where. D'you think he might be one of those theatrical people that's been after settling down towards Blair's Cove?'

'Could be, Maeve. Did he say whether he'd be back?'

'That he did. Not that I'm holding my breath. Heard it all before, so I have. Mind you, he was a lovely dresser. There's money in his pocket, that's for sure. Which could be what you're after, Maurice, is it right I am?'

'You know my weakness, Maeve. Speaking of which, would it be too early for the day's first drop?' Mrs Rafferty's brandy measures were famed for their generosity. He gossiped for a while before returning to his private quarters in order to make another 'phone call to the newsagent in Bandon.

Around noon, the not-quite Englishman arrived at Shannon Airport, deposited his hired car and checked with Onaping Enterprises, the London Office of which he used, inter alia, to filter enquiries and transmit messages.

'Yes, Mr Tull. Well before ten this morning. Mr Colclough was most anxious to speak to you.'

'That's encouraging. If he contacts you again, tell him that one of my associates will telephone him later this week to confirm my interest and to find out whether he has established ownership.'

'Certainly, Mr Tull.'

He hesitated a moment but knew he had to ask. 'Have you heard from Miss Norton?'

'No, Mr Tull. Do you want us to pass a message on to her?'

'Thanks, but I'll handle it myself.'

He was surprised to discover how badly he had wanted Phyllis to have telephoned, but was unsure whether his disappointment signified much more than wounded vanity. Perhaps she had written him off as an unwise investment, a lesson learnt, and had moved on decisively in search of richer rewards; but he doubted it. Some instinct told him that she would be waiting for a sign. He recalled her parting words: 'I'll give you time, James. Not, maybe, as much as you want, but ample. I know you're afraid of commitment, Aren't we all? But we'll work our way through the doubts, given half a chance. Don't you think so? Anyway you'll know where to find me.'

It was late afternoon when he boarded the aircraft at Shannon. He ordered champagne in a doomed attempt to raise his spirits but soon found the sombre mood that had descended upon him the previous evening returning, a burgeoning sense of inner emptiness, of not belonging. He had, of late, become obsessed by a deeply subversive observation of Stephen Hawking whose words he had copied down inside the cover of de Chardin's book:

'The human race is just a chemical scum on a moderate-sized planet orbiting around an average star in the outer suburbs of one among a hundred million galaxies.'

Tull was, after having devoted several hours to a contemplation of Hawking's more accessible writings, still unsure whether this account of mankind was intended to be deflatingly bleak, or whether even a chemical scum could be interpreted as having been created, however mockingly, in the image of God. He wanted to believe the latter, to be convinced of the reality of a purposive universe, but remained awash with doubt. In his worst moments, at his soul's midnight, he would experience a dread hollowness in the pit of his belly as he confronted dark images of a condition of universal meaninglessness, the terrorising possibility of an ultimate futility at the core of things. The fear that this might be so, the certainty that such fear could never be dismissed as an impossibility, had on occasions brought him close to panic. But against this stood de Chardin, holy optimist, with his conviction of evolutionary consciousness, and his clear-eyed vision that man could aspire, through accumulative acts of will and intellect, to transform Hawking's genetic slime into a transcendental entity which, for lack of a better word, one might call God. Without such hope, however provisional, how could one construct, or justify, any firm structure of morality?

He watched the land slide away beneath the Boeing's wing, a gleaming sea supplanting it but soon to be lost in shrouds of cloud, the colour of fleece, shouldering eastwards from Labrador.

CHAPTER TWO

Phyllis Norton saw no reason to condemn Wagner's anti-Semitism despite Hugh Jennings's provocations. She simply considered it as beside the point.

'As long as his operas are aesthetically sublime it really wouldn't matter were we to discover that he had been granted some precognition that his music might serve to motivate workers on the production line at Dachau. Indeed, had he actually anticipated such a possible future use it could well have enhanced the quality of his harmonics, given the added enthusiasm with which he would have embraced the project.'

'Isn't that rather extreme?' Jennings enquired owlishly.

The young woman would not yield. 'Surely the only reasonable requirement of art is that it delivers, in some balanced and disciplined fashion, both technical excellence and emotional charge. We're not looking for moral treatises, are we? Who cares if the artist is a total shit in his private life? Or in public life for that matter.'

Jennings, in search of a rebuttal, stared from the Festival Hall terrace across the slick-running Thames towards the curvatures of Terry Farrell's Charing Cross: a temple to transportation. There were times, he reflected, when the sharp edges of her personality almost invited some physical chamfering. He was conscious of her body stiffening at his elbow, poised to counter-punch whatever his response might be. Around them the interval crowd, drinks in hand, chattered agreeably in the mild September air, tensionless, enjoying their evening, colourful and animated. Phyllis, however, maintained an unbreachable embargo on relaxation.

It was his mistake for having steered her towards the small exhibition in the concert hall's foyer, a collection of prints and assorted documents designed to illustrate Jewish influences on late nineteenth- and early twentieth-century Viennese culture. Had he not made what he took to be a commonplace observation about

Wagner's ethnic atavism he too might now have been lapping his wine contentedly, gossiping lightly about the latest sexual indiscretions surfacing in Westminster or Washington, instead of finding himself thrashing around in intellectually choppy waters. Or perhaps not. Phyllis was a woman around whom contention flourished. Even if he had not impaled himself upon her sharp tines, this woman who irritated and fascinated him by turns would doubtless have conjured up some other issue with which to rake him.

Before the interval – hence the exhibition – it had been the Siegfried Idyll and a Mozart aria (*Non più … non temer*; Felicity Lott in great voice) with Richard Strauss's Metamorphosen to follow, allusion to which would be unlikely to extricate him from the debate in which he was temporarily enmeshed. Diversion was the only possible solution. He waved a proprietary hand towards the Thames: Palace of Westminster to their left framed by a deepening September sky; Somerset House to their right; the Savoy's rosy windows; the vaulted mouth of Charing Cross; extravagances of swooping angles and pinnacles; the entire panoply of power and possession of which he felt himself to be a part, and not the least.

'Isn't London wonderful.'

'Hugh, you're evading the issue.'

'Trying hard I admit.' He adjusted his spectacles. 'Look, the fact that Wagner might well have relished writing a musical accompaniment to gas chamber horrors damns him in my opinion, even when measured against your own criteria. Not all emotional charges can be condoned. Some are repugnant. Wagner's creepy personality poisoned everything he produced. I fail him on the grounds of invalid content.' Jennings, who could never resist parading his grasp of historical detail, continued, 'Think about it. Here we have a man whose early career had depended critically upon Meyerbeer's patronage, a Jew whose favours he had obtained through obsequious flattery. Later, ashamed of his outrageous brown-nosing, Tricky Dickie converted his self-disgust into a virulent hatred of all things touched by Jewry. The only emotions he projects are despicable ones.'

She examined his flushed features, the film of perspiration above his gold-rimmed spectacles, his moist but compressed mouth. She said, 'You must have difficulty with a great many artists.'

'Discrimination is, I acknowledge, an unfashionable virtue.' He half-turned away from her to acknowledge a passing Commons Member who had, *en route* to snatching a quick second glass of wine before the interval bell, made some jocular comment into Jennings's right ear. Normally he would have seized the chance to harvest the Member's current views on the proposed common European currency or any other timely political issue; but he knew that the tense woman at his elbow would not have easily forgiven any slackening in the attention paid to her. She was, he realised, still in turmoil as a result of Tull's unanticipated departure a few weeks ago. Although she had never been, in anyone's experience, the most serene of women – one of his colleagues having dubbed her K2: unsurmountable save by the nerveless or suicidal – her present prickliness was extreme. He had refrained from contacting her in the days immediately following Tull's exodus. Mutual acquaintances had told him that she had been taking it badly and he had judged that his association with Tull, through whom he had first met Phyllis, might render any early approach on his part unwelcome. Last week, however, he had contacted her on the pretext of commissioning a review of a new biography of Tobias Smollett, a writer on whom he knew she had previously published a couple of well-regarded critiques, the eighteenth century novel having been the subject on which she had secured her Doctorate, a distinction to which she drew no particular attention.

He had first met her at a reception thrown by the BBC to mark some award or another. She had arrived on Tull's arm and the cool appraisal to which she had subjected him made an immediate impression. Tull had soon swanned off to converse with a Home Office civil servant he had known at Oxford, leaving Phyllis in Jennings's sole company for several minutes during which he had found his normally reliable skills of seduction wholly unavailing. He had later established that she was a product of Benenden and Durham University with a First in English Literature followed by post-graduate study at Cambridge. Her parents lived in Kent and were comfortably, but not notably, prosperous. After a brief, unsatisfactory spell as an academic at Hull she had taken a position as reader at Longstaff's publishing house where she was highly regarded. If she harboured ambitions as a creative writer she had never mentioned it, but several tautly-phrased exegeses on Fielding, Richardson, Smollett and Sterne had appeared from time to time in unfashionable but intellectually accredited journals. Jennings considered her apparent lack of interest in building a substantial career to be part of her oblique charm. In this signal respect she was wholly unthreatening to male contemporaries: undriven, seemingly agenda-less.

He allowed her to move ahead of him as they returned to their seats. She held herself well, head erect, elegant in her olive-hued Jean Muir suit, dark hair drawn back to emphasise her strong cheekbones, grey eyes staring straight ahead in characteristic expressionless self-containment. His earlier favourable assessment of the social advantages of being seen in her company remained intact, but he found himself speculating uneasily as to the nature of her sentiments on that subject. What, he imagined her thinking, am I doing here with this overweight, short-sighted, disagreeably perspiring and opinionated middle-aged married man whose attentions are almost certainly less than honourable?

Later, post-Strauss, as they eased their knees under a corner table at Carafini's, that worrying mist of self-doubt rose again in his mind, removing some of the edge from his normally rapacious appetite. She silently contemplated the menu, her long untinted fingernails running up and down the stem of her wine-glass, effectively controlling the occasion in a manner he would have found intolerable in other women of his acquaintance, certainly any with her lack of influential connections.

Their tagliatelle arrived. He decided it was time to raise the subject which both had hitherto been avoiding. 'Have you heard from James? I gather he's been on a trip to Ireland.'

'Long gone. He's in Toronto. Or was. I had a 'phone call to that effect a couple of days ago.'

'Really? Not the most beguiling of cities.'

'He has family there, I believe.' She raised her eyebrows. 'You did know he is Canadian?'

'I'm astonished. His Home County accent seems entirely genuine. And I'm sure he said he was educated at Dulwich College.'

'So he was. Nevertheless he is a colonial. But I'm not surprised he has not admitted to the fact to you. He is a maestro of evasiveness, particularly when his personal life comes under scrutiny.'

Jennings forked his pasta furiously. 'I've never worked out how you and he met.'

'Ditto,' she said evenly.

'That's easily explained. I was introduced to him by Sylvia Edgcombe, the so-called artist who made her name by producing outrageous representations of female genitalia. It was, if you'll pardon the obvious pun, at a private view, and Tull was about to purchase a canvas of quite revolting intimacy.'

'I've seen it. He hung it initially in his bathroom but it didn't enjoy a steamy atmosphere, so he removed it to God knows where.'

Jennings smirked. 'Not a thing I'd care to take home but James was much attracted. And Sylvia evidently took a shine to him for reasons not entirely related to the size of his … ah … cheque. I seem to recall we three ended up at some wine bar in Covent Garden. It must have been about three years ago. Of course, I'd heard of him vaguely before then. He'd been producing occasional stuff in the financial pages and dabbling in politics. I remember someone telling me, around the time that I contracted him for *The Mercury*, that he'd acted as some kind of unpaid researcher for one of these political think-tanks. Not that I hold it against him. All this must have been shortly before you and he became … what's the term? … an item.'

'Possibly. I met him, purely by chance, when I was on holiday in Florence in May 1992. I was under the impression that he held some kind of vague diplomatic position. At any rate, he took me to a couple of functions organised by the Canadian Consulate.'

'That fits. I was told he had experience in promoting certain trade deals in Italy.'

She stared into the half-distance, speaking quietly. 'I confess to having been flattered when it seemed … not that he ever admitted as much … that he had returned to London to seek me out.'

'And why not?' he oiled. 'A better reason than most.'

They fell silent again, concentrating on their food. But he could not let the opportunity slip. Clearing his mouth, adjusting his spectacles, he launched into his rehearsed speech framed to offer her a permanent reviewer's slot on his paper, dignified with the title of Assistant Literary Editor. He was disappointed by her lack of immediate enthusiasm.

'The money would, of course, be very welcome, but why are you doing this?'

'I genuinely believe you would bring a fresh and rigorous judgement to bear on contemporary literature. Too much of our so-called criticism in these post-modernist days strikes me as flashy masturbatory stuff. We need something sterner. And you always express yourself, how shall I put it …?'

'Abrasively?' she suggested.

'Uncompromisingly. Succinctly.' He poured more wine into her glass, disturbingly aware that her grey eyes had locked fixedly onto his face, scanning for ulterior signs.

She said, 'It's very flattering, Hugh, but given that such talent as I have is far from extraordinary, I need to be absolutely clear about the basis on which this offer has come my way. Forgive me, but you do have something of a reputation as a sexual adventurer, and one has to speculate whether you might have it in mind to insert certain sub-clauses in my job description.'

He leant back to glance around the now-emptying restaurant. 'Parallel tracks,' he murmured. 'Unrelated objectives.'

She smiled thinly, candlelight accentuating the shadows under her cheekbones. Once again she had moved onto the offensive, as naturally as inhaling.

She said, 'If you're planning to bed me tonight, perhaps you could call for the bill. Once we get the sweaty stuff out of the way I might – having paid my dues in advance – be able to consider your parallel offer with greater clarity.'

Half an hour later he dropped her off on the corner by the Pimlico Wine Vaults, pointedly a hundred yards or so from her flat, in an attempt to regain the initiative. He had been at pains to ensure she understood that his reticence was stylistic, not substantive: a matter only of timing; pleasure postponed. If it was to be a question of debt collection, he preferred the obligation to mature beyond the point at which it would be resented. And if word of the eventual liaison were to reach Tull, as he intended, how much sweeter it would be were the act to be seen as wholly considered on her part, rather than as a mere exercise in therapy to assuage the pain of abandonment.

She drank cocoa before disrobing, selecting from her small collection of CDs the Adagio from Shostakovich's 14th String Quartet, to quieten her nerves, careful to activate the repeat control before her machine rotated the disc into the jagged chords of the final movement. Further agitation she did not need.

She could not believe how foolishly, impulsively, she had behaved. With Jennings of all people! She imagined him indulging in one of those chuckling masculine exchanges of confidences, 'Oh, by the way, have I told you …? Naturally I let her down gently. Some conventions just have to be maintained, don't you think …?'

It was, she knew, anger. 'It is the cause, it is the cause, my soul.' She had been angry for weeks, with herself, with the world at large. James Tull sat at the core of her disequilibrium, his memory goading her, his absence a constant source of pain, a misery made deeper by her sense that it was probably her own doing. Probably. Why had she rejected – so coldly – his offer to accompany him to Ireland? She had known, by a succession of small signs over several weeks, that he had become restless with London, that some pressure from his family had been unsettling him. Yet she had offered no sympathy, no understanding, not a shard of soft compromise when his moment of decision had arrived. He had not rejected her. Although his manner of presenting his intentions to her had been almost offensively casual, she had come to recognise that to be his style, an element of his highly developed self-protectiveness. She had chosen to make no allowance, to stand firmly on her principled ground of independence, a young woman to whom nobody could dictate. So they had parted coolly, since when there had been a single telephone message, left on her answering machine, brief and non-committal, indicating that he was intending to remain in Canada on family business for the remainder of the year, a message that served to refuel her vexation.

There had been other men in her life, with most of whom she had dallied beyond the point of platonic propriety, but Tull had always been – continued to be – different. His absence had affected her, in ways that she had found to be unexpectedly adverse. She had become moody; she knew it; and her tendency towards stridency had been reinforced, had taken on an even sharper edge.

She turned off the CD player, lit a cigarette – a consolation to which she turned only at moments of stress – and stared thoughtfully at her carpet, regretting – not for the first time – its greyness, its accumulation of even greyer stains, a metaphor for those qualities she had begun to recognise as quintessentially modern English: a leaden society concerned above all to go through life as comfortably – and to leave it as painlessly – as possible, its politicians motivated only by an ambition to achieve the greatest apathy for the greatest number; a selfish, self-absorbed people turning in on themselves, losing definition, wallowing in a multi-cultural soup where all values merged seamlessly into grey muddy relativity.

The following morning, Friday, she rang Jennings. 'I put you in an unforgivably awkward situation. It was stupid of me. Hormonal, I suppose. And you'd been so kind, providing such an agreeable evening. I truly enjoyed the concert.'

'There's really no need ...'

'I feel badly about it, and you were so considerate in allowing me to slip off the hook of my own making.'

He giggled. 'I wouldn't trust your luck on a second occasion. In my circles a man benefits on the whole from being known as something of a stud. And I was, of course, immensely flattered.'

'That's really kind, Hugh. But you must realise that my accepting your job offer is now quite out of the question.'

There was a protracted silence. Finally: 'We must talk about this. I went to considerable lengths with my literary editor – '

'I can guess. I don't delude myself that I would be anyone's unbiased choice.'

An even longer silence. 'As you wish, dear girl.'

'I do. Sorry.'

She imagined him grinding his expensively immaculate teeth. Which were, however, sharp. He said, thinly, 'There is one thing you might do to redeem yourself. Do you by any chance have a contact number for James? A small legal matter has arisen on an article he wrote in June, and I need to clear it up. You said that he'd phoned you from Toronto.'

'Actually, he didn't speak to me in person. For some reason, he just wanted me to know his whereabouts. All I had was a message on my answerphone.' Why was she divulging this to him? She steadied herself. 'But I have a New York number somewhere. I'll let your secretary have it once I dig it out.'

'I would be most grateful.'

'No trouble, Hugh. And again, sorry.' As she replaced the receiver she wondered whether she had – once again – allowed her self-esteem to sabotage her self-interest.

Jennings, during what would be an autumnal evening in Manhattan, made contact with Joseph Marotti, the name supplied, as promised, by Phyllis Norton. It was his intention to tap into Tull's memory concerning an article the latter had written about a controversial civil case that had been the subject of a court of appeal judgment, a piece which latterly had given rise to the threat of litigation against *The Mercury*; but it would be convenient if, as a bi-product, he could ascertain whether Tull had any plans for an early return to London, a démarche that could complicate his vaguely-focussed pursuit of the Norton girl.

Marotti expressed at length much delight at having been sought out by the editor of such a distinguished British newspaper. When eventually brought around to the subject of Tull, however, his response was not particularly helpful.

'Was here until Wednesday. Then left for Toronto, but I guess may be already *en route* for Vancouver. His schedule is pretty hectic this month.'

'Would you by any chance have any number on which we might reach him? It's quite important that we speak.'

'Can't help you there, Mr Jennings. But when he checks back – which he often does – I'll certainly let him know of your interest.'

'I'd be most grateful. Incidentally, Mr Marotti, could you possibly enlighten me as to the nature of your relationship with James? I'm afraid your name didn't crop up during his work on the paper.' In the ensuing pause Jennings's journalistic antennae informed him that shutters were falling.

'Mainly professional. The Trust, you know. I handle some of its major investments. You'll realise that I'm not about to breach any confidences.'

'Of course not.' Jennings manufactured a light laugh, unready to admit that Marotti's reference to a Trust carried no meaning for him. 'It's good to know that his interests are being looked after so competently. Please feel free to look me up when you're next in London.'

'I might just do that, Mr Jennings, although my travel to Europe these days is usually confined to extending the Trust's range of assets, and I guess *The Mercury* isn't ripe for grabbing just yet.'

'Ah, a nice thought, but a little beyond your reach, I would have thought.' Marotti heard a chuckle thick with complacency.

'Well, that's for you to assume, Mr Jennings. Me, I'm a cautious guy. Anyway, nice speaking to you.' Marotti, replacing his telephone, stared pensively at the windowed view of Central Park. Had he reacted a tad too revealingly to provocation? Either way, prudence dictated that the conversation be reported.

Phyllis strode into Kensington Gardens, pulling up her collar to shield her from September's first chill wind. She headed initially northwards up the Broad Walk, noting the red helicopter on the palace's greensward poised to hurry some royal to a chicken lunch.

She made a brief detour into the Italian Gardens at the tip of Long Water, its fountains passive, stonework crumbling with the melancholy of a half-forgotten memory. An early fall of leaves drifted from the avenues of plane and lime. She loved this park, its moods and subtle variations, its history. Sheep had, up to the 1960s, grazed on this stretch ahead of her – the former hunting chase of St Peter's Monastery.

To reach the matching island of natural pasture in the north east quadrant of Hyde Park she was obliged to exit by Marlborough Gate, brave the choking flow of traffic slicing down West Carriage Drive and re-enter by Victoria Gate. Tourists and joggers who tended to hug the banks of the Serpentine rarely penetrated this quiet ungardened corner. She reminded herself of the incident when Cromwell, having sold off the entire park in three lots, allowed one of the entrepreneurial purchasers to levy an entry toll for coaches and horses. Partial – in Phyllis's view, too partial – retribution for this early exercise in privatisation had been narrowly averted when Cromwell – whilst whipping with excessive zeal the six horses drawing his coach across the park – had been thrown from the driving seat, the impact of republican buttocks upon expropriated earth resulting in the accidental, albeit harmless, discharge of his pistol.

She quickened her pace past the Nursery and Police Station, criss-crossing the pathways towards the ugly accumulation of under-passes at Speakers' Corner through which she threaded before hurrying down Park Lane, then eastwards towards the pub in Shepherd Market where, most Saturdays at noon, she met Emily, her oldest friend. She was in danger of being late. Her stride lengthened. When, glowing with exertion, she finally sank into her customary seat adjacent to the bar at the King's Arms, she was feeling more cheerful than she had been for days. She admitted as much.

'Thank God,' said Emily Barton. Ten years Phyllis's senior, she eyed the flushed young woman across their vodka and tonics. 'You were beginning to become a pain in my butt. All that angst! Does this mean that you're over James, or merely in remission?' A successful divorce lawyer, Emily had dealt with too much self-inflicted damage to sympathise with anyone displaying tendencies in that direction.

'It's not as simple as that, Emily. If I didn't care for him, well …' she shrugged – 'perhaps I wouldn't be driven to act, on occasions, with such stupidity.' She proceeded to describe her passage of arms with Jennings.

'Well now, I think we can agree that *was* stupid,' murmured Emily. 'Not like you at all. I don't care to admit to having dumb friends. Lowers the tone.'

'Sorry. I'll try to do better.'

'And it wasn't too clever declining the job offer, whatever his motives. I'm sure you could cope.'

'With him or the assignment?'

'Both. If I might offer free counsel, I suggest you should attempt to retrieve the situation. And sooner rather than later.'

'I think not. Anyway, I'm now committed to spending a few days with my parents next week. I 'phoned Mother this morning. I'm in need of a break.'

Oddly, Joan Norton had been uncharacteristically incurious when her daughter had enquired whether her visit would be convenient. 'Tuesday would be fine, dear, unless you'd like to join me for golf on Monday.'

'I think not.'

'Tuesday, then. Very timely in fact. There's a family matter I do rather need to talk over with you.'

'Oh?'

'It can wait until next week. It'll be lovely to see you.'

The King's Arms was beginning to fill with other drinkers including a noisy group of blue-scarfed soccer supporters warming up for their afternoon of catharsis at Stamford Bridge. Phyllis knew nothing of football, her interest in sport of any variety being restricted to an occasional social day at the races, but many of the aficionados, throwing their first lager of the day down their gullets, were regulars at the pub and she had grown to enjoy their harmless banter, their semi–innocent chat-up lines which Emily, shameless as ever, did nothing to discourage. Phyllis had learnt to appreciate such intercourse as an essential element of the alchemy possessed by good drinking establishments: a relaxed, unthreatening atmosphere which fosters unrecriminatory exchanges of a piquant saltiness rarely experienced by citizens of more sober habits. She had once attempted to educate a French friend to appreciate the peculiar charms of London's pubs but had wholly failed to convince her that the social inclusiveness of places like the King's Arms were infinitely superior to the misogynistic, narrowly-structured, downwardly-mobile bars of Paris, Marseilles or any other Gallic city; that barmen like Marcus (now cheerfully anticipating their need for further vodkas) were much more than mere servitors but would happily fill the rôles of confidantes, father confessors, occasional bankers in moments of emergency, and patient recipients of tired jokes.

Later, after several drinks, when the pub had begun to empty again, the two women – with Marcus in close attendance – found themselves returning to the subject of James Tull.

'When he said that he was leaving for Ireland, did he give you to understand that it would be months before he planned to return to London?' enquired Emily.

'More or less. But I don't think his intentions were wholly clear even to himself. I do know that his family had been applying pressure for him to return to Canada. And he'd certainly become disenchanted with *The Mercury* job.'

'But he expected you to drop everything and follow him into the blue yonder?'

'It would, I suppose, have been an adventure.'

'Sod that! I know he has money, but that wouldn't have been much of a consolation if things had turned sour between you after a couple of weeks and you'd found yourself stranded and jobless.' Emily, single mother of two, spoke from experience.

'Nevertheless, given the choice again ...' Phyllis shook her head. 'Perhaps it was some kind of test. Commitment and so forth. All I know is that I've never before experienced such a feeling of hollowness, of loss.' She stabbed a finger at Marcus. 'Bloody men! Why do we put up with them?'

'It's some form of occult chemistry,' said Emily. 'Some itchy, peppery, wet-knickerish chemistry.'

'Nice one,' commented Marcus.

'I have a theory that there are simply too many of them around,' Emily continued. 'Fewer would be much more manageable. We could share them out, each male given a rating in terms of sensitivity, wit, penetrative intensity, whatever.' She was becoming expansive, waving her cigarette-festooned hand above her cropped hair. 'We should reduce their number, definitely, in the interests of improving the average quality.'

'Could be good,' said Marcus, whose appetite for lusty men probably matched Emily's.

'Darlings, I've worked it all out. The National Lottery exists to finance all those wonderful projects that the tax-payer would baulk at in normal circumstances. Why not this? The secular response to a maiden's prayer!' She was inspired. 'Believe me, I've thought about this, not least when being regularly touched up on the Northern Line.'

'Tell me about it,' said Marcus.

'I will, dear boy, I will. Now, do you think it wholly fortuitous that as we speak, China has fifteen males under the age of forty for every woman of comparable immaturity? Of course not! These matters can be arranged if they are held to be of sufficient importance. Not that I'm recommending the Sinic approach. State-directed abortions of inappropriate foetuses – female in China's case, male in mine – has to be costly, painful for women and capable of manipulation. Genetic cleansing and all that. No, the West can surely come up with a more sophisticated solution, one that removes the risk of malign selectivity and at the same time avoids both physical and psychological trauma.'

'Absolutely,' agreed Marcus. 'But what?'

'I've worked it all out. The Lottery could pump money into the development of some kind of implant painlessly inserted at birth into a randomly-selected percentage of male infants. What could be simpler? The implant would, of course, be pre-programmed to release an irreversibly fatal sleeping draught some time before puberty.'

Marcus began to display alarm. 'Hang on a minute. Wouldn't the kids involved be a bit pissed off?'

'Ah, that's the beauty of it. They wouldn't know. Nor would their parents. It would be just a simple, invisible operation carried out behind the scenes in maternity wards. That's where the need for research comes into it – to develop a sufficiently subtle, non-alarmist technology.' Emily leant back, smiling triumphantly.

The three of them pondered the possibility in silence for a couple of minutes. Then, 'Sorry, it won't work,' concluded Phyllis. 'It would keep the numbers down nicely, I'll grant you. But random selection means by definition that you can't guarantee quality control. We could end up disposing of all the better blokes by accident.'

'Shit!' Emily wrinkled her brow. 'Perhaps we could make a start by tackling all those whose fathers were called Nigel. I've never known a Nigel who wasn't a bastard.'

The conversation steadily deteriorated from this point, as successive vodkas took their toll. Marcus kept a solicitous eye on them and judged to a nicety the moment at which to suggest that he might summon their cabs. After taking their leave with customary displays of affection, the two women were driven their separate ways, Emily northwards to tree-lined Maida Vale, Phyllis back to her Pimlico flat near the bus depot and the prospect of an evening in front of her television. She ate a micro-waved lasagne whilst watching the early evening news with its account of fresh outbreaks of internal Tory dissension over Europe, an issue which interested her not at all, and a brief review of the interminable negotiations about what was laughably described as 'the peace process' in Northern Ireland. Bored and restless, she scanned her newspaper to check whether any later programmes might offer some diversion, feeling too drunk to contemplate returning to the latest Rushdie novel, the remorseless playfulness of which had failed to engage her. A screening of *Cape Fear* with deNiro looked promising but how was she to occupy herself during the two hour interval before the film commenced so as to avoid the affliction of brooding further about James? She switched off the set angrily, deciding to take a stroll before darkness fell. Her apartment had begun to oppress her; she needed to feel a sense of unwalled space. She marched determinedly down Rochester Row towards the Embankment, before turning right, past the mouth of Lambeth Bridge and onwards towards the Tate Gallery now emptied of visitors, the curious configuration of the MI5 Headquarters to her left on the river's south bank. Although she had no fixed purpose, her stride, as ever, projected a don't-mess-with-me feistiness, every inch a professional, post-modern woman making her independent way in the world. Nobody observing her progress could have discerned the extent to which she was no longer assured of the solidity of the ground beneath her feet.

CHAPTER THREE

Colclough had neither anticipated nor appreciated either having been diverted from his *Irish Times* or delayed from enjoying his mid-morning brandy with Maeve Rafferty across the road. His peaceable routine had, however, been invaded by an untimely telephone call from New York. He was not looking for any further perturbation. The day had begun sourly: Annie in a strop over some difference of opinion with her husband; the weather miserable; the potentially lucrative sale of a farmhouse over in Durrus having fallen through because the prospective purchaser, a German, had picked up on the adverse publicity about the recent murder of what the locals termed a 'blow-in' – some French woman – in her cottage over at Schull. And now this rasping baritone disrupting his reflections, reinforcing his disquiet.

'And what might I be doing for you? I don't get too many calls from the USA. Quite an occasion!'

'I guess so.' His caller was in no mood for pleasantries. He cut directly to business. 'Do you recall meeting my associate, Mr James Tull, a month or so ago? He expressed an interest in a certain property on ... have I got this right? ... the Rossbrin Road.'

'Let me see now. Didn't I contact somebody in London a while back to explain –'

'Yeah. I know about that. You'd been checking out the willingness of the owner to sell. And getting nowhere.'

'I've had a real problem reaching them. They've moved away, you see.'

'So I understand, Mr Colclough. But may I take that you do know precisely where Mr Kierney might be contacted, the authorities permitting?'

Colclough sucked his teeth. He was beginning to dislike with some passion this transatlantic voice which, he correctly divined, carried an undertone of contempt; and he was distinctly unsettled by the

New Yorker's use of Tom Kierney's name. Someone had been busy. He said, 'Ah, well, that's part of the difficulty, don't you know.'

'Not entirely, given that the property's title is actually vested in his wife. A very practical arrangement from our point of view since Mr Kierney is not likely to be moving in polite society for a heap of time.' The voice paused to allow Colclough to reassess the situation; then 'Would it surprise you to learn that Mrs Kierney is ... as we speak ... in the USA?'

'It would. It surely would.' Matters were moving too quickly for Colclough's comfort. 'Hey, it's just struck me. Isn't it the middle of the night over there?'

'Early morning. Very early. Time to catch worms.' A faint gust of laughter breathed down the wire. 'Let me level with you, Colclough.' All politeness gone. 'I really want that you understand where I'm coming from. We ... that is, Mr Tull's associates ... are set on buying the house ... what's its goddam name? ... Bracken Point. And Moira Kierney wants to sell. Christ, does she want to sell! Like yesterday. So we have a deal made in heaven.'

Colclough held back his irritation. 'You're absolutely sure she's able ... that is, legally in a position ... to sell?'

'Do I make that kind of mistake? And, what d'you know, there's no mortgage on the place. Either the Kierneys are richer than they seem or they have generous friends.'

'Their friends may want their donation back.'

'Are you saying there is a donation, Colclough?'

'Just guessing.'

'Thought so.' Another sarcastic laugh. 'Let me be as clear as I can. Whoever lent the Kierneys the money to buy the place is no concern of mine. Bracken Point is incontrovertibly in the wife's name. She's wetting herself to sell. And she knows we'll take care of her. She's had enough of the husband, and of Ireland.' The voice rolled over Colclough like a dark rip-tide. 'We could handle the whole thing from here. We're deeply professional. Deeply! How else would we have tracked down the Kierneys? How else would we have spirited the lady from Limerick? At her insistence, let me add. And we've settled on a price. Three hundred thousand dollars. Generous in the circumstances, doncha think?'

Colclough, now greatly concerned, broke in, ' So, what do you want of me? You seem to have everything sewn up. But there'll be consequences. People will soon find out what's happening. Around here if you fart in Ballydehob they'll know in Crosshaven within the hour what you had for breakfast.'

'That's kinda what Moira tells us. And that's why we're having this conversation, Colclough. Personally, I see no reason to keep you in the frame but others reckon you might serve to ease things along locally in the early stages, talk to the right people, know what I mean? We guess it's worthwhile buying goodwill. So you end up with a fat cheque for what we'll call a handling fee although whether it would exactly be clever to keep it all in your personal account is your call.'

Colclough struggled for coherence. 'So what exactly …?'

'There's work to be done on the place. We need plans and a detailed survey. The woman has given us written authorisation for immediate access. Get someone reliable to handle it. All documentation will be with you within twenty-four hours. The legalities will be handled by our London associates. You won't be involved in any of that stuff. Your job is to help us make the place habitable by Christmas. So are you on board, or not?'

Trouble had finally flooded up to Maurice Colclough's doorstep but he was beginning to discern where safe ground might be found. After all, he had done nothing to promote the sale. Far from it. Surely, that would be understood. And it was more sensible to remain within the loop than to be wholly uninvolved in whatever was happening at Bracken Point. That too would be appreciated. As for the money, he could work out the angles in his own good time. What worried him more immediately was his total vagueness about the identity of the people with whom he was being obliged to deal. He phrased his response with due care.

'Would you kindly convey to Mr Tull just how much I appreciate his remembering me in this way. I … ah … take it that the documents you'll be after sending will also confirm your status and that sort of thing. One has, as you'll appreciate, to be so careful these days. So, subject to that detail, naturally I'll try to meet his requirements.'

'Mr Tull will be real glad to hear it. He's told me you're exactly the kind of guy we need to look after our interests on the ground. And incidentally, feel free to cut deals locally within whatever budget we eventually settle on. Can't say we aren't generous. And we want an immediate start on the basic stuff, like fixing the roof. We'll decide what improvements to make when we've had a chance to look over the place. Some of our people will be visiting with you real soon.'

'And Mr Tull? Will I be seeing him?'

'In time, I guess. He's pretty well tied up at present. But he did ask me to say how much he'd enjoyed meeting with you, and he especially wanted to say "Hi" to Annie. You'll do that for me, won't you? Incidentally, my name's Marotti. Joseph Marotti.' A valedictory gust of mirth terminated the conversation.

Colclough, at his obsessively tidy desk in the small office above the bar, adjacent to his comfortable living quarters, stared for several minutes at the cascades of October rain conjuring the gunnels of Ballydehob's steep streets into rivers of near-continental grandeur. Clouds the colour of milk edged with caramel bullied their way inland from the Atlantic, unforgiving in their intensity. He watched two women struggling to load shopping into the boot of a mud-streaked Ford Escort, head-scarves unfurling in an ecstasy of whipped motion.

He knew them both. Each would, if squeezed over a glass of lager and blackcurrant, have tales to tell of Moira Kierney. They would have witnessed her at communion, or at Duggan's, the grocers, on her weekly shop or less frequently here in Colclough's own beerhouse: a sour, barren creature of little conversation with, he recalled, a preference for brandy. Her husband, electrician by trade, demolition expert by choice, had often been away, rumoured to be chasing employment on building sites in Prague or Budapest, but now known to be residing in Albany Prison on the Isle of Wight. Tom Kierney would not be best pleased to learn of Moira's venture into property dealing. Before being lifted in Kilburn, following what locals referred to as an incident in Birmingham, he would – on his irregular visits to West Cork – be seen in company only when accompanying Moira to Casey's, a hard man hunched uncommunicatively over his Guinness, effortlessly spreading unease among the regulars, putting a damper on the evening's *craic*.

Colclough had been told that, whereas Moira's father had been a well-to-do dentist from Omagh, Tom had sprung from the wilder mountains of Donegal, a farmer's son born near Slieve Snacht, who had obtained his basic technical education in Galway, and his more advanced applied skills in Libya. It had never been established how he had met Moira, but gossip had it that she had abandoned a university course in Belfast to waitress in Belgium and Holland before returning to Ireland a married woman. She had made few friends in West Cork and there would now be even fewer who would own up to that status. Once he broke the news, that is; a task he was not relishing and certainly not one to be discharged casually. Sighing, he took his raincoat from its cupboard. In this weather it would be a cold and miserable journey to Bandon but it would not be prudent to delay.

He descended to the bar where Annie had been cleaning out the pipes, her cheeks pink with effort. A single customer, old Brendan Mulcahy, was occupying his usual seat nearest the uncurtained window from where he could keep a rheumy eye on the town.

'I'll be out for the rest of the day. Can you manage?'

She shrugged. 'Have to. Not that we're being run off our feet.' She took in the tension on his face, the stiff set of his shoulders. Not a time to trifle with him. He turned his back on Brendan and spoke quietly, although she judged not softly enough.

'Just heard about Bracken Point. Looks as though the sale's going ahead. Unfortunately. Which means I've a few things that need sorting.'

''Tis a shame to have to be abroad on a morning like this. Look at that rain; it's delving down. I wouldn't put out a milk bottle in such weather.'

He shrugged, staring morosely around the shadowed bar, grey light seeping through high slats of windows to reveal gouged table surfaces still stained with last night's beer. He trailed a meaningful finger across a film of dust on a nearby chair-back, sniffed, then stepped out into the slanting downpour. Annie watched his short-arsed figure dipping into the wind, as he scurried the few yards to his car. One of the reasons she fancied him was the whiff of ambiguity that hung around him like a trace of his musk aftershave emanating from obscure recesses, simultaneously beckoning and menacing. She knew most Ballydehob people disliked him, distrusting his Welsh genes, his professional egregiousness, his shady connections, his general cockiness. That wasn't a problem for Annie. She knew his weaknesses well enough, but they were shared by so few other men in that part of West Cork that, to her eyes, Colclough achieved a tasty distinctiveness.

Still, he was not at the forefront of her preoccupations on this particularly miserable morning. She had problems of her own: a husband arriving unexpectedly at the house and she unprepared altogether, with the smell of another man still on her and the bed cold. Somehow she had diverted him with a not wholly feigned show of anger, her housewifely panic over lack of notice, her eventual melting absolution of his thoughtlessness. She hoped that Colclough would not unduly delay his return from Bandon – for she knew well enough what he was about – because she was keen not to keep Eamonn waiting for his supper.

Brendan tapped his glass with a far-from-clean finger, the less to indicate his need for a refill than to demonstrate his alertness. 'So Moira Kierney's on the move, permanent like?'

'What would you be knowing about anything, Brendan?'

'I have a bloody sharp nose about me, woman, sharp as scissors.' He twitched his thin lips. 'Someone was after telling me he drove Moira from Glengarriff to Shannon last Tuesday. With a fair load of baggage and all, so he did.'

Annie sighed. 'That would be your Padraig. God help me if I ever need to do a quiet flit from these parts. I'd have to charter a fucking helicopter to pick me up from the back of the mountain, and even so I'd probably find that one of your damn blow-offs was flying the thing, so I would.'

He cackled and again tapped his jar. During her ritual preparation of his next Guinness Brendan offered the opinion that the Kierneys would not be greatly missed, and indeed that he'd welcome his ears no longer having to suffer the woman's barbaric Ulster accent.

Annie could not remember a time when Brendan, long a widower, had not monopolised that seat by the window, morning and evening. Newspaper across his knees, studying form, pronouncing judgement on his peers, making no apparent difference but fixedly occupying his determined space in Ballydehob's diurnal passages. He had been retired from the cement factory since before she had left school, had sunk pints with her father, dead these five years, had outlived most of the town. His seven children and their innumerable offspring lived close by, colonising a council house terrace along the rise along the Durrus Road. Each of his sons now took a turn at collecting Brendan towards dinner time when his steady intake of booze made a directional hand essential. Last year, prior to the institution of this support system, he had on several occasions been found crawling on hands and knees up the hill, perfectly civil but presenting something of an embarrassing challenge to the conscience of those stumbling over him. Shamed, his boys had, despite his objections, assumed a duty of care, monitoring his few movements, ensuring that he was properly clad and fed.

He had few friends still alive, but he was always active on the fringe of others' conversations, putting in his sour comments, picking up shards of gossip. He was humoured as was proper for a man of his years, but not with affection. Few willingly parked themselves next to him or bought him a pint: there was a former colleague at the factory who would yarn about distant grievances, and an insurance broker from Cork City who called in when his business brought him in this direction and who seemed to take a peculiar delight in prompting Brendan into recounting his scurrilous sagas of petty misdemeanours and disasters. But otherwise Brendan was left to himself and his sharp observances.

As Annie handed him his fresh glass he adjusted the woollen cap which he wore, indoors and out, in all weathers, fitted snugly over his protruding ears. She had read somewhere that a man's ears continued to grow throughout his life; Brendan's were startling tributes to longevity. Beneath the cap – one of an ancient pair he had bought during his time with the fishing fleet off Iceland – he was magnificently hairless, a gleaming condition in which he took inordinate pride. 'No grass grows on a busy track,' he would boast on those rare occasions when his pate was accidentally exposed. Now he sat before her, licking his thin lips, moist with stout, weighing the significance of Moira Kierney's departure. Speculation around such happenings brought substance and pleasure into his narrowed existence. He said, 'I remember that Englishman. Looked as though he had deep pockets. 'Tis a fact he'll need a bob or two to put Bracken Point in a decent way again.'

'Maurice says he isn't English.'

The old man ignored her intervention, focusing on his own line of thought. 'I allus wondered how them Kierneys could afford that place, for certain it was a grand house when they first moved in. And by all the saints we had the answer to that when the British took Tom.'

'Good riddance, says I. Them Kierneys are trouble through and through. Let them take their mischief somewheres else.' She swished her towel dismissively.

He fixed her with a sharp look. 'Let's hope to Jasus the mischief has moved with 'em, but I doubt it so. Might that be the business that's taken Maurice out of doors in such weather instead of being comfortably tucked up in Maeve Rafferty's snug!'

'And why should you be thinking such a thing?'

'Ah now, it's a well-connected fella he is, so. And you'd be after knowing his connections better than most.' The old man rose to ease himself in the direction of the bog, rubbing his nostrils slyly as he passed her.

Annie shrugged. She could survive his insinuations. There were greater problems in her life. Eamonn had not been a demanding husband, until now. She had wondered occasionally whether he knew a great deal more about her infidelity than he ever cared to show but had chosen not to argue with having to share the good fortune of his wifely possession with another, provided his charity went unremarked upon. But, given his high temper, that seemed unlikely. Moreover he had recently let her know that he craved a child, a secular epiphany that she, for her part, would sooner avoid. Evasion, however, was demanding a degree of artfulness that she found it increasingly difficult to supply, what with Father Dominic dropping leaden hints, and with Eamonn springing sudden visitations upon her, and with her mother's crude promptings.

Brendan reappeared, adjusting his flies with deliberate carelessness, offering her a glimpse of his pale and shrivelled manhood. This was not a unique occurrence. He possibly regarded it as her treat.

'Did you wash your hands, so?' she demanded.

'At my time of life, who cares?'

'In that case, you won't find me giving them a warm.'

He raised his finger-tips to his nostrils. 'Better than roses, my girl.'

'Dandelions, more like!'

'Ten years younger and I'd be after getting you into trouble.'

She snorted. 'Try thirty!'

He stared at his glass. Thirty years. In 1965 he'd been in his mid-forties, in his pomp, well known in Liverpool and Glasgow, having been over the water, or on it, or under it, since his twenties, sending good money regularly to his wife in Wexford, reaping the sea and proud of his wiry muscularity. But somewhere along the way, he couldn't calculate when or how, he'd caved in, become undemanding, diminished, ceased outfacing the devil. He had eventually returned to Ireland like a dying salmon, although still physically vigorous; had moved his family to County Cork; had taken the bloody job in the cement works; had discovered Casey's; had grown old.

Outside, he observed the rain slackening. It was approaching noon. Others began to enter the bar. Some he greeted; a couple he ignored, maintaining standards. Annie kept her eye on him, seeing to his supply of Guinness, exchanging the occasional unserious insult. After a while he ordered fish pie and ate it noisily.

Three hours later Colclough returned. His humour had not improved, nor did a rapidly-consumed couple of Powers mellow him. He did not react kindly to the news that Annie would be leaving early and that he would have to man the bar until Declan, the usual Tuesday night replacement, arrived at six. Damn and blast! It was proving to be a real bitch of a day.

The meeting in Bandon had gone badly. They had reacted with a ferocity that he had not anticipated. Hadn't he thought it odd that some hot-shot Yank would have bothered to telephone at some God-awful early hour, New York time? Where were his fucking antennae? How did he know that the call hadn't been made from just around the corner? Had it not occurred to him that someone might have been watching to see how he responded to having his cage rattled? Had he taken the trouble to check whether anyone had followed him to Bandon? Colclough had sweated hard, twisting in his chair, inwardly cursing himself for his unpreparedness to deal with such questioning; but had slowly begun to fight back, his colour rising.

Wasn't it the case that nobody had been able to trace Moira Kierney since Paddy Mulcahy drove her to Shannon last week? Didn't that support the proposition that she was indeed over the big water? And if the promised documentation materialised, wouldn't that cast doubt on any conspiracy theory? And what would be more natural than his prompt visit to a well-known building contractor to check on their willingness to carry out work at Bracken Point? Anyway, why should the Brits or the Gardai be interested in the place any longer? There was nothing to be learnt from the house; it was clean, and the old van and dinghy had been disposed of shortly after they had learnt of Tull's initial enquiry, just in case.

After an interminable hour they had begun to be persuaded. They had noted the name of the New Yorker and one of them, a blond man unknown to Colclough, had left the room to make a few telephone calls. Before Colclough had been dismissed it seemed they had received some confirmation of Marotti's existence. He had, however, been severely warned about his lack of prudence, an admonition he had taken the more badly because he knew it was deserved. He had been jerked into precipitate action. He had been manipulated. It hurt.

On the way home he had driven by the house, to curse it. Damn the Kierneys to hell! Damn James Tull! He had stared morosely at the green wreck of its surrounds, a wilderness of bushes heavy with glistening moisture, beyond which the building squatted defensively, warding off angry squalls whipping in from the bay. Spikes of wild irises, their leaves fractured and angled, shivered under their beating. Brambles snatched at his trousers as he stepped out of his Land Rover to take a clearer, malign, look at the place. The gutters, he noted, would require early attention; a black slick of dampness extended from the roof down to the front door. Beyond the house he could just make out, through an enveloping mist, a fishing smack beating its way to harbour. Not a day to be in open water. Not a day for any manner of exposure.

He tried to imagine what had moved Tull to act so determinedly to acquire the place. A man with his means might have been expected to look for somewhere less unremarkable, unless – and the thought brought him no comfort – he had been searching for a property with exactly those qualities that had brought the Kierneys there in the first instance. He climbed back into his car, damp, cold and tired; and arrived back at Casey's in low spirits.

Nursing his third whiskey he watched Annie putting on her raincoat and took what comfort he could from the sight of her thick auburn hair being tucked protectively inside her yellow scarf, and of her shapely rear as she bent to don her outdoor shoes. His proprietorial satisfaction was, however, short-lived. Her husband shouldering in at the door, wind at his back, had driven around in his lorry to spare Annie a longish walk home in the wet. Colclough controlled his irritation at Eamonn's unlooked-for arrival, conscious of Annie's mild embarrassment and Brendan's sly smirk. He busied himself with unwashed glasses until the couple was ready to depart, addressing his forced jocular remarks to a quartet of regulars playing brag in their usual smoky corner.

Annie said, 'See you in the morning.'

'As ever.'

'Thanks for letting me off early.'

'As if I had a choice.'

He fingered his control to activate the television in a gesture of dismissal. He was becoming too dependent on the woman's attentions. At first it had been nothing but a bit of selfish convenience, a way of giving each other a modicum of animal comfort during long nights which would otherwise have been spent in pointless solitude; no harm in it for anybody. But he now knew it had evolved into something darker, a witch's brew that gave off pain as well as pleasure; a novel sensation for a man who had prided himself on his painted butterfly reputation among ladies along the Republic's southern seaboard: a charmer who gave momentary delight wherever he settled but who never lingered, and who was prized for the reliability of his transitoriness. Others may have offered a less complimentary interpretation of his behaviour but most were agreed that Maurice Colclough was not someone who overstayed his welcome. He had made a virtue of superficiality, of never having to be taken seriously except, naturally, when money was involved. Nobody was altogether clear as to how he had managed to accumulate enough in his bank account to acquire both Casey's and another small hotel in Kenmare which his sister managed on his behalf, but general opinion had it that he had speculated successfully in property, catching the tide which had, during the eighties, swept a pile of Euro money into Ireland. He talked openly of his Welsh antecedents, a condition to which people found it difficult to take exception, however much they were tempted to do so, because it was a heritage he shared with Saint Patrick; but of his early life in Wexford not much was known, and his sister was not famed for loquacity. The only thing that could be said with confidence about Colclough, which was indeed frequently said, was that he was a man with connections. He knew everyone in Cork, Waterford and beyond; and they all seemed to know him, although few were certain of the advantages of doing so. Very few detected the traces of exoticism and ambiguity that Annie had divined; but then very few knew him as intimately. Which is how he preferred it.

He stared at the TV. The early news programme was highlighting the blocked peace negotiations in Ulster. He shook his head. What a monster surprise! Did turkeys vote for Christmas?

The bar was slowly filling with its normal evening trade. On most Fridays and weekends he had introduced musicians and the place became crowded, but today being Tuesday he did not expect much by way of business. Nevertheless he was much relieved when Declan Feeney arrived to take over. He poured himself another Powers and, after an abbreviated tour of his clientele, slouched upstairs to take a shower in an attempt to sluice away the day's frustrations. Cleansed, he watched a porno video for an hour, penis in hand, thinking of Annie.

CHAPTER FOUR

Driving faster than was prudent down the motorway, Leeds Castle glimmering distantly westwards, Phyllis found herself as usual reflecting upon the unhappy historical relationship between her parents' adopted county and the continental mainland: for example, Jutish Hengest scrambling from his black longboat at Thanet, ostensibly to succour, but all too readily thereafter to supplant hapless Vortigern. She always derived pleasure from the remembrance that the Jutes had fixed the value of their currency – the shilling – by reference to the price of a cow in Kent but to a sheep elsewhere. Her memory summoned up Caius Julius Caesar probing with his legions from Deal; and Dover's chalky palisades, the sight of which had persuaded William the Bastard to shift his rapacious Normans westwards to Pevensey; and Tom Beckett bleeding in St Augustine's Canterbury for having stuck to pan-European attitudes in defiance of Henry's modish concept of national sovereignty; and Biggin Hill's Spitfires and Hurricanes clearing the Luftwaffe from London's approaches. And, now, the more subtle French imperialists establishing their tunneled beach-heads at Ashford and Folkestone. What might Dickens, who had once lived just over there, to her left in Rochester, have made of this Gallic incursion? Or, more pertinently Henry V whose invasion fleet had been assembled not far to her right in the long-lost wharves of Small Hythe, the anvil of Agincourt.

She found herself recalling a half-drunken debate between Tull and Jennings, some four months earlier at a drinks party in Blackheath hosted by June Templeton, an upwardly-motivated Labour Member of the European Parliament. Jennings had been in ebullient form, buoyed up by a conviction that his paper's steady drip-feed of sceptical opinion had begun to swing Government Ministers away from further entanglements with Brussels, fragile though the Tory's hold on power was becoming. He had long seen the late twentieth century's drift towards federalism in Europe as a threat to the values that he held to be quintessentially English, and regarded the French in particular as the malign authors of this strategy. His spectacles misted as his assertions grew more heated, his vivid aquamarine braces seemingly thrusting forward over his well-fleshed pectorals like a pair of martial insignias.

'The French are less distressed by their successive humiliations at the hands of the Germans than by their awareness of indebtedness to the British for having rescued them twice this century. They know their La Rochefoucauld – "Diligence in returning good for good becomes a form of servitude loathesome to tolerate." The French can never forgive any nation that does them a favour.'

Tull had bridled. 'Whilst the English continue to complain that nothing but ill comes your way from across the channel. Here you are, unloved and unlovable, the sterile maiden aunt of Europe, censorious, self-absorbed, quick to take offence, vaguely aware that others take little pleasure in your company but uncomprehending of the reasons for such lack of popularity.' Tull had gone dangerously close, by the manner in which he delivered these remarks, to associating Jennings with this catalogue of national traits. There had been a moment of coolness during which Jennings had stared owlishly at his journalist colleague in a silent display of gravitas calculated to establish, in the eyes of onlookers, his editorial pre-eminence.

June Templeton had attempted to ease the awkwardness with some light remark about Margaret Thatcher, a comment which led someone to refer to Bruges and thence to Waterloo and finally to Wellington, thus allowing Jennings to re-launch himself. He could never resist an opportunity to parade his credentials as a lecturer in 19th Century European History, a career path he had trod briefly on graduating from Oxford, before being seduced by journalism.

'The curious thing is that Wellington, when he was merely the impecunious and unpromising Arthur Wesley, was enrolled by his parents at a French military academy, Angers, as "*un gentilhomme Irlandais*". So you see, Tull, I am prepared to concede that we occasionally benefit from exposure to French influences. Oddly enough' – Jennings was now in irresistible flow – 'Wellington arrived in Angers only two years after a chap called Bonaparte had graduated from a sister academy a few miles distant at Champagne.' He went on, unconscious of his listeners' wavering attention, to relate the familiar story of how the adolescent Arthur had desired above all to devote himself not to the arts of war but to the violin, a talent inherited from his father. It was at this point that Tull, with a shake of his head, had taken Phyllis by her elbow to steer her towards the garden, exercising a degree of proprietorial firmness she had found not wholly welcome. She now remembered that Tull had muttered something about his French genes being offended, a statement which puzzled her since she had always thought of him as an émigré Scots-Canadian, but she had responded by pointing out that she did not take kindly to masterful behaviour and moreover had no great affection for hydrangeas. He had laughed stonily before temporarily abandoning her amid the damp foliage.

Had that been the moment at which the seed of their later parting was sown? They had, she calculated, been lovers for eight months by the date of June Templeton's party, her sense of the solidity of their relationship deepening week by week, but his brief display of peevishness, combined with his cavalier attempt to control her, could well have triggered one of those subtle, scarcely recognisable, seismic shifts of feeling; an instant in which irritation supplanted attraction. She had seen the flash of antagonism in his green eyes even as he had laughed at her protest. He was, she realised, unused to being checked.

She was still reflecting on that experience when the sign for Ashford Junction brought her back to more imminent concerns. What particular item of family business might it be that her mother wished to discuss? Not again, she hoped, that wretched issue of inheritance. Two years ago a protracted negotiation over the terms of her father's proposed disposition of spoils had been deeply distasteful. Her parents' declared aim was to equalise over time the financial benefits accruing to their son and two daughters, a process weighted and complicated by the anticipatory consumption of a substantial slice of assets by the cost of educating three grandchildren: one fathered by her brother, Peter; and two produced out of wedlock, by different lovers, by her younger sister, Susan. Phyllis devoutly hoped that nothing had happened to destabilise the delicate accommodation that, after much debate, had been reached with barely-concealed rancour. Surely Sue could not be pregnant again! If so, Phyllis was determined to resist any further pandering to Arnold's favourite little girl. It had always rankled that her father treated Susan's misdemeanours so lightly, not least when he fondled her fractious kids (one boy with an Iranian father, the older girl with Jamaican antecedents) and dared to make comparisons with Phyllis's lack of procreative progress.

She turned north-east on to the A28 before diverting right again through Wye. Home, if such it was, lay in the next valley, its deeply-wooded approaches displaying the first onset of winter, leaves shredding from the branches in a keen wind, the invasive pines standing out ever darker against their fading neighbours of sycamore and ash. The nearer she drew to her parents' house, the more disquieted she became. She could not recall a time when she had been wholly at ease in this place. *Urbe in rus*, an unconvincing transplantation of suburban attitudes into the Kentish landscape, had always jarred her sensibilities. The countryside, she felt, should be something other, something wilder, than a steady aggregation of lovingly tended gardens.

She had been in her mid-teens when her father had moved them from Eltham to the converted parsonage considered by him to be a more suitable environment in which to bring children to maturity. He had, his career thriving, also shrewdly taken a pied-à-terre near the Isle of Dogs, a neighbourhood shortly to be transformed – to his intense satisfaction – by the brash revival of London's Docklands. He thereafter stayed in town most evenings during the week, normally rejoining his semi-detached family on Friday evenings. Gradually he had ceased to be the familiar reassuring presence, snorting over breakfast at some offensive passage in the *Daily Telegraph*; complaining at his delayed access to the bathroom; hunting for his golf socks; chiding Peter for his less-than-perfect school results; pottering, awkward among privets, around the garden with his mis-applied secateurs.

This division of Arnold's life between the City and the hamlet had somehow altered the chemistry of his relationship with the family, had objectified him, turning him into a figure that could be observed more distantly in emotional terms; had thrown into sharper relief those selfish corners of his personality which, Phyllis now observed, had never quite bent to meet their domestic concerns. Phyllis recalled some blazing rows as he had begun to wrestle with the onset of her womanhood. She had been much relieved when, at the age of fifteen, she had obtained a scholarship at an agreeably distant boarding school. Three years later she had moved to Durham, then Cambridge and, after obtaining her Doctorate, had made it clear that she intended to live independently in London. She was inclined to take for granted the generous allowance which her father had willingly provided, and continued to provide, an emolument enabling her to live comfortably beyond the confines of her salary.

Arnold Norton was now semi-retired. Phyllis would meet him for occasional lunches in the City, usually with her brother sharing the experience, but her trips to Kent were infrequent. Her mother referred to them as 'Phyllis's swift forays, taking no prisoners'. But her parents made few serious complaints about her inattentiveness despite her siblings' superior performance in that respect. Susan, she knew, was always trekking across from Brighton with her brood, whilst first-born Peter, to whom Phyllis spoke on the telephone at regular intervals, remained close to their father, sharing an enthusiasm for cricket, real ale, pipe tobacco and Mensa, a combination she regarded as unacceptable to the power of four. Moreover, she made no effort to visit the homes of either Peter or Susan, certainly not the latter who shared with her raucous offspring a disorganised and not particularly clean housing association flat in a 1960s tower block with an intimate view of Brighton station. Peter frequently invited Phyllis for Sunday lunches at his neat semi-detached in Ruislip but the prospect of protracted conversation with his rancorous wife, Sandra, invariably encouraged Phyllis to invent some passable excuse. Peter, she felt, had prematurely settled for a life of comfortable mediocrity; he himself had described his existence as 'second-class suburban'. He was some kind of civil servant in Customs and Excise – she had never been sufficiently interested to probe him for details – having entered Whitehall immediately upon having secured his First in Law at Cambridge. And although she was saddened by his loss of the youthful blond attractiveness and the intellectual fizz she had once so much admired, he retained a warm corner in her affections; unlike Susan whose untidy affairs and feckless life-style she found irritating.

She had almost reached the end of her journey. Her Ford turned off the narrow road some half mile beyond the public house and jolted down the final stretch of unmade track, woodland on either side rising to the Weald's crest, bringing her at last to the white gates of the former rectory. She discerned her mother's outline through the kitchen window, doubtless fussing over preparations for lunch. The engine's sound brought both parents to their front porch.

'Darling, you look so well.' Joan Norton was perpetually surprised by the capital's inability to induce in her daughter a wanness she assumed to be obligatory among metro-dwellers. 'Was the journey dreadful?'

'Not in the least.'

'We didn't know whether you would remember how to get here.' Her father's opening remark was typically waspish, but he placed his arm around her shoulders before attending to her baggage.

Phyllis made an effort. 'The garden is still lovely, Mother. How were the apples this year?'

'Not marvellous. It's been unbelievably dry. You really should have come down to enjoy some of our summer. I know it's been intolerable in town. You could have brought James too, you know. How is he by the way?'

'Abroad at the moment.' Phyllis did not elaborate.

Joan's grey eyes – all three women in the family shared her colouring – scanned her daughter's face for signs of trouble and found them. After all, what else would have brought her from London mid-week? But she had come to a house where trouble was already installed.

She was a tall woman, stately, approaching sixty but still handsome; attractive in a riding-to-hounds fashion. Hailing originally from Dorset, she had felt truly fulfilled when Arnold had moved the household from south-east London some two decades ago. Over those subsequent largely untroubled years she had moulded the house and garden in her image. It had become inseparable from her, from all that she held dear.

She knew it would never be her daughters' home. Phyllis was an urban creature, moving among sophisticates, needing to be immersed in the flux of ideas which only cities can generate; whilst Susan was simply too wild, unpredictable. Moreover her younger daughter had a taste for life by the sea, revelling in its restless physicality, its changeable moods. As for Peter, the prospect of his wife moving proprietorially among the house's delights and inflicting her barbarisms upon them was too unpleasant for Joan to countenance, a possibility only to be lit upon for it to be immediately rejected. No, this place was hers, hers alone, to be nurtured by her broad competent hands whose shape suggested a degree of assurance that belied her inner uncertainties. She ran those practical fingers through her cropped, now-whitening hair, watching Arnold hauling two suitcases into the hallway.

He was a tall, well-preserved 62 year old, bald these many Octobers, prow-nosed above a strong but petulant mouth. His powerful buttocks preceded Phyllis up the stairs to the primrose-hued room she had occupied as a child. She smelt the familiar odours but experienced no nostalgia. He stood, framed by the lace-shrouded window, face in shadow. 'You'll need a wash before lunch, I expect. I'm just off to the Mucky Duck for my usual but I'll be back about one-thirty.' She observed the sallowness around his faded blue eyes. 'Mother will doubtless be glad of your company.'

Left alone, she sat in the window-seat, watching him stride up the lane, shoulders hunched against the wind. It would take him twenty minutes to reach the pub on foot, the same to return, leaving an hour's drinking. Not excessive, although she guessed he had already sampled the household Scotch. He had, she noted, not kissed her cheek, his customary greeting, nor squeezed her hand. His figure lost definition as it moved away through the bare bones of syca-mores. Not really a smile, either.

Her mother brought up a cup of coffee and sat at the bed's foot. She observed, 'You've begun to smoke again.'

'Occasionally. When I feel unloved.'

'Darling! What a thing to say! You know how dear you are to us.' Joan's hands flapped in protest. Then, 'Or was it someone else you have in mind?'

'Well, you must have guessed that it needed some minor crisis to bring me down here.'

Joan rose to hold her stiffening daughter close. 'I suppose it's James.' This was not a situation on which she felt capable of making adequate comment. Not now. Not today. But she hugged Phyllis tightly. 'Is it over? I had thought that, at last, you ... '

'I don't know. He's moved out of London. Suddenly. He asked me to go with him, but I couldn't convince myself that he meant it.' For the first time since Tull's departure she began to consider the possibility that his absence might be permanent. She shivered.

Joan drew back a little, questioningly. 'It's not one of those Victorian situations, is it, darling?'

'Good God, no!' She forced a smile. 'One single mother in this family is quite sufficient.'

'Actually,' said Joan, 'we already have a second.' She could not believe the words had slipped out. Stunned by her indiscipline, she sat down heavily, catching her breath. 'In a manner of speaking.'

Silence settled on the two women as they avoided each other's eyes. Phyllis drew on her cigarette. Joan fiddled with a coffee cup. A fly huzzahed behind the curtains, celebrating its survival in such an immaculate setting. Finally the daughter, who realised that she might be drawing close to the source of the unaccustomed coolness she had sensed in the household, said cautiously, 'I'm not sure I'm following you.'

Joan attempted to select her words with care. ' It seems, my dear, that we belong to an extending family.'

'What on earth – please speak plainly – I still don't understand.'

'Neither do I. Nothing makes much sense any more. Do you know that when Arnold first told me, I took to composing rather savage limericks. Quite unlike me.

There is a young woman in Harrow

Whose cunt is arousingly narrow ...'

'Mother!'

'Oh, I know, darling. I know. It's all in the worst possible taste.' She tasted tears, fought them back.

Phyllis was gripped by indignation. Harrow was the clue, wrongly, she seized upon. 'Christ, it's too bad. I know Sandra is a miserable cow ... she'd drive most men to it ... but Peter knew perfectly well what he was marrying. How could he? What does Sue call him? Captain Sensible! The safe older brother. How could he be so stupid?'

Joan smiled grimly. 'He hasn't ... isn't ... my dear. If only. I'm not talking about Peter.'

Lunch was consumed in silence. Light conversation was quite impossible. Arnold kept his eyes on the crossword at his elbow throughout. It was only when he rose, with absolute normality, to pour himself a digestive whisky that Phyllis's restraint collapsed.

'Why couldn't you use a whore or subscribe to a porn channel like other middle-aged men with your problem?' She was aware that her voice was resonating harshly around the walls of this normally well-ordered and sedate house. 'Or did you positively want to inflict pain on your family?'

He stiffened. 'When did you last give a damn about this family, may I ask?'

Joan sat amid the ruins of her apple pie, white-knuckled above the starched tablecloth, watching her husband, dark against the late sunlight slanting through a narrow window and splintering the room's gloom. She wanted to escape to the garden, to leave behind the conflict and recrimination fermenting around her, to lose herself amid the shadowed leaves and the deep scents of autumn; but her daughter now stood behind her, fingers gripping her shoulders, converting her into a bastion of silently outraged womanhood from which Phyllis hurled her barbs at the man who now represented to her more, much more, than merely an errant father. Arnold, however, refused to buckle.

'Such astounding prudery from a child of the sixties. I've slept with only two women in my entire life. May I enquire after your tally to date?'

'I'm not married.'

'Indeed not. But I believe you've had lovers who were. I even remember one or two of them having been brought down here for an occasional weekend. No moral outrage then that I can recall.' His voice was steady, rehearsed. 'You must know how distressing exchanges of this nature are for your mother. I see no need for it.'

'So you're not prepared to apologise?'

'Not, my dear, to you.'

There had been a time when Phyllis would have intimidated him, but her capacity to do so had diminished over the years of her adulthood as he had come to recognise the extent to which she had progressively distanced herself from him. He did not know why the estrangement had occurred but had adapted to it, acknowledging its probable permanence. He did not flinch, therefore, when, ignoring his plea to spare Joan's feelings, she snarled her next question.

'And you're still seeing this woman?'

'Her name is Helen. Please use it. And yes, I visit her regularly. And our child, whose name is Alex.'

'What do Peter and Sue make of this adventure?'

He shrugged. 'Peter has known for some time. It doesn't seem to perturb him. Susan will doubtless learn of it soon enough. But again, why should she care, given her track record?'

'She will care quickly enough when she realises your financial support for her kids is threatened. No doubt you're paying for this latest addition to the Norton collection of bastards.'

Joan broke free of her daughter's grip. 'That's enough!' She was nauseous, clutching her stomach. 'I can't bear any more of this.'

Arnold had also endured sufficient taunts from this mordant accuser into whom his once engaging and companionable daughter had metamorphosed; and he suspected that even had an explanation for her antagonism offered itself he might now prove indifferent to it. 'We can discuss money matters – my money, incidentally – at some other time, when you've succeeded in curbing your tongue.

And if you can't curb it, you'd better prepare to take yourself back to London tonight, my girl.' With which he left the room with an assurance Phyllis found crushing.

About an hour later Peter Norton, slightly unnerved by the importunate call to his office from his sister, sought refuge in evasion. 'Really, Sis, I can't talk about it now. I'm about to be summoned to a meeting. Yes, I know I should have put you in the picture before now, but it seemed more appropriate to leave it to Mum' – a style of address Phyllis regarded with distaste – 'and it's not my fault you don't get in touch with her for weeks on end. What? Well, I do know a little about his intentions.'

'Which are?'

'It's clear that he's not ducking his responsibilities towards Helen. In fact, he's being so generous as to drive Sandra into ballistic mode. Yes, of course I've discussed it with Sandra. She's endlessly badgering me to talk some sense into Dad – as she puts it – or to warn off Helen, which is even more ridiculous. Trouble is, she's such an agreeable woman. What's that? No, not Sandra. Helen. Yes, of course I've met her. She's an accountant working for a firm of management consultants. Her team was brought in to do a hatchet job on our Personnel Division. Actually they installed a rather good information system. What? Oh, I know you're not interested in her job but it was because of her involvement here that she happened to meet Dad. I introduced them over a drink one evening. Hey, calm down! How was I to know that his testosterone could go into overdrive? I wouldn't have guessed she was his type at all, although she has an attractive personality. For Godsake don't mention that to Sandra or she'll think this is some kind of joint enterprise. Oh come on, I know this isn't a laughing matter. Let's meet for lunch next week and talk things over. But I really must go now, Sis. And stop worrying. The whole affair doesn't rank highly on any standard scale of human misery. Anyway, you don't exactly yearn for Dad's company these days, so why should you assume Mum continues to do so? With that thought, as they say. Speak to you anon.'

Phyllis stared frozenly out of the hall window at the shadowed garden where her mother was busying herself, well-wrapped against the chill, sweeping together a mound of dead leaves and attempting to persuade them to burn. Thin smoke from the smouldering pile spiralled lazily into a cyclamen sky. Her father had taken himself off for a long walk, and Joan had made it obvious that she was unready for further analysis of the situation until such time as Phyllis was able to display more restraint. An unquiet silence had fallen on the house.

Perhaps her mother was wise in seeking temporary refuge in work. Phyllis went to her bedroom and collected one of the manuscripts she had brought down from Longstaff's. She remembered that her laptop was still in the car, which prompted another thought. She put on her leather coat and let herself out of the house. Joan ceased forking the leaves as she approached and looked up with a worried expression.

'You're not leaving, surely?'

'Only temporarily. I'm better out of harm's way for the evening. I'm off to find a quiet corner at the Tickled Trout. Could I borrow your key to let myself in later? You needn't wait up for me.'

Joan rummaged through her pockets for her key-ring. 'As you wish, darling. Perhaps it's for the best.'

'I've spoken to Peter. He sends his love.'

'How kind.' Joan turned her clenched face towards a pallid quarter moon. 'It must be difficult for him. He's very close to his father. But I expect he does, occasionally, think of me with affection.'

'More than occasionally. And with more than affection.' Phyllis felt her anger reviving. 'Listen, don't allow them to rob you of your self-esteem, the shits!'

'Oh, please!' Joan was again fighting back agitation.

'OK. I'm leaving. But we'll get you through this mess, believe me.'

Joan poked her fire's margins with her toe. 'We haven't talked about James. That's really why you came, isn't it? I'm not being much use to you, am I?'

'Time enough for that. I'll see you at breakfast.'

As she reversed into the narrow lane she glanced back at the wounded but still resilient woman, her sturdy figure employed once more in raking the year's detritus across the darkening earth. Idleness, Joan had always instructed her children, only makes bad worse and good less than satisfactory. Her mother's arms moved in a steady rhythm, her legs braced to the task.

CHAPTER FIVE

Annie Fogharty cycled towards Rossbrin on a fine late October Sunday afternoon, propelled by curiosity, dead cats or no dead cats, triggered by the arrival of those two Americans at Casey's the previous evening. They had come in like they owned the place, especially the woman with a face like a clenched fist and a taste for vodka, more or less demanding to see Maurice. Just as well he had been over at Kenmare with his sister; he was not one to enjoy surprises unless he was the one springing them. Surely it was the same woman who had been telephoning about the Kierney place over the past two weeks, a transaction that had been giving Maurice too many uneasy nights of late.

They had not been at all happy about his absence. Unpleasant comments had been made by the woman who hadn't given her name, but Annie had heard the man call her Morag. They had taken their drinks to the corner by the TV, having demanded that the sound be turned down. They hadn't spoken to the regulars once, staying for about an hour, leaving when the band began to tune their fiddles. Even they didn't dare to defy the locals' appetite for music. After their departure she had spoken to Colclough's sister on the 'phone, himself not being back from the golf club. Knowing that Maurice was not planning to return to Ballydehob until late on Sunday, she had decided to check for herself whether the couple were hanging around the house. If so, it would confirm that they were Tull's people. Not that they'd be at all comfortable: the place wasn't anyway near ready for occupation yet. Sean O'Leary had said as much when he'd been in for a drink last Wednesday, complaining about some complicated electrical parts that hadn't been delivered on time.

Annie felt a trickle of sweat between her breasts as she pushed down hard on the pedals to master the rise hiding Bracken Point from a view of the town, but a wind off Roaringwater Bay rapidly cooled her skin as she pulled over to stare through the new wrought-iron gate controlling access to the debatable property. A handsome piece of metalwork it was: cheeky-looking dolphins weaving through complicated clusters of bladder-wrack. It had cost a fortune from a workshop over in Waterford.

Beyond the gate a freshly-laid gravel drive led her eyes to the repainted house beyond which she knew a new jetty extended in place of the rotting stumps to which Tom Kierney had once tied his dinghy. Looking right through the seaweed gates, she could see that work was well-advanced on the laying of ten square metres of heavy concrete on the property's western edge, a requirement necessitating the sacrifice of several hawthorns. That innovation had really set Maurice's nerves dancing a jig. He couldn't guess how his friends in Bandon would react to the idea of a helicopter drumming along the inlets from Kinsale to Crookhaven. She also noted the security cameras swivel-mounted on their supporting columns following the line of the eight-foot high and spike-topped perimeter wall which had supplanted the once-familiar bramble-tangled wire boundary. The O'Leary brothers, with whom Maurice had cut a deal, had been busy for sure.

Finally, she registered the red BMW standing in the spot where garages had yet to be erected, the self-same car that had been parked outside Casey's last night. No doubt about it; Tull's people were in possession. She thought, when Maurice drags himself back from his weekend's boozing he's surely in for some hard grilling by that sour-faced bitch about deadlines and such. Annie felt a twinge of sympathy for him. It would have been better for him not to have got himself involved at all, but he couldn't resist the idea of a fat cheque. He had told her that he was expecting a minimum of £10,000 plus whatever commission he'd exacted from the contractors, although it wasn't certain that he'd be able to keep all of it. The trouble was that he'd put himself in the middle between a pair of powerful interests and was now having to juggle his obligations with a delicacy that would have challenged a man with much greater facility in the serpentine art of diplomacy than Colclough could summon up. He was shrewd enough in the running of his business – many would say too shrewd – but he had always hitherto ducked his head a fraction below the point of significant contact with those obsessive values that drive others well beyond rationality. Colclough's competence in the skills required to survive when afloat the harsher oceans of men's ambitions could scarcely have been lessened by decapitation. He could manage to paddle in the shallows with some style, but there was something in his nature – the quality that drew her to him – that tempted him to venture sufficiently close to the deeps to endow him with a reputation as a chancer, even though he would always draw back from genuine peril. She knew him to be a poseur but somehow that knowledge did not reduce – and possibly even reinforced – his appeal. He brought a little colour and romance into her otherwise predictable world.

Momentarily absorbed in her thoughts she did not immediately notice the dark-haired man emerge from behind the house. He was approaching with deliberate tread and was upon her before she could affect a dignified retreat. She recognised him well enough as the fellow who'd been in Casey's the previous evening. He was smiling, so she waved back in friendly fashion until she caught the steeliness of his eyes as he drew close. He boldly examined her old-fashioned sit-up-and-beg bike before raising his gaze to take in her ample breasts, her strong features pink from exertion, framed by loose-hanging brown hair. Anticipating him, she said, 'In the bar, last night.'

'I remember.'

'But you didn't let on that you work for Mr Tull.'

'Any reason why we should?'

Annie shrugged. 'Well, it would've been polite. I've been taking a parcel of messages about the work here, from America. And I'm not thick. I can add two and two.'

He opened the gate to come within touching distance. 'So you thought you'd take a closer look? To protect Colclough's interests?' He spoke softly but with an edge. She was reminded of some actor who specialised in quiet menace; what was his name? Out-of-synch eyes. Malkovich, that was it!

'So, is the work going well enough for you?' she asked.

'I guess.' He lit a cigarette but refrained from offering her one. 'You've met Mr Tull, then?'

'But the once. I thought he'd have been back before now.'

'Life is full of disappointments.'

''Tis so.' She decided it was time to be moving on, but he put a hand on her handlebars, casually but with white-knuckled firmness. Pretending not to have noticed, she continued, 'Maurice will be pleased to learn of your arrival when he gets back tonight. But he'll be less than thrilled if I'm not behind the bar within the hour.'

'We can't have that, can we.' He smiled thinly but did not release his grip. 'May I ask just one question? I can't help but be a mite curious about how things really work around these parts.'

Beyond him she now saw the woman coming up from the water's edge, saw her halt and stare, head thrown back, the low-glancing sunlight catching her streaked helmet of hair.

'It's a simple enough question,' he persisted. 'I know Mr Tull would appreciate some honest advice.'

'Ask away, then.'

'Fine.' He too now noticed his female companion. Although the woman made no sign of joining them, her distant scrutiny seemed to make him more cautious. He stood back a little, scratching his chin. 'It's just that we don't know how neighbourly people are around here. Like, did the previous owners have many friends in town? Apart from Colclough, that is.'

Annie snorted with laughter. 'Maurice was no friend of the Kierneys. What a notion! Sure, someone's been winding you up. Tom and Moira Kierney weren't close to anyone at all around here. Not what you'd call a convivial pair.' She shook her head, suddenly sober. 'I know what 'tis you're after, and you're legging it down the wrong road. Ballydehob isn't that kind of place. We have our villains like anywheres else but not many of that persuasion. You can put Mr Tull's mind at rest if he's having worries on that account.'

'But this *was* a Republican house?'

'I wouldn't be after knowing about that. To be sure Tom Kierney's got a black reputation although whether he's done the things the Brits took him for I couldn't say.' Annie mounted her cycle, rewarding him with a full view of her lower thighs. For the first time he seemed to relax. His thin smile returned.

'Thanks. That's good to know. You did say that Colclough will be back this evening? We'll probably be along to see him. You will be sure to let him know?'

Annie took a final look at the restored house. Its windows, spruce in their freshly-whitened frames, caught the westering sun. She could distantly smell the benison of newly-cut timber. The man was securing the gate behind him as she applied her weight to the pedals, and she knew he would be watching her all the way to the bend, skirt tight across her arse. When she reached the old abandoned schoolhouse, half a mile towards the town, she braked to light a fag, to collect herself, to quell the sensation of something alien having entered her life. Two kids were kicking a ball around in the weed-infested playground, raucous in their rivalry. A thrush chortled in the blackthorn. A normal Sunday afternoon. Only it wasn't, some-how.

Brendan was, as usual, installed in his corner when she reached the bar. He and Declan, the relief barman, exchanged quips about her lack of punctuality, which she ignored.

'Himself is back.' Brendan pointed upwards. 'These thirty minutes. Asking for you, he was.'

'In a good mood?'

'Couldn't say that.'

The bar was beginning to fill, as it always did once the prescribed period of Sunday abstinence had concluded. She busied herself about the place, pulling pints, washing glasses, exchanging pleasantries, feeding the brassy rectangular spaces of Colclough's till with coin and note, putting off the moment when his ill humour had to be confronted. This was customarily her favourite time of the week when the smell of tobacco mingled with that of ale, when the *craic* was at its juiciest and when Father Dominic, a regular user of Casey's at this hour, often led the singing. But the mood had not yet taken hold of the cleric and Annie could not shake off her uncharacteristic apprehension.

It was a little after six o'clock when Colclough appeared. He had taken a nap and a shower. A red carnation sported itself in his lapel and he had donned his most brilliant waistcoat, an expanse of peacock blue. If he was out of temper, as alleged, she thought he was disguising it admirably. He worked the room jauntily, shaking hands, talking of Kerry and golf, his laughter deep-throated. Annie waited until he came to the bar to pour himself a stiff whiskey before unloading on him an account of her exchanges with the Yank. He examined his fingernails.

'I've been expecting this. Everything's under control. All squared away. Nose beautifully clean. So, they're calling in tonight?'

'That's what he said. I didn't ask his name. But the woman seems to be in charge. Unpleasant cow.'

'Ambrose, she's called. Morag Ambrose. Assuming she's the one that's been telephoning me.' He shrugged. 'I can cope with her.'

Annie stared hard at him. 'I hope you're right about that. It was a foul temper she was in last night. Isn't the work up to scratch?'

'Well enough. At any rate it's well enough advanced for me to be getting out from under. I reckon another couple of weeks and it'll all be behind me.' He knocked back his Powers. 'The money's as good as in the bank.' He grinned, agitating his eyebrows clownishly.

She knew that his bonhomous behaviour was artificial. She could almost share the sensation of his nerve-ends pulsing beneath the skin. His eyes flickered towards the bar's entrance as more customers elbowed in from the street; not the Americans this time. He poured another whiskey.

Annie said, 'The fella this afternoon. He was asking about Tom Kierney.'

She became aware of old Brendan at her elbow. He leered over his empty glass. 'If it's them Americans you're after talking about, I happen to know that they spent the morning nosing around the town dropping Maurice's name into chat about Bracken Point. Not that it did 'em much good. A final half of Guinness, m'darlin', if you please.' He tapped Maurice's arm. 'Shit stirrers, if you ask me. Spot 'em a mile away.'

'Duly noted, Brendan.' Colclough smiled thinly. He thought: what the hell; they've already got all they need to know from Moira Kierney. He turned to Annie. 'Am I right in thinking Eamonn is away?'

'That he is. On his way to Düsseldorf. Chemicals.'

'There's a thing,' said Brendan. 'So you'll be after trailing home to a cold bed. A criminal waste, I call it. Isn't that so, Maurice?'

Annie broke in, 'It's a smutty minded bugger you are, Brendan Mulcahy. Get back to your seat, so, and hold your whist. I'll bring your beer over this minute.'

They watched him weave through the other drinkers, scratching around the frayed rim of his cap. Colclough said, 'He sees too much. His eyesight, and his lip, will be the death of him, wouldn't you say? There are times when I think Brendan has overstayed his time on God's earth, despite his pissing his pension straight into my pocket.' He rapidly switched on his most affable expression as Father Dominic breasted the bar. 'Another port is it, Father? I've a true tale for you from Kenmare. I met this fella who was telling a local farmer that he was over for his grandson's christening and that the priest who'd originally married his boy and his bride some three years back had travelled all the way down from Sligo to perform the ceremony. And d'you know what the farmer said? I'll give you his exact words. "Ah, now, that marriage must be going along real fine. But if I could find the priest who married me I'd give him a right hammering." Isn't that a grand one?'

Father Dominic enjoyed the joke, and the laughter was still hanging in the smoky air when Morag Ambrose came through the door, followed by the dark-haired man to whom Annie had spoken earlier. Annie's head went back in involuntary challenge. Morag was wearing a grey trouser suit that would have cost Annie a year's wages, beneath a shimmering black shawl of matching opulence. She surveyed the occupants of the bar with obvious disdain before moving towards Colclough. She ignored the priest, ignored Annie, ignored everyone except the focus of her attention.

'Where might we talk?'

Maurice made an attempt to hold his ground. 'And who might you be?'

'Don't frig me about, Colclough. Where's your office?'

Slowly he said, 'Annie, can you look after things for a while?'

'I'm sure Annie can cope,' the woman said.

Father Dominic was moved to comment quietly on the intruder's extraordinary rudeness. Before she could react, her companion interjected, 'Sorry about this.' He smiled all round. 'You can sure tell Morag didn't have the benefit of a convent education.'

She stared at him coldly. 'Always the diplomat, Leo. Can we get on?'

Colclough addressed the priest. 'Will you excuse me, Father? Business, you know, even though it is a Sunday. Mea culpa. Mea maxima culpa.' Annie admired his show of composure. He pointed to the green door to the left of the bar area. 'Shall we go up then?'

'Oh let's,' the woman said, her voice gravid with sarcasm. She led the way, twitching her shawl which glimmered as it caught the beams of Casey's recessed lighting. The dark man, Leo, closed in behind them but his watchful eyes lingered upon Annie's upper body as he moved away. She was aware of his interest but spun sharply away to attend to her regulars' thirst. Father Dominic was agitated. He had been suddenly isolated, left with nobody to whom he might immediately converse, and was troubled by the behaviour of those two blow-ins. He saw Brendan squatting in his habitual spot chatting to a couple of his sons; and moved uncertainly across to them. 'And how are you all?'

Brendan's face registered surprise, annoyance, reconciliation, in that order. 'Fine, Father, just fine. The boys were just about to take me home. They reckon I've supped my fill.'

''Tis probably right they are, Brendan. Your face has a grand pinkiness about it.' He sank into a vacant chair. 'So, what d'you think is going on with Maurice, then?'

'What should I know?'

'Brendan, we both know you've the sharpest nose in Ballydehob.'

The old man grinned. 'Well, Father, I expect it's something to do with the sale of Bracken Point. You've probably just had your first sight of our new neighbours, so.'

The priest was thoughtful. 'A right tartar, she seems.'

'That she does.' With which Brendan began to climb into his overcoat, assisted by one of his lads.'Colclough will be getting on a real sweat, I reckon. The Lord be with ye, Father.'

Dominic watched him depart a little unsteadily. A gust of chill air swept around his ankles as the Mulcahys shouldered through the open door into the darkening evening, a harbinger of winter. The priest would have liked to hang around until the Americans re-appeared, the better to gauge the quality of trouble they might be bringing to his town, but he had other duties that evening to which he must attend. With a sigh he downed his port and followed the Mulcahys into the dusk.

Fifteen minutes later the dark newcomer, Leo, returned to order a round of drinks. Annie wished he could erase that ingratiating smile he assumed whenever he was around her; she wanted none of him.

'A large vodka, an orange juice for me and whatever your boss fancies. They're on their way down.' As she failed to respond, he added, 'Didn't take long to sort everything out.'

'Nothing to do with me at all.'

'That's not the impression you gave this afternoon.'

'Impressions can be misleading, I suppose. Just what sort of impression d'you think she wants to make?' Annie jerked her head in the direction of the stairs down which Morag Ambrose was descending, followed by Maurice, grinning nervously. Putting on a show, thought Annie. Him, not her. With her, what do you see is what you get. Unfortunately. In your face. Up your snout. Not to mention your arse.

Casey's was slowly thinning out as customers began to return to their families for their Sunday dinner. Colclough had once or twice thought of serving food in the bar, but had decided to draw the line at nuts and crisps. Too much hassle for too little return. Besides he didn't want to rob Maeve Rafferty of business. Had a soft spot for Maeve, he had. As she fiddled with the optics Annie again wished it could be just another customary Sunday with her few regulars, sharing gossip, enjoying the singing or half-watching the TV in the corner which, she noticed, was now showing soundless images of the early evening news: Gerry Adams being interviewed somewhere in Belfast; saturnine, flick-eyed. She didn't need to turn up the volume to know what was being said. Peace process. Plenty of process. Not so much of the other. Annie didn't, however, appreciate her unspoken views being endorsed by that bloody woman alongside her, jewellery glinting chunkily around her mannish wrists. She had followed the line of Annie's eyes to the screen and jerked a derisive thumb in that direction.

'Waste of time. Why give that piss-artist valuable air-time?'

'What do you know about it?' Annie demanded, ignoring Maurice's imploring expression.

'Enough.' Her penetrative nasal delivery was already turning heads reacting with a mixture of curiosity and disapproval. 'We live in a global village, don'tcha know? What you people don't seem to register is the scale of things.' Again she indicated the screen. 'Let me ask you, do you know how many people were murdered in New York alone last year? Over two thousand. In a single city. The stuff that goes on in Ulster is minor league, hardly worth bothering about. Nobody should take it seriously unless things get a good deal heavier. And then, of course, they'd probably be too heavy for that fucker Adams to handle. What d'you say to that, lady?'

Colclough broke in. 'She's not paid to express opinions. But if you're interested in my view, anything that keeps the ceasefire going must be worth it, wouldn't you say? Even for half-a-dozen lives.'

'Re-armament time. *Reculer pour mieux sauter*. Big mistake by the Brits. Unless, that is, the cunning bastards are looking for a good excuse to unload Ulster, to dump the problem in Dublin's lap. Come to think of it, that's not a bad idea.' 'She chortled throatily.

Annie could remain silent no longer, but was determined not lose her rag. Sweetly she said, 'D'you know, when I met Mr Tull he struck me as a very discreet, very quiet sort of fella. Not at all the sort to be coming out with the powerful thoughts we've just been hearing from you, would you say? Not that we don't find them stimulating. Makes a change from the usual chat about fishing and the price of a pint.' She saw that the man appreciated her impudence, but Morag Ambrose stared frostily before knocking back her vodka.

'C'mon, Leo. We're outa here.' She gathered her shawl around her shoulders before addressing Annie again. 'I wouldn't trade too much on familiarity with James Tull if I were you, lady. You'll be seeing rather more of me than of him.'

Annie was about to say, not if I can help it, but thought better of it, to Colclough's evident relief. He ushered them to the door, and although there were no handshakes Leo threw her a slow wink. Colclough was not appeased.

'All right, you didn't take to her but you needn't have made it so bloody obvious.'

'She's a three-flush floater.'

'Maybe, but your attitude doesn't help.' He poured himself another whiskey. 'I'm off upstairs. Leave you to it.'

'Shall I come up later?'

'Suit yourself.'

She thought about leaving him alone for the rest of the night, and returning to her cold house on the other side of town, but the prospect was unappealing. And she was curious about whatever had transpired in the office upstairs. She knew she could wheedle it out of him. His sour moods rarely lasted for long. She would make it up to him.

It was two of the morning – she squinted at her wristwatch illuminated by the orange glow from the streetlight filtering through the window – when she at last asked him if everything was OK. He rolled away from her warm body to light a cigarette. She stroked his buttocks; they were, she thought, pretty trim for a man of his age. He was wearing well. Nothing like as muscular as Eamonn, but then her husband's solidity and weight sometimes intimidated her. She never knew for sure what went on in Maurice's head but his body never worried her; with Eamonn it was the other way round. Ideal combination, some would say.

Colclough got to his feet. 'I need a pee.' She watched his dim shape edge towards the door with short dapper movements. When he returned she had put on his woollen dressing gown and turned on the bedside lamp. She stroked his white skin. Another contrast. Eamonn was as brown as a nut. She told herself to stop making comparisons with Eamonn at times like this. A distraction. She stroked on.

Eventually Colclough said, 'My sister's not well. She's finding it a bit of a strain running the hotel on her own. She needs help. I may have to spend more time up there.'

'Sorry to hear that. Not serious?'

'Arthritis mainly.' He rolled over to face her. 'Now that I'm pretty well out of the Bracken Point business I can afford to spend more time at Kenmare.' Almost as an afterthought he added, 'You can take on a bit more down here. I'll up your wages, naturally.'

'Oh, gee, thanks! Magic!'

Noting the sarcasm, he said, 'I promise not to be away too often.'

'Is this to do with your sister entirely? That bloody woman Ambrose wouldn't be after rattling your cage?'

He sighed. 'You really don't like her, do you? Well, nor do I. But it's only business. And well paid, too. They handed over a grand wad tonight, more than I expected.'

'So they're happy? Didn't give that impression.'

'She'd anticipated the garaging to be more advanced. And the helipad isn't where she wants it. Too visible from the road, she says. But I told her, put it further back and you get a risk of flooding. Anyway, she's going to think more about it.'

'Won't Tull have an opinion?'

'Seemingly not. I don't know where he fits in. All the paperwork's in the name of Onaping Enterprises. What the hell! They're bringing in their own people to finish the house inside. My part in it's nearly zero from now onwards. And, Jesus, I'm not sorry.'

'So it's over then?'

'Hope so, but I've a queer feeling it may be only a beginning.'

'Have you squared it away with the fellas in Bandon?'

He turned off the light. 'That's another funny thing. When I 'phoned tonight I had an impression that they already knew what was happening. Anyway, they were easy about it.'

He began to stroke her breasts but without passion, still lost in speculation.

She said softly, 'It's Monday already. A new week. Turn the page, wee man.' But he did not respond. The remembered sneer on Morag Ambrose's lips as she slipped him the envelope containing £15,000 in cash, treating him like a common casual labourer, fuelled his sense of redundancy.

CHAPTER SIX

Hugh Jennings stared with displeasure at the fax which his secretary had just deposited by his elbow, his draft editorial momentarily abandoned. Not a word from Tull in over three months, not a single response to his earlier request for advice on that troublesome litigation, and suddenly this impertinent communication; one of those odd coincidences that he experienced from time to time and which he had learnt to recognise as harbingers of some disquieting turn of events: not necessarily disastrous, for few disasters had disrupted Jennings's smooth progress through life; but certainly unsettling.

October sunlight, strangely intense for this time of year, thrust through his windows. He rose to take in the comforting panorama of aspiring towers and spirals, the river's easy curvature towards Blackfriars. Nothing else like it, he told himself; nothing so noble and fine; nothing at any rate that had crossed his line of vision on his recent journeyings through the Far East; certainly not to his English eye. But, but ...

He returned to peer, spectacles lowered, at his word processor, its screen reflecting his recorded impressions of the tigerish aggression of Asian economic growth, its growing threat to Western dominance. There was no doubt it about. Britain would have to pull up its socks if it was to avoid financial decline. He had never seen so much concrete being poured, vast tons of the stuff mounting above a forest of tower cranes, the entire region buoyed upwards by a seemingly unstoppable wave of expansionist investment fuelled by the international banking community's notion of some bottomless pool of intelligent quick-fingered but cheap labour driving the whole greedy caravanserai onwards in an irresistible quest for betterment. Jennings's confident, name-dropping prose reflected his persuasion of the certainty of a dawning of a fearsome eastern challenge.

It had been profoundly gratifying to have been the object of such attention on his tour, to have been feted at numerous excellent restaurants across Hong Kong, Tokyo, Bangkok, Kuala Lumpur, all triggered by his having been invited to deliver a paper on the Thatcherite Legacy at a symposium organised by the Taiwanese government in Taipei. Not that he considered the enjoyment of such hospitality wholly undeserved.

Three years into his editorship he was beginning to harvest the fruits befitting his status. Jollies such as his oriental odyssey merely represented a pleasing layer of cream atop the rich chocolate of his carefully-selected non-executive Directorships, his Deputy Chairmanship of the Arts Council, his appointment to various Committees of Inquiry; all pointing the way – with such delicate and fastidious gestures – towards a knighthood, even perhaps to ermined splendour; all serving to keep his wife more than adequately possessed of designer accoutrements and frequent opportunities to display them. Not bad, as he complimented himself frequently, for a product of Blackburn Grammar School whose father still struggled to sell life insurance to the increasingly Islamicised inhabitants of that borough, and whose mother had once peddled cosmetics around its council estates; a progress perhaps not quite as remarkable as achieving the Premiership with barely any academic qualifications and with a promiscuous street performer for one's sire. Nevertheless, he assured himself, a palpable indentation on the fabric of British society.

But, even so, he was still insufficiently august to avoid the invasive irritation of gratuitous advice from people like Tull to whom he had scarcely directed a thought in weeks (other than as a by-product of his half-hearted pursuit of Phyllis Norton) until yesterday when his name had cropped up in conversation over lunch at the Athenaeum with Sir Edward Dutton, Second Permanent Secretary to the Treasury. Hence the ominous coincidence.

He fingered the fax with scrupulous distaste, reading again, 'Are you wise to so demonise Labour? Blair's agents are brown-nosing the City with their strap-line that if Big Business liked Maggie it will love Tony. You must be aware of the effect this message is having. So take care. As the Chinese say, never kick the beggar outside your door; he may prove to be your landlord. Think on these things. James.'

Jennings snorted. He was not about to take advice on editorial policy from Tull of all people. Under other circumstances he might have fired off a waspish rejoinder (he noted that the fax had originated in Ottawa) but the context in which Sir Edward had woven his reference to Tull suggested that a more cautious response might be called for. Over their steak and kidney pies – Jennings had found the quantity of viscous gravy excessive – the topic under discussion had been a rumour picked up by the Treasury of imminent and significant dealings in the equity holdings of the World Tidings media group of which *The Mercury* was the UK flagship.

'You will appreciate that any such transactions would be of immense interest to HMG for all manner of reasons. Competition policy, not least. And, of course, the possible political fall-out.'

It had irked Jennings that the civil servant had felt it necessary to rehearse the obvious. 'We are aware that an election is only eighteen months away.'

'Indeed so. Inconvenient things, elections. They do so get in the way of effective government. And, if I may say so, they tend to gift the press an undue influence.'

'You wouldn't expect me to agree with that.'

'Of course not.' Sir Edward had smiled, between bites. 'A very fine thing: a free press. Every nation should have one. Indeed, I look upon all forms of the media rather as the Romans regarded religion. Do you know your Gibbon? Something like, "All modes of worship were considered by the people as equally true; by the philosopher as equally false; and by the magistrate as equally useful." But I digress. These rumours?'

'Precisely that, as far as I'm aware. Neither more nor less.'

'Ah.' Sir Edward appeared unconvinced. 'Let's hope so.'

Jennings's irritation had grown. 'Look here, I don't know where you are picking up these stories; and I'm prepared to accept that the sources for your information may be better than mine; but rumours of this sort are common currency. I've heard them too. But I've no reason to believe that there's any substance to them.'

'That's most reassuring.' With which Sir Edward had moved their conversation on to unrelated matters with an adroitness and felicity of tone which betokened years of schooling in the ways of Whitehall; but as they were completing the demolition of their respective puddings, and with the disinterested air of someone seeking no more than to bridge an unwanted hiatus in the flow of chat, he laid the foundation for the following day's coincidence. 'That fellow, James Tull, no longer writes for *The Mercury*, I gather?'

'Resigned a couple of months ago. Didn't really settle. A bit of a dilettante.'

'But quite talented. I recall one particularly amusing piece just before the last Budget which tweaked the Chancellor's nose with some vigour. I suppose one ought not to enjoy the discomforture of one's political master, but Tull's description of Ken Clarke's taste in footwear as a metaphor for more serious failures of judgement was a neat conceit. How did you come across him?'

'As far as I can recall, he was initially recommended by one of our Group Vice-Presidents. He'd been writing occasional free-lance articles for the *Economist* on Euro-politics and was working out of Rome and Paris where he seems to have garnered a fair number of useful diplomatic contacts. I believe our chap had come across him when Tull was covering one of those over-rated and somewhat masturbatory conferences at Davos. I saw no reason for not trying him out.'

'My dear chap, I'd say you displayed your characteristic felicity of judgement.' Sir Edward distributed the Club port. 'So, where is he now? I haven't seen any of his pieces in a rival paper.'

Jennings had begun to divine some purpose, as yet unclear to him, behind the civil servant's apparently casual enquiries. 'We didn't drop him, you know. It was entirely his decision to move on. In fact, it was inconveniently sprung on me. And I don't really know what he's currently doing with himself. He does, of course, have private means.'

'Ah, yes. The famously discreet Tulliver Trust.'

Jennings had managed to remember the references to a Trust made by that unhelpful fellow Marotti during their telephone conversation some weeks previously. It had meant nothing to him then, and over the subsequent passage of time he had felt no need to relieve his ignorance. He decided to chance his arm. 'Canadian-based, isn't it, this Trust?'

'Just so.' Dutton had pursed his lips. 'Or at least Canadian in origin. Precisely where it pays its taxes, if any, is rather more obscure.'

'James never spoke of it to me; not once.'

'I did, I believe, indicate the family's obsession with discretion.'

Jennings had fiddled with his napkin. 'Come to think of it, I know remarkably little about his personal details. Odd, really, given that I often enjoyed his company socially. He had an amusingly wide circle of acquaintances, some of them decidedly away from the mainstream, and I found it fun to mingle. But he rarely spoke of his private life. I suppose I was remiss in being so incurious. He certainly had expensive tastes. As far as I know, he still owns a well-appointed house just off the Kings Road. But it never occurred to me to enquire where the money came from. Indeed, it was only recently that I learnt of his Canadian connections when his former girl-friend told me something of it.' Jennings had paused, suddenly aware of a subtle increase in the Permanent Secretary's attentiveness. He said, cautiously, 'Do I take it that it would have been advisable to be better informed?'

'It might have been prudent. We were really most intrigued when he showed up on your pages. Not that he is thought to be a particularly dominant figure in the Trust's affairs. It's generally accepted that his older, reclusive brother takes all major decisions.'

'But this Trust is significant enough to warrant Treasury attention?'

'I think you may safely make such an assumption. Time for a final coffee?' As Sir Edward poured, he added gently, 'You mentioned a girl-friend.'

'Former, I rather think. When he left in August … it was, as I've already indicated, very unexpected … I fear she was unceremoniously dumped. I feel sorry for her. One minute he was rarely out of her company; the next he was off to Ireland, with barely a farewell.'

'Ireland?'

'A holiday, I understand. But he then took himself off across the Atlantic and, as far as I know, he's still there. Back to base, I imagine.'

Their exchanges had then moved on to other matters, not least some salacious gossip about the latest Ministerial indiscretions, before faint intimations of business pressures had drawn them from their table. As they parted at the foot of the priapic Duke of York statue, Sir Edward had murmured, 'My dear Hugh, to revert to our earlier topic, it may well turn out to be mere rumour which, as we all know, can circumnavigate the globe whilst truth is still lacing up its walking boots. But should you happen to come across news of significant share acquisitions, if anything of that nature shows the teeniest sign of emerging – the faintest scintilla of a vague probability – you will alert me, won't you? National interest and all that. You know the form.'

Jennings had perceived that he was receiving some kind of friendly warning. People like Sir Edward rarely asked a question of Whitehall outsiders unless they were reasonably certain of the predicted response. Some realistic assessment of a predatory bid must already exist within the Treasury. Jennings was not unduly disturbed by the prospect, being sufficiently confident that eminent journals such as that which he headed relied for their reputation upon maintaining a firm distinction between ownership and editorial control. Of course, he had occasionally been gently advised to soften his line on, say, human rights in China but such guidance had fallen well short of dictation; and although he had invariably taken heed of the silken suggestions he had never found it difficult to persuade himself that no significant principle had been breached.

On this October Thursday, however, with Tull's fax in front of him, an unwelcome possibility began to seep into his consciousness. He was obliged to devote the next hour to a presentation by his Design Manager and her staff of the lay-out for a re-launch of their weekend colour supplement, enjoying his prerogative of demonstrating a capriciousness appropriate to his status, polished shoes on polished desk, carping and magnanimous by turns; but once they had been dismissed he telephoned the financial desk to commission a piece of research into the Tulliver Trust. 'It could provide the basis of a major story if we can pierce its veil of secrecy.' Increasingly he found himself using journalistic clichés in his common speech and made a mental note to discipline his tongue. 'I want its history, ramifications, holdings, ambitions, failures, and especially stuff about the Trust's involvement, if any, in the communications business. And I expect an initial report in 48 hours.'

He then attempted to contact Phyllis Norton at her office only to discover that she was again visiting her parents. Twice in a month, he noted; not her usual style at all, and damnably inconvenient. He tasked his secretary to persuade Longstaff's of his need to speak urgently with Phyllis and, having eventually been provided with her Canterbury number, he found himself speaking to her mother.

'I'm afraid she's out for a walk. Could I ask her to call you back, Mr ...?'

'Jennings. *The Mercury*. She knows my number. Will she return shortly? I'm about to lunch.'

'Within the hour, I expect. But things down here have been rather unpredictable of late. Is this a business matter, Mr Jennings?'

'Absolutely. And I've had some difficulty in tracking her down. I take it she's not unwell? I mean to say ... how should I put this? ... that it's somewhat unusual for her to spend so much time out of London, isn't it?'

'How perceptive of you, Mr Jennings. But she is, happily, in perfect health. And I'm sure she will be delighted to learn that you've 'phoned.' The receiver was replaced, a trifle forcefully, he judged.

It was not until around five o'clock that Phyllis returned his call. Her repeat visit to her parents, an attempt at reconciliation on her part, had been penitential, her mother oscillating between discreet tearfulness and brittle jollity, her father largely uncommunicative. Her dissatisfaction was transmitted by her tone of voice.

Jennings said, 'I fear I offended your mother.'

'Easily done these days.'

'Is something amiss?'

She ignored his question. 'What do you want of me, Hugh?'

'I would really like to meet you as soon as possible. A matter has cropped up on which I'd greatly value your advice.'

'It's not the job offer again?'

'That might arise, but it's not the main item on my immediate agenda. I prefer not to be more explicit on the 'phone.'

'How mysterious.' She sounded thoroughly bored. 'I'll be back in town by Monday. Perhaps, when I've sorted out my schedule for the week, I could be in touch to fix a time before next Friday. Can't commit right now. I know my workload is stacking up because of the extra leave I've been taking.'

Jennings swore. 'I'd hoped to see you more quickly. Look, why don't I come down to join you at some convenient hostelry over the weekend? It is important, I promise.'

'I suppose so.' She was unenthusiastic but temporarily incapable of producing a sufficiently convincing deflection. 'OK. You probably know the Tickled Trout at Wye? Yes? Mid-day on Saturday then? But not for long.' As she spoke she recalled her escape to that establishment, some three weeks earlier when she had been seeking a brief refuge from the tension between herself and her parents, a respite that had solved nothing, done nothing to lessen the confused anger which obstructed all her efforts to reconcile herself to her sense of displacement; of the decay of certitude, comforts, anchorages. Jennings's eager confirmation of their weekend appointment seemed to reach her from some increasingly alien and unreal world of business engagements, word processors, letters to be opened, decisions to be taken, bargains to be struck, insurances to be obtained.

'OK. Until Saturday, then.'

As she replaced the receiver she saw that her father had been observing her from the door of the small front room he described as his inner sanctum, a space heavy with pipe smoke where he stored his collection of books and discs, his computer, his private correspondence. He said, 'So, we're to enjoy your company for a few more days, I gather. Or, rather, your mother will. I'm intending to spend most of tomorrow and Saturday in London. You'll probably have left by the time I'm back on Sunday morning. We could wave at each other on the motorway.'

'It's time for your weekly shag, is it?'

'You can't imagine how much I'm looking forward to it,' he replied steadily, his gaze unyielding. As she flushed, he raised a hand. 'Look here, let's not have another row. I'm about to walk up to the Mucky Duck. Why don't you join me? We'll be back in plenty of time for dinner. Joan won't be inconvenienced. She won't be back from the golf club until six-thirty or thereabouts. And you've been stuck into that manuscript for far too long.'

She had spent the last two hours completing a report for Longstaff's on a text she had brought from London, a reasonably competent but unriveting biography of Keats drawing on some newly-unearthed correspondence between Fanny Brawne and one of her cousins. Phyllis doubted whether the expensive shelf-space of the shortly-to-be-completed British Library really needed to be burdened by yet another account of Keats's final days in Italy, however worthy and diligent the work. Her analysis reflected both her view of the essential redundancy of the exercise and a feeling that her own talents, such as they were, had been expended gratuitously. She felt she deserved a few vodkas. Nevertheless, she drew back. 'I'm irritable and tired. I'll be poor company.'

'Still, the best immediately available.' He unhooked her coat from the bentwood hallstand and draped it around her shoulders. Briefly she felt the man's heaviness, his solidity, and drew in the male odour from his hands as he propelled her irresistibly towards the front door. He pocketed his torch. 'It might be dark in the lane later. Better to be safe than sorry.'

They stepped out into a dank evening smelling of damp leaves and distant bonfires, acrid and weighted with nostalgia. A wood pigeon heaved itself through the shredding sycamores and horse-chestnuts at their approach. A deep melancholy had settled over the valley. Their feet scuffed in the gravel and seer leaves as they climbed the unmade track before gaining the metalled road. Above the hill's shoulder a sky solid with pewter-coloured cloud pressed down upon them. Her father slashed at brambles with his walking stick, humming tunelessly. They were within sight of the pub before he broke their silence. 'We've both been speaking too cruelly. It upsets Joan terribly. Let's try harder to be kind.'

'Isn't it rather too late for that? And isn't kindness of that variety a form of dishonesty?'

'Not necessarily.' He wondered again what experiences had 'engendered such an appetite for combat in his daughter. He tried once more. 'Our situation is far from unique. Others manage to come to terms with it, usually by smoothing awkward corners by a process approximating to kindness. Dishonesty would be not admitting to the reality of relationships, especially to oneself.'

Phyllis stared fiercely straight ahead. 'So you think I should be more accommodating, do you? Is some kind of bonding expected?' Before he could respond, she answered her own questions. 'I think not. My loyalties lie elsewhere.'

The Black Swan, characterised by locals as the Mucky Duck, was surrounded by a cluster of distinctly kempt cottages comprising the heart of the snug hamlet of Hastingleigh. The pub's lights, red and gold, along its frontage anticipated the onset of dusk. Arnold's spirits rose as he approached its cheery windows. He said, 'I really do appreciate the effort you've made to keep close to Joan, particularly your having taken time out to come down here again this week.'

'The least I could do. For her.' They had reached the entrance when she managed to raise the issue that had to be addressed before they joined the company of others. 'One thing I need to know: do you intend to divorce?'

He halted and stared at the dimming sky. 'The clocks will be put back soon. Next week, I think.' He grinned and shook his head. 'Sorry. My mind had drifted for a moment in the direction of normality. As to divorce, it's up to Joan. I've made it clear to her that it's not what I want. I regard divorce as rather unnecessary at our time of life.'

'Not to mention the expense.'

He shrugged. 'It would effectively be your money going into the lawyers' pockets, not mine. And if you're worried that I'll be diverting your inheritance to Helen, you should know that by far the largest amount of our capital has been in your mother's name for years. For tax avoidance. Technically I'm quite a poor man.'

'So you expect Mother to share your favours?'

'As I said, that's a matter for her. And, of course, for Helen.' To her astonishment he broke into a self-satisfied giggle. 'I'm a hostage to fortune. A new and rather exciting experience.'

Later, over drinks, Arnold attempted to assume a more typical fatherly role. 'We haven't spoken of your problems. I gather from Joan that your affair with that fellow Tull is not going swimmingly. Sorry to hear it. From the two or three times we met, I rather took to him. A cut above your usual, if I may say so.'

'If you must.' She knew it had been a mistake to expose herself to her father's observations; and that he would doubtless proceed to hint that her separation from James could be laid at the door of her temperamental inadequacies.

'Have you had a row?'

'He's abroad. Let's leave it at that, please.'

'What a pity.'

They finished their drinks in ruminative silence. As Arnold was about to order his second, she said, 'Look here, Father, one of the lesser reasons for my concern over your stupid affair is ... I'll admit – wholly selfish. I've been given a chance to change my job. That 'phone call you overheard was partly about that possibility. But the new position, although well-paid, would be less secure. I can't make a move that carries too much financial risk. I'm not someone who lives for the moment. I value stability in the way I order my life, perhaps more than I should, but there you are.'

'I'm not sure that I see the relevance.'

She ran her fingers through her hair in frustration. He was forcing her to expose her mean streak, and she hated him for it.

'It's simply that I need to know where I stand, financially. I can't ... won't ... take a leap into the unknown without knowing that I have some kind of lifeline.'

'Ah, the monthly allowance.' He reached over and patted her arm, a gesture into which she read condescension rather than affection. 'Well, nothing lasts for ever, but I see no immediate threat to our present arrangement. Helen is not a greedy woman.' He smiled thinly. 'We are going to remain good friends, aren't we? Now, tell me more about this new job opportunity.'

Phyllis was still seething at the unsubtle warning when, two days later, she found herself seated, in a not wholly dissimilar establishment, across a pseudo-rustic table from Hugh Jennings.

He had stepped blinking from his chauffeured BMW into bright mid-day sunlight, the diamond-edged autumnal brilliance seeking to reconcile the English to the imminent prospect of months of elegiac greyness. At first they had made small talk, chardonnays in hand, in the beer-garden, watching the Stour's brown ripples gurgle towards Canterbury and thence to Pegwell Bay; but a cool breeze suddenly arose, persuading them indoors where he guided her to a nooky corner adorned with well-burnished brasses and willow-patterned platters. He was dressed casually, sweater and chinos, a mode to which his softly-padded frame adapted itself uncertainly, whimpering for the security of well-tailored suit and tie. She recognised a couple standing at the bar, a farmer and his wife from Bodsham; she responded to their wave of acknowledgement with a cool nod. Doubtless they would be speculating upon the identity of her companion, striving to recall where they had previously come across him, his features being vaguely familiar. Phyllis resented being the indirect object of such ruminations. She said, 'Where does Candida believe you to be?'

'Oddly enough, with you. And she knows why. And she isn't in the least perturbed. She would find it difficult to perceive of you as one of my quarries. Not my usual style at all.'

She considered his remark carefully, noting its ambiguities. 'Then, what has brought you down here?'

'James Tull.' Observing her frisson, he hastily added, 'I've no wish to intrude into your private affairs. Not today at any rate. My interest is professional, *tout court*. It's just that I think you're best placed to help me on this particular matter.'

'What precisely do you want of me, Hugh?'

'I need to make contact with James rather urgently. An issue has cropped up concerning his family business about which I really must talk to him on an informal basis. I want to avoid normal channels if at all possible. That New York number you gave me last month is no help. You're my best hope.'

'But I've no idea where he is. I last heard from him, by letter, some two weeks ago. Just a brief note.' She remembered only too sharply the sick excitement of tearing open the flimsy airmail with a Brazilian stamp to read Tull's solicitous but hardly impassioned enquiries into her well-being.

'There must have been an address.'

'He was in South America. Passing through. He could be anywhere by now.'

Jennings rubbed his nose thoughtfully. 'And you have no way of contacting him? At a personal level, that is?'

'I don't think he'd welcome it. Anyway, why is it so crucial that you reach him?'

'I'd prefer not to burden you with that, if you don't mind.' He assumed what he hoped was a gnomic expression. 'But in general terms I'd very much like to find out rather more about his family firm, the Tulliver Trust. Has he ever spoken to you about it?'

'Never. The name means nothing to me. I've told you before, Hugh, that he always drew a veil over his background. To be honest, I suppose that this slight aura of mystery was part of his attractiveness.'

Jennings went to the bar to replenish their drinks. She stared at his broad buttocks speculatively. Whatever had brought him down to Wye it must have been important to him professionally for she was now persuaded that his motive for meeting her owed little to sexual ambition, although she knew that spark still glowed. She found herself anxious to discover more about his reasons, to allow their conversation to dwell – however vicariously – within Tull's sphere of influence. She followed him to the bar.

'Look, we clearly have things to talk about. Why don't you stay for lunch? The food here is passable.'

He smirked. 'That would be very pleasant. I'll have a word with my driver.' Who, she noted, was seated before his orange juice in a distant corner of the room. Having made his dispositions, Jennings returned with a bottle of claret and clean glasses. 'Let's move on to a decent red, shall we? Let's make it a splendid Kentish occasion.' He snuggled into his seat, drawing it closer to her knees. 'Sackville West country, isn't it?'

'Twenty miles further west. As is H. E. Bates. And Kipling was just over the county boundary. Not much to boast about around here.'

'Never mind. An opportunity for some decent writer to make a mark, then, wouldn't you say?' He poured copiously. 'May I return to business? James and his whereabouts? Since I spoke to you on Thursday I've discovered that there's some screening agency in London that routes messages to him. I'm surprised you don't know of it, but there we are. I'd be very grateful if you would write to him, via this agency … Onaping Enterprises … and plead for an opportunity for me to meet him. Of course, feel free to add whatever other personal stuff you may wish; but the main thing is to let him know that I'm ready to travel to see him anywhere within reason.'

They had been in the midst of their first course – bowls of hot carrot and tomato soup – when she ventured to demand a good reason why she should put herself out on his behalf. He pursed his lips.

'I've already told you that it's all rather sensitive but there could be a major story in it, somewhere along the line.' Noting her stony features, he went on, 'But I can divulge something about the Tulliver Trust which may interest you, especially as it may add to, rather than detract from, James's air of mystery.' He paused conspiratorially. 'Provided, of course, you are prepared to help.'

'Why don't you write the damned letter?'

'Because it would be filtered out of the system. Have you come across Consigliere Marotti? I see from your expression that you've had the pleasure. So you know what I'm up against. But I'm sure that a skilfully worded letter from you would reach him.'

Phyllis stared fiercely at her soup-bowl. Eventually she raised her head. 'So, tell me about this Trust.'

CHAPTER SEVEN

Jenning's account of the Tulliver Trust's history was understandably incomplete and, in several respects, inaccurate owing to the steady accretion of obfuscation skeined around its multi-layered activities, none of which, could have been foreseen when, in 1887, Hamish Tulliver first made his mark in Western Ontario.

Hamish's own father had emigrated from Skye to Newfoundland in 1851 with his young wife and two year old son to take up a position with the Hudson Bay Company.

For nearly two hundred years the Company of Adventurers had enjoyed a trading monopoly in Rupert's Land – 'in whatsoever latitude they shall bee that lye within the entrance of the Streightes commonly called Hudson's Streightes'. By the date of the Tullivers' arrival, the Company effectively ruled over whatever passed for civilisation, and several settlements that could not be said to have achieved that status, in the vastness between the Great Lakes and the Pacific; and where it did not absolutely rule it still decisively influenced the execution of trade. Its ten Council members, predominantly Scots, provided the only enforceable system of governance north of the USA border, each of the ten administering a territory which could have swallowed their native Scotland several times over, but all subject to the will of the Governor-in-Chief, Sir George Simpson, who lorded it in Company House at Lachine on the St Lawrence, his orders being carried by horse, canoe and foot across endless tracts of forest, peaks and plain from his table surmounted by the Adventurers' armorial bearings: beavers in quarters, fox sejant proper, elks supporting.

To this enterprise young Duncan Tulliver bequeathed his abundant energy, dour Presbyterian values and navigational skills honed in the world's most treacherous waters off Cape Wrath. He was responsible for piloting Company vessels through the Gulf and Cabot Strait, schooners carrying prodigious cargoes of fur to distant

Gravesend and returning with a weighty array of manufactured goods to be distributed through Company posts across an expanding hinterland. Duncan prospered. His competence earned him, within seven years, a preferment that brought him to Lachine itself. His first-born, however, had never – since reaching the age of discretion – been inclined to follow his father into factorship, unlike most sons of Company employees who saw themselves as members of a proud clan, a loyalty never to be forsworn. Hamish though had been shrewd enough to recognise that the findings of a Parliamentary Select Committee in 1857 had set in train a process that was, within a generation, to remove the Company's monopoly and encourage others to seize their share of whatever riches this still largely virgin domain could offer. Accordingly, at the age of 19 Hamish took leave of his family. Duncan, coldly disapproving, distant and within four years of his death from swamp-fever was destined never to see his son again.

Hamish, shrugging off his mother's protestations, drove his canoe westwards up the Ottawa River, hauling his provisions over the Sturgeon Falls to North Bay, then on again through a hard winter to Onaping Lake, some 50 miles north of Sudbury where he decided it was worth halting to look around, a decision he found no reason to fault during the long years remaining to him until his fatal aneurysm in 1923.

There, near Laforest, he founded a logging business with the enthusiastic support of a Metis partner he had acquired at North Bay and whose sister – three-quarters French, the remainder Cree – he married in 1875. A faded photograph on the dining-room wall of the solid log and stone house which still punctuated the pine-fringed southern shores of Lake Onaping revealed a stern, unyielding character, ruddy-faced and balding, looking much older than his then 26 years, towering over a dark, sparrow-boned Marie-Louise who grasped, in nervous gloved hands, a tremulous sheaf of white lilies.

Their union produced three children: a first-born daughter, Jeanne-Marie, who was to marry happily at nineteen into the Leplange banking family from Sudbury; a much-adored Gregory who did not survive a rock-fall in his twentieth year; and a final son, Gordon, born in 1897 when Marie-Louise was held to be dangerously mature for such an enterprise.

It had not been a jocund household in which Gordon spent his childhood. Marie-Louise, who owned a frail mental disposition, was doomed always to struggle with her maternal responsibilities. She leant heavily on her strong-willed, wild-eyed grandmother who had arrived unbidden from the Red River wilderness to buttress her ill-equipped descendant through her third pregnancy, unbidden that is by any agency other than some weird spirit-borne premonition of Marie-Louise's need. This remarkable woman, once having set foot in Laforest, was to cast her gloomy shadow there until her health failed conclusively at the age of 101, nearly three years into her grand-daughter's widowhood. She brought with her a power-fully primitive Catholicism, an overwhelming awareness of man's propensity to sin, a sensibility amply nourished by Hamish's excellent example. He had, on leaving Lachine, jettisoned his father's heavy Presbyterian morality, no longer acknowledging the relevance of religion of whatever colour to what he had determined to make of his world. His steady accumulation of wealth owed little to observance of Christian charity and he shrugged off with a harsh laugh the old woman's minatory demands that he should render occasional signs of penitence.

Gordon's late birth had been unwelcome to both parents: to Marie-Louise who, fearful of her ability to cope with another child (despite the fact that, at core, she had inherited a Metis tough stringiness which enabled her to outlive her husband by five years) treated Gordon as a burden to be endured; and to Hamish who, far from seeing the boy as a solace following Gregory's untimely death, regarded him as a painful memory of what might have been. Hamish therefore wholly devoted himself, with almost fanatical fervour, to expanding his business interests, divorcing himself from any significant family responsibilities, a strategy facilitated by his daughter, Jeanne-Marie, having been taken off his hands shortly after Gordon's birth in a most agreeable – and financially convenient – manner. The lad was, by default, shunted into the crepuscular care of his great-grandmother throughout his formative years, a woman whose ferocious Catholicism was not only fuelled and discoloured by a primal animism derived from her Cree ancestors but also inflamed by a deep resentment of the Anglo-Irish treachery that had destroyed the independent Metis province of Manitoba less than twenty years earlier. Gordon's memory of his childhood was, in consequence, of loneliness, long silences, harsh winters, imprisonment by pallisades of impenetrable thicknesses of larch and spruce, the inescapable sick sweetness of conifer sap and of little laughter, his only solace being the romantic novels sent to him regularly by his distant sister.

It had been an occasion for celebration when, at the age of ten, he had been transported by wagon and steamboat to the St Xavier School for Catholic Youths at Montreal. Such an education did not come cheaply but Hamish was by then conspicuously prosperous, a sturdy fellow of 58 summers, well *en route* to becoming one of the most influential citizens of North-Eastern Ontario, dabbling in Provincial politics, his establishment in Sudbury to which he had moved the previous year being noted for its high Victorian splendours, its rich furnishings, the excellence of its southerly aspect, its ample table. His business had long outgrown its timber base and now encompassed interests in haulage and mining, an expansion financed at critical phases – when Hamish's ambitions temporarily outstripped his self-generated means -- by his son-in-law's bank. The Leplange connection had been particularly crucial when buying out his partner in 1901 and again when he hazarded most of his capital in promoting explorations for deposits of nickel, cobalt and tungsten in the wild terrain towards Mount Collins, searches that had eventually yielded more than satisfactory profits for all concerned.

Belatedly, Hamish had begun to experience dynastic longings and recognised – albeit reluctantly – that the changing world in which he now moved would require qualities and skills which he wholly lacked, attributes of learning, polish, social grace that had not been much in demand above Sturgeon Falls. It never occurred to him to doubt that Gordon would eventually join him in the running of what was then known as Onaping Enterprises, faint traces of which could still be found in the labyrinthine structure of the Tulliver Trust; but he insisted that a careful preparation for his son's assumption of that role, away from the stifling influence of Marie-Louise and her Cree forebear, was essential.

Gordon proved to be an assiduous student but ungregarious, scarcely remembered by his teachers, almost anonymously acquiring the qualifications that took him – after some negotiation and exchanges of money – to Oxford where he began to develop a passion for the law. His studies, however, suffered a painful interruption in 1916 when – on an impulse he could not subsequently rationalise – he enlisted and served for eight months on the Western front before sustaining a shrapnel wound at Vimy which left him with a permanent limp but spared him any further exposure to military action. He returned to Canada, at last, in 1921 upon which, to Hamish's dismay, he insisted upon settling in Toronto where he joined a small but respected firm of solicitors specialising in company law. Prior to renting his own apartment in a fashionable quarter convenient for the financial district, he had briefly accepted the hospitality of the Leplange household. He had not seen his sister, Jeanne-Marie, since leaving for University in 1914 and had almost forgotten the existence of her three children, not least that of his niece, Caroline, a spirited and intelligent girl, born at the turn of the century, for whom Gordon, to his great puzzlement, conceived an inconvenient and wholly improper passion. She in turn was fascinated by this youthful uncle who had seen so much of the world and who, perhaps because of the scars, psychic and fleshly, he had collected, distanced himself fastidiously from most company but avidly sought hers. Henri Leplange, having correctly identified the cause of his daughter's unprecedented and uncharacteristic oscillations between rapture and despair, banned Gordon from further contact, but by then it was too late.

The product of their liaison came into the world in 1923 prior to which Caroline had already quit her parents' home to share a form of unconventional domesticity with Gordon. Both sets of appalled parents found the scandal hard to bear. Hamish, by now a stooping patriarch of 74, discovered that his son's misdemeanour exposed him to the discreet but smirking sympathy of his peers, a novel but intolerable sensation. Already provoked by Gordon's apparent reluctance to apply his expensively-acquired education to the increasingly demanding management of Onaping Enterprises he told Marie-Louise of his resolve to transfer his exclusive ownership of the Company to Henri Leplange but suffered a massive, terminal stroke before he was able to put his punitive intentions into effect.

Thus, at the age of 26, Gordon found himself in possession of substantial wealth, extensive corporate responsibilities, a permanent mistress, an illegitimate son and ostracism from polite society, a heady inheritance calculated to drive an already introverted and limping man ever deeper inside his carapace of studied indifference. He swiftly resigned from the law firm and removed his household to Sault St Marie on the outfall of Lake Superior, a town in which his father had already made significant investments but where recent Tulliver history was little commented upon. He also adopted Tull as the family name, presenting Caroline to all concerned, not least to his son, Robert, as his wife. He made no effort to uproot Marie-Louise from Sudbury but provided for her care unstintingly; not that his mother made many demands upon him, dying alone in the cavernous house (which he promptly razed) in 1928, two years after her sour grandmother had gone the way of all flesh.

From his new base Gordon set about the task of rationalising the tangled ragbag of activities that then constituted Onaping Enterprises. There followed a number of disposals, sackings, strikes ruthlessly suppressed. He began the process of detaching his fortunes from those of the Leplange Bank, his long-term aim being total self-sufficiency, finally achieved in the early 1960s. He also applied his expertise in corporate law to draw up a Trust structure that was simultaneously coherent and opaque. Steadily he reduced his direct involvement in running his various concerns, opting instead to create networks of holding companies over which he exercised control through financial mechanisms. Most of his senior managers never met him. He developed a talent for searching out a few highly-motivated men who became his 'Guardians' and upon whose shoulders he placed well-rewarded responsibility to promote his interests, to which their own were tightly bound. He was, from the outset, prepared to abide by his own definition of the permissible. He exploited Sault St Marie's proximity to the Michigan shoreline by arranging for the export of substantial quantities of distilled products not at that time readily available in the States. Through this trade he was, for some years, able to draw upon unconventional sources of finance, to the mutual satisfaction of both supplier and customer, which he was able to put to uses that the orthodox banking system – not least the Leplanges – would have been embarrassed to underwrite. He deployed the proceeds to acquire interests in activities – some of a dubious nature, and invariably calling for bribery – in the Middle East and Latin America, oil and shale concessions proving particularly rewarding. A foray into movie production in California was less so. This latter experience triggered in him an anti-semitic instinct, derived possibly from the Frankish strain in his blood, that was later to prompt certain investments in a chemical plant in Düsseldorf during the 1940s.

Throughout these years Caroline showed herself to be a woman of no small consequence. There were to be no more children, the risk of adverse outcome being agreed by both to be excessive; but the bond between them never slackened. Although her features were too powerfully delineated to allow her to claim the title of beauty she possessed a sparky stylishness that was profoundly attractive to men and a strength of will that fortified her against her unyielding rejection by her parents. These qualities were supplemented by a feminine shrewdness (on which Gordon drew whenever uncertain of the trustworthiness of an acquaintance) spiced by an acquired cynicism regarding mankind's condition. As Joseph Marotti, Robert's only childhood friend, was once to observe, 'Your mother isn't great on the human race, is she?' Always ready to assume the worst of people, she knew instinctively which way to jump should a choice arise between the pursuit of commercial advantage and some inconvenience (at best) to others. She taught Robert to act on the assumption that at all times men's actions would be governed by venal self-interest but that, moreover, it was entirely appropriate that this should be so. She would declare, 'The whole of economic theory rests on precisely this principle, only people don't care to admit it, so don't be fooled by moralists who try to tell you otherwise.' As for the law: 'It's there to protect the clever ones who've made it from the stupid ones who don't know how.' By extension, she asserted that openness of purpose was a fool's tactic, and that unseen exercise of power over others provided the highest degree of pleasure.

As a child Robert was shielded from the skin-thickening experiences that inevitably accompany enforced mingling with assorted contemporaries at school. Instead, a small brigade of well-qualified tutors was hired to ground his education, Caroline's conceptual model being Alexander at Aristotle's knee. Large-boned and sinewy with a ruddy stubborn expression, Robert demonstrated early a phenomenally retentive capacity: few facts, once received, escaped his memory as certain of his associates were later to discover, to their disadvantage. His schooling was shared only with Joseph Marotti, the son of Salvatore, a talented, if sly, immigrant from Genoa whom Gordon Tull had initially appointed to handle his investments in Venezuela but whose adroit financial manoeuvres had led, after suitable inducements had been settled upon, to his transplantation to the cooler climate of Ontario.

Only a year separated the two youths, Joseph being the elder. For the best part of a decade they were inseparable. In 1939, however, external events began to threaten the protective shield which Caroline had erected around her son. She had always recognised that Robert's intended entry to university would mark the end of her direct dominion, but had provisionally agreed with her husband that she would accompany the boy, to Oxford naturally, for at least his initial months 'to keep him straight'. With the outbreak of war, however, and with any colonial at risk of being sucked into the conflict, particularly if based in England, all concerned agreed that an alternative strategy had to be adopted.

Gordon took to staring at his russet-haired offspring while thoughtfully scratching his increasingly arthritic thigh. Having experienced war at close quarters, he discounted any claim for its character-building properties. It fell to Salvatore Marotti to suggest Madrid as suitably neutral territory with a decent, if not deeply resonant, academic pedigree; he intended to send Joseph there as soon as possible in order to hone his Spanish, a language of which his son had some basic command following his early childhood in Venezuela. Gordon made enquiries and satisfied himself that the Mathematics Department in Madrid had a more than adequate reputation. Thus it followed that, in March 1940, Robert and Joseph travelled by cruise liner from New York to Bilbao, under Caroline's close supervision. They rented a villa initially in Leganes, south-west of Madrid, where they spent the spring and summer studying the language and familiarising themselves with the forms of behaviour expected of foreign visitors to Franco's Spain. Joseph, having already reached the age of eighteen, secured a place for himself to read Economics, and moved to an apartment in the city that autumn. Robert whiled away a lonely year, seeing Joseph occasionally at weekends and during vacations, but mainly being subject once more to force feeding by private tutors when he was not being exhorted by Caroline to admire the splendours of Castile and Aragon. What really excited him however – much to his mother's alarm – were the majestic Sierras in which he insisted he be allowed to wander in the company of local guides, following high trails across verti-ginous ravines above snow-swollen rivers.

When, finally, Robert entered university Caroline succumbed to the pleading of her husband and returned, not without great fore-bodings, via Cape Town and Rio de Janeiro, to the rain-spattered shores of Lake Superior.

To his mother's surprise, tinged with an unwelcome sense of her redundancy, Robert managed to survive with occasional support from the ever-willing Joseph. After completing his studies satisfac-torily he made haste to take passage across the South Atlantic, not without hazard, on a cargo vessel to Buenos Aires. His parents met him to discover a son who had thickened physically and developed a toughness of character beyond any potentiality hinted at during his tender years. He had also acquired an unattractive offhandedness, an air of cold detachment. He did not choose to relate easily to others and showed no sign that the resulting social isolation occasioned him any discomfort.

Gordon arranged for him to be apprenticed to Salvatore Marotti who had returned to South America in 1943 to look after the Trust's investments in copper, tin, coffee, beef and other less overt enterprises in Colombia and Bolivia. Robert opted to live in an apartment above the Trust's Buenos Aires office, fastidious in his habits, frugal in expenditures, his sole admitted passion being scaling whatever peaks he felt lay within his slowly improving level of competence, his aptitude for which had been developed by solitary expeditions during his university vacations to the Picos de Europa and eastwards into Andorra. Now he took himself off to the southern Andes, to Copahue, Tinguiririca and mighty Tupungato; or to the Peruvian Huayhuash Cordillera where he tested himself on the perilous glaciers of Yerupaja and Rasac. Caroline protested but was politely ignored. Finally she brought her apprehensions to her husband's attention with a vehemence that could not be brushed aside. Gordon flew to Buenos Aires and peremptorily ordered Robert back to Canada. His son briefly contemplated rebellion; harsh words were exchanged. Eventually, however, the debt owed to his parents was acknowledged, a sense of obligation that was reinforced as Gordon's dynastic ambitions were firmly pressed upon him. A secure succession, it was forcibly pointed out, required more than a sole heir, particularly if the latter happened to possess an unfortunate taste for life-threatening pursuits. Thus, in 1946, with a graceless show of reluctance, Robert returned to Sault St Marie where, in accordance with his parents' promptings, and in cold blood, he began to pay court to a childless widow of French-Canadian stock, some four years his senior, whose husband had been killed in a bombing raid over Cologne, a woman to whom he had been introduced at one of his mother's musical evenings.

Francine, a pragmatic soul, had taken up a post as primary school teacher in her home town of Glendale some twenty miles north of the Trust's centre of operations but close enough for its inhabitants to be aware of the Tulls and their wealth. Certainly Francine was wholly seized of the material advantages that Robert was offering her, and had no illusions that deep attachment might accompany them. He was not, however, unprepossessing with his ruddy vigour, and she found herself charmed by Caroline's frankness, unflagging vivacity and sense of style. A bond of understanding was forged between the two women which encouraged the younger to enter into serious negotiations with Gordon about the terms on which she might entertain his son's proposal. It was accepted that Francine could – if she wished – continue in her profession until motherhood was achieved, but that immediately on marriage, she would receive a not-ungenerous independent income to be subsequently aug-mented in tranches of 25% of the initial value for each child of their union up to a maximum of four. If, however, no progeny were achieved by Francine's 40th birthday, divorce would not be contested and her stipend, although continuing to be paid throughout her life, would be reduced by half. These terms were acceptable to Francine subject to a caveat being entered which would negate any reduction in her entitlement should it be established that Robert was sterile or should he suffer an untimely death. This sub-clause was reluctantly acceded to by Gordon who saw it as a possible indication that the circumstances of his son's birth might have been more widely appreciated than he found it comfortable to contemplate. Negotia-tions completed, a sparsely-attended wedding ceremony was followed within a year by the birth of a daughter, Morag. After a worrying interval of six years Colin arrived, to his grandfather's excessive delight, and finally – a distressingly late afterthought – James emerged blinking into a pale November sky in 1964. This last delivery, a most painful, complex and exhausting triumph, took its toll on Francine's hitherto robust health. James was to know little of his mother. Cancer spreading from the womb robbed him of her care before his second birthday, thereby providing Gordon – not that he allowed himself to take comfort from the outcome – with an admirable return from his pre-nuptial contract.

The arrival of these grandchildren not only enabled Caroline to lay confident claim to possession of a conventional household but also released in Gordon a renewed surge of ambition. He became expert, ahead of the game, in off-shore trading and in what came to be known as money-laundering. He arranged for his companies to be wrapped within companies, their transactions sliding invisibly across frontiers. His principal aides throughout these manoeuvres remained the Marottis: Salvatore who managed the South American connections until his death in 1959, and Joseph who was based in New York and handled most of the European business.

On Colin's birth, his grandfather had seen fit to create a charitable foundation, the Glendale Trust, named in tribute to his daughter-in-law, Francine. He placed Robert in charge of its affairs, trusting that the public profile his son would establish as a consequence of the

Trust's benefactions would enable him to acquire a patina of acceptability to which he himself had never felt sufficiently bullish to lay claim, but of which he believed old Hamish, over fifty years beneath the sod, would have approved. He also hoped, as did Caroline (whose idea it was), that exposure to the petty audit of community response to the Trust's initiatives might help Robert to overcome his reclusivity which marriage had done little to soften. The ploy did not succeed. Robert remained happy only when on lonely treks into the wilderness. Several weeks each year were devoted to rigorous explorations of the peaks around Banff and Jasper, or further north along the South Nahanni River into the remote Selwyn Range where he established a cabin retreat near Mount Hunt. Robert's interest in his children was, at best, perfunctory; he had displayed no apparent distress at Francine's painful death, nor – within a year of that event – his mother's fatal crash on an icy road outside Toronto. Gordon, by then beyond his 70th birthday, was left – at a time when he found his emotions closer to the surface of his skin than had ever previously been the case – to provide front-line support to his three grandchildren. No amount of raillery on his part, however pointed, moved Robert to attend seriously to his offspring's needs.

Morag was the least pressing problem. Nearly seventeen when her mother died, and being a girl of tough disposition, she bore her grief easily and was soon to depart for Chicago to study structural engineering. The younger boys were a wholly different matter, James in particular, being a demanding infant badly in need of a woman's attention. Another intense debate between Gordon and Robert forced the latter to concede that a surrogate mother had to be acquired. Robert, however, was adamant that any candidate for his hand had to accept that no further progeny were to be countenanced; and he was notably reluctant to participate in courtly pursuit. Joseph Marotti was to provide the solution. He spoke to Robert of his illegitimate daughter, Constanza, an accidental result of an ill-fated adventure during his final year in Madrid, a child for whom old Salvatore had accepted a duty of care. After Salvatore's death she had lived uncomfortably in Joseph's household, a deeply unattractive girl in her mid-twenties, resented by Joseph's wife and his legitimate son, Leo, but schooled since infancy to accept subservience as her natural condition. Her Catholicism presented no problem given that the Tullivers had been dipping into and out of alternative religious affiliations for a century. Moreover, Constanza would need no lengthy instruction in the company's idiosyncratic customs and practices. Thus it came about that an even closer bond was forged between the Tullivers and the Marottis, Scots and Genoese: dangerous conjunction.

The pine-shrouded mansion on a bluff overlooking the junction of Wabos River and the Soo Canal was not a notably convivial establishment. Gordon, whose ancient leg wound increasingly plagued him, tended to confine himself to a ground-floor apartment from which he continued obsessively to attend to the Trust's affairs, attended upon by the assiduous Joseph and, progressively, by his careful grandson, Colin, who from the earliest age had shown an ardour for the business that his cold and indifferent father wholly lacked. It was not that Robert neglected his responsibilities. He played his part in the empire's growth, but only as required. He was competent and reliable, his primary concern being the Trust's wholly legitimate holdings in Canada, principally in extractive industries. All murkier aspects were left to the Marottis. Gordon handled the big issues, the take-overs, the dynamics. Robert was happy to be sidelined. He considered that two marriages of convenience were a sufficient demonstration of a commitment that exceeded normal familial requirements. He had no complaint to lodge against Constanza whose gentle, compliant and serene nature had been of great comfort to his younger son; and her undemanding acceptance of his tepid sexuality had earned Robert's respect. He remained genuinely attached to Joseph, once his fellow student, now his father-in-law, and acknowledged without rancour Marotti's superior energy and ambition. He also approved of the extent to which Colin had fallen under Joseph's tutelage, recognising in his older son that virulent strain of Tulliver acquisitiveness which he himself had never possessed, a fact which did not escape Gordon's keen eye.

Robert and his family occupied the upper reaches of the echoing house (little altered since Caroline's day) while the intermediate floor – providing some degree of *cordon sanitaire* between the generations – was given over to communal eating spaces and secure offices. It was in one of the latter that, shortly before his death in 1977, Gordon handed his son the sheet of paper which effectively conveyed control of the entire Tulliver empire to Colin, lesser interests being vested in equal parts to Joseph Marotti, to Robert and to the latter's two other children, James's to be held in trust until he reached the age of 21. These minority shares fell short – even in combination – of Colin's portion.

Robert had barely blinked but had immediately made a will ensuring that his inheritance would be divided, on his death, between Morag and James, save for a generous endowment to Constanza. He thereafter scaled down his involvement in the Trust's affairs, devoting himself principally for the next fifteen years to his abiding love affair with empty spaces until his ultimate appointment with an avalanche on the north face of the inappropriately named Mount Joy in the Yukon. Constanza mourned him but his passing was of little consequence, other than financial, to his children. Robert could not, nor would have wished to, lay claim to having been loved, other than by his mother who came to see in him a hunger for impersonal epiphanies that could perhaps be traced back to his remote Indian antecedents. From this point onwards, Jennings's account of the Tulliver history had been broadly accurate: a chronicle of a secretive Trust Company controlled by James's reclusive elder brother; rumours of not-wholly legitimate involvement in recent dealings in Eastern Europe; financial interests across half the universe characterised by brutal but skilled manipulation of currency exchanges across electronic banking systems; a steadily growing ownership of media enterprises.

Colin had apparently spurned university education and was rarely seen outside Ontario, abjuring public exposure. James had been sent abroad at eleven to Dulwich College, thereafter to Oxford – following in his grandfather's footsteps – and finally to Harvard where he completed his study of history and philosophy. Little was known of Morag who would now be in her late 40s; Jennings had surmised that she had settled, after graduating as an engineer, into a quiet marriage. As over so many aspects of the Tulliver's affairs, guided by the well-nigh invisible hands of Colin Tull and Joseph Marotti, a close-woven veil of discretion had been drawn.

CHAPTER EIGHT

6 November

Dear James,

I'm not going to attempt to reach you via that creature Marotti any further. I'm not even sure that he passes my messages on. Hence this letter. If this doesn't bring a response I'll regard all contact at an end. And get on with the rest of my life. Don't fret. I expect I'll survive.

If we were eyeball to eyeball I'd say much more than I'm prepared to commit to paper. I don't know who might be reading this, and I'm not much given to baring my soul at the best of times, that is at the most intimate of times. But I do miss you – shameful admission – and I regret not having swallowed my pride and accompanied you to Ireland. But it didn't seem a good idea at the time.

So now you know; or somebody does.

To business. Hugh Jennings is most anxious to meet you, so anxious that he has recruited my help in an attempt to reach you. Could you – not Marotti – give him a call? I'm sure you haven't forgotten his number. I've no idea what's bothering him but he seemed very interested in the Tulliver Trust, a subject on which he was much more informative than you have ever been. I suspect that his paper is about to produce an exposé. Someone must have prompted him. Any guesses? At any rate, until he briefed me about the Trust I'd no idea of the scale of your family's enterprise.

Incidentally, Hugh has offered me a job. I'm tempted. What else have I to do with my life? Of course I know he has mixed motives, but who hasn't? Poor Hugh. In affairs of the trousers he's not to be taken seriously. Certainly his wife doesn't.

I hope your life is going to plan, whatever that may be. If you deign to reply, perhaps you could give me some news that I might convey to the many enquirers after your well-being.

Please telephone Jennings.

Love, Phyllis.

P. S. I've taken a copy of this letter in case I ever need to prove to you that it was actually written. You may judge from this how persecuted I'm feeling!

17 November

Dear Phyl,

Abject apologies for having been elusive. I have no valid excuse. Joseph Marotti (who, incidentally, is my stepmother's father and a major share-holder in the Trust) has been religiously conveying your approaches to me but I've been strangely reluctant to respond. At first I didn't know quite what to say, and then as weeks passed it became more difficult to say anything. Time is not invariably healing.

As you can see from the postmark I'm back in Canada. In the event, I spent very little time in Ireland. I discharged some family business there, reluctantly, and returned within two weeks to New York where, after some discussion with my brother, I've assumed control of the charitable activities of the Trust; low key but tolerably rewarding.

I suspect I know what Jennings wishes to discuss with me, but I'm the wrong person to handle it. I've drawn his request to the attention of my brother who is considering how best to proceed. If Jennings doesn't hear from Colin within, say, a month he should contact me directly at the above e-mail address.

I'm not planning to return to Europe for a while, but perhaps you could contemplate meeting me in New York? Should I send you air tickets? I know we need to talk, but I'm going through an acute phase of what has become a semi-permanent condition of doubt and confusion, partly self-induced, partly family-related. Although I didn't recognise these symptoms at the time, such uncertainties must have precipitated my flight from London, and from you, in the summer. I'm not sure that, even now, I'm ready to unburden myself by confessing the scale of my problems even to you, but if I can bring myself to do so I accept that it will have to be 'eyeball to eyeball'. Already I feel that I've committed too much to paper.

Believe it or not, I'm missing you too. Greatly.

James.

29 November

Dear James

Now I'm really worried. Hence the e-mail. What on earth is going on? There's no way at present I can cross the Atlantic. I too have family problems. My father, you'll be astonished to learn, has become involved in a truly stupid liaison, and I really have to be around to support Mother. Are you sure you can't come to London?

More moans from Hugh. He still hasn't heard from your brother, and sounds increasingly depressed. He was banging on again about the Tulliver billions. I'm beginning to feel out of my depth simply writing to you. Basically I'm a simple suburban soul. Can I afford you?

I'm also much intrigued by your glimmerings of information about your family. What a secretive creature you are! You told me of your mother's early death, but never once have you previously mentioned a stepmother. Who must be quite youthful. If we do ever manage to see each other again I shall insist upon being allowed to tweak the curtain which has hitherto concealed all these shadowy matters. If we are to have any future together, that is.

James, dear, I do understand that you're labouring under some severe pressure, even though I have little conception of its nature or source. Perhaps because I too have begun of late to experience the decay of once-familiar certainties I am better able to sympathise with others who find themselves in a similar predicament, a capacity for sympathy not being a trait of which I've yielded much evidence in the past. Some, including Father, would doubtless argue that there has been no perceptible change in my attitude, but I can sense my internal softening. There are times when I even accuse myself of sentimentality.

Speaking of which, I visited your dusty house last week. I still have a key, as you do to my flat. I haven't been around since August but I remembered that some of my books were stacked amongst yours (more sentimentality) including my copy of *Advancement of Learning* from which I needed to lift a quotation: 'In civil actions he is the greater and deeper politique that can make other men the instruments of his will and ends, and yet never acquaint them with his purpose.' Which fits well with a piece I'm writing on Machiavelli's impact on Elizabethan attitudes.

Incidentally there were signs of more recent occupation in the house: a pair of woman's slippers; a half-empty bottle of face cream (expensive); a used towel. I remain surprised by the intensity of feeling which these mundane objects aroused in me. Any explanation? (Not that I'm owed one.)

Back to my starting point. Can't you manage a trip to London? (I almost wrote 'another' – imagination playing around the towel. Sorry.) Please, let's meet soon.

Love

Phyllis.

2 December

Dearest Phyl

A compromise. I can manage Ireland over the New Year. We've acquired a house in County Cork which is currently being refurbished and which Colin wants me to inspect. We'd be, more or less, alone. Lots of explanations on the agenda. Please say yes.

Colin has promised to contact Jennings before Christmas.

Cream, slippers, towel etc – down to my sister. She uses the place occasionally.

Still missing you – even more.

James

3 December

Dear Tull,

Phyllis gave me this e-mail number, for which I'm grateful. I apologise for being importunate, but events are pressing in upon me and I fear I'll have to risk this communication not being entirely secure.

My Whitehall sources (eminently reliable) have led me to believe that the Tulliver Trust may be interested in acquiring *The Mercury*. You should know that HMG will resist the Trust taking a majority share, although a lesser holding may be nodded through. Please advise your brother accordingly.

I would have vouchsafed this information earlier had he, or you, deigned to have contacted me. Reasons for HMG's nervousness (verging upon hostility) could be provided if required of me; and I hereby offer my services as intermediary should the Trust see any advantage in making use of me – assuming, of course, that my intelligence is as well-founded as I believe it to be. I would also expect my pivotal position to be (appropriately) acknowledged.

Regards,

Jennings.

5 December

My dear Jennings,

We are most appreciative of your communication which – my brother advises me – confirms much of the assessment our analysts have already 'fed into the decision matrix'. Quite what will emerge from this arcane process is unknown to me. Colin makes all the key executive judgements on Trust business. I merely wave a congratulatory flag on those few occasions where I feel my approbation is warranted.

I do hope your dear wife is well.

Regards,

James.

5 December

Dear Tull,

Well, thanks!

Jennings.

7 December

Dearest James,

Yes.

Phyllis.

CHAPTER NINE

She took her time in the village store, not needing much beyond four pounds of potatoes, bread and a packet of cornflakes, but being in no hurry to return home with its prospect of further clashes with Eamonn. The weekend had been purgatory and although more miseries stretched out ahead of her she was now reconciled to the necessity of enduring them, even the slaps to her head he had winged her way, especially after a few glasses of Paddy. Her heavy woollen scarf disguised most of the bruising but the swollen lips caused her to mumble as she exchanged the barest number of words with young Aileen at the till. What she couldn't yet get her mind around was how she would tell Colclough that she would not be behind his bar that evening, or ever again as far as she could see.

As she left the shop, plastic bag in hand, the sharp December wind stung her eyes, forcing involuntary tears. She turned up the hill, recognising as she did so Colclough's Land Rover outside the Ballydehob Arms. He would be taking his regular morning brandy with Maeve Rafferty, having returned from a visit to the brewery where she knew he had intended to lodge a complaint about the recent irregularity of deliveries. He would be chirpy after a show of masterful stewardship, a minor resurgence of his old ebullience which he had been at pains of demonstrating ever since the cheque from Onaping Enterprises had boosted his bank account and, more to the point, had disengaged him from further involvement in what-ever might be happening out at Bracken Point. She knew he had declared his fee to the Fenians, and it seems that they had waived any claim upon it. He had confessed to being nonplussed by their relaxed attitude. Perhaps, he had speculated – elbow on pillow, his whiskey breath close to her ear – they had tracked down Moira Kierney and had clawed their money back. They had powerful connections in the States. Annie had her own ideas on that matter but had kept them to herself.

A few days earlier she had been walking home from Casey's when she had encountered the American with the dark, crooked smile. He had pulled his car over just on the town side of the estuary, wound down his window and offered to drive her home. They had, by then, established an uneasy rapport during the few occasions he had called in the bar for a drink, attempting – with limited success – to ingratiate himself with the regulars. Annie too found him discomfiting with his metropolitan ways and his ambiguous relationship with the woman, Morag, who had shown herself but rarely in the town and whose undisguised dislike of its inhabitants was now legendary.

'C'mon, take the weight off your legs.'

'It's out of your way.'

'No problem.' Again that slow, hungry smile. 'I'm not contagious, Annie.'

She had squeezed into the passenger seat, taking care to keep her skirt low around her knees, avoiding risk of transmitting misleading signals. She said, 'So, how are things going, then? I understand there's a chance of the work not being finished by Christmas.'

'Is there anything the guy doesn't tell you?' He started the engine but kept his dark eyes upon her.

'That's common knowledge. Everyone, the builders, the suppliers, everyone, knows that Maurice was told by that fella Marotti in New York to have the house made ready by the end of the year, but that there's been some hitches. And I've heard that Morag bitch say as much.'

'Well, things have much improved. A few arses have been booted hard and you'll be pleased to hear we're almost back on schedule. I'll soon be heading off to the Big Apple, thank God. Nothing much more to keep me here.' He grinned at some private joke. 'Incidentally, that Marotti fellow of whom you spoke just now is my father.'

'Someone had to be, I suppose. And the bitch? Is she leaving too?'

'Before me. Her end of the business is pretty well tied up.'

'And what end would that be, so?'

'Aren't you the nosy one.' He had laughed throatily. 'Like Colclough, you're better advised to keep out of it.'

She persisted, sensing he was in a good humour. 'So will James Tull be after moving in soon, then?'

'Doubt it, Annie, although I expect he'll be visiting with you from time to time. But don't wet your pants in anticipation of seeing much of him. The Tulls are a migratory breed.'

As they pulled into her street – parallel rows of council terraced dwellings, greyish brick, uniform green paint on doors and windows, yellowing roof tiles – he had wrinkled his nose in perceptible disapproval. She said, 'Not much to look at, is it? Beggars can't be choosers.'

'You could do better. You're a bright one. I like your style.'

''Tis a wicked devil you are, trying to unsettle a happily married woman.'

'Not so happy, I guess, from what I hear.'

'So who's been gabbing, then? Spreading rumours?' She stared at him aggressively.

He shrugged, 'Part of my job is to talk to people, to find out what gives in any place we're investing in. So I've been picking up morsels of information from a whole bundle of neighbourly folk, including from guys along the coast who seem to know your friend Colclough pretty well. And what he gets up to in his spare time.'

She was now angry, reddening below her thick brown hair. 'And what exactly do you mean by that?'

'Easy, easy. I'm not planning to speak out of turn.'

'You already bloody have!'

He had parked immediately outside her door. It was not until later that she came to wonder how he had known her address.

He asked, 'May I come in? I'd enjoy a coffee, or something. I don't want to upset you, leave you upset.'

'Not a good idea.'

'Husband home?'

'Fuck off!'

'Hey, don't be so hard on me. Can't blame a guy for trying. It's the American way.'

'Marotti sounds more Italian than American.'

'Melting pot of nations. Confusion of cultures. Still melting; still confused. That's why we need a whole lot of forgiving.' He laughed again.

'Was that an apology?'

'One of my rules: never apologise, never explain. *Qui s'excuse, s'accuse.*'

'Come again?'

But he had merely smiled, shrugged and departed. She hadn't seen him since but had, too late, recognised that their having met by the bridge had not been at all coincidental. Some form of negotiation had been taking place, at least on his part, not wholly or even mainly sexual, the significance of which remained unclear to her. Then, three days ago, Eamonn had returned after a long thirsty haul from Istanbul via Vienna. First he had slept, then made a few 'phone calls and, come evening, had gone drinking in a fisherman's bar beyond Rossbrin where he'd arranged to meet friends of long-standing recently back from Icelandic waters. The next day he had confronted her with scarlet accusations. She couldn't prise from him the name of his informant. It was unlikely to have been his friends. There must have been someone else in the bar. When he had come home from boozing he had been silent, cold, morose. Nothing had happened in bed, which was unusual after his long absence. He had turned his back to her and had seemed to have fallen asleep. She had put it down to weariness combined with the drink. She had been wrong.

Next morning she had been first downstairs, to put on the kettle. The tea had not even brewed when she saw the sweat on him as he shouldered his way into her kitchen, an icy sweat. He had not waited for explanations, denials, mitigations. There had followed two days of raw anger: first violence, then a retreat into glacial silences punctuated by random outcrops of jagged, volcanic contempt. He had not left the house for a second, keeping her under his cold eye, but he had made a couple of telephone calls, one of them to Father Dominic, the other she knew not to whom. Finally she had drawn attention to the need for a few household essen-tials, and he had raised no objection to her expedition. But she guessed that she was being tested and that someone would report her movements.

Accordingly, shopping completed, she turned away from the corner of the hill where the Ballydehob Arms faced Casey's, noting as he did so Brendan Mulcahy gesturing to her from the bar's entrance, indicating it was time to unlock the doors. She ignored him, resolved to set her feet nowhere but on the path home. But she had reckoned without Morag Ambrose whose rasping voice suddenly cut through the raw air. She must have been talking to Brendan. To be sure, she was waltzing across the road from that direction as though she owned the town. Annie couldn't understand how she had failed to notice the woman immediately. Maybe she had unconsciously not wanted to see her. Maybe it was the last thing she had wanted. The damned bitch had been putting herself about these past six weeks, winning no marks in the local popularity stakes, snarling at the O'Leary brothers for their workmanship, complaining at every restaurant within miles about their offerings, parading her designer clothes under the noses of women whose husbands couldn't sweat enough in a month to pay for the fabrics around her none-too-beautiful shoulders.

She had been visiting Casey's every week, knocking back the vodka. Sometimes she had been accompanied by Leo: more often she drank alone. She took particular pleasure in directing snide observations towards Annie who, out of loyalty to Colclough, had bitten her tongue most of the time, but had on a few notable occasions snapped back, hoping the cow might in consequence take her custom elsewhere, a hope unfulfilled. And here she was again, throat full of bile.

Morag was clad in a conspicuously expensive coat, daffodil-coloured with a high black collar, her sharp nose and powerful chin protruding above an Armani scarf. She moved fast, overtaking Annie with ease, and touched her on the elbow.

'Well, look here! My favourite bar-person. I've come into town especially to catch you. I just couldn't leave without saying goodbye. Wouldn't be polite.'

Annie remained poised for flight. 'I heard you were off. Today, is it?'

'Me today, Leo next week. All neatly wrapped up in time for Christmas. Tomorrow I'll be making waves in the Russian Tea-room.'

Annie looked blank. 'I hope you'll enjoy it so.'

'Believe me, I will.' Morag twisted her lips in a thin smile. 'Actually I'd hoped to see Colclough too.'

'I'm sure Brendan's told you that he'll be just yonder in the hotel. There's his car. He'll be delighted to see you. Sorry I can't take you to him but I must be about my shopping.'

'I do understand. You have a husband to look after. You can't be forever running after Maurice Colclough.'

Anne struggled to remain calm. 'So, have yourself a safe journey. I don't expect we'll see you again.'

'Who knows? Life is full of surprises. Six months ago I'd no notion where Ballydehob might be.'

'James Tull has much to answer for.' Annie was beginning to feel the devil troubling her blood. This woman, she knew with a sudden adamantine certainty, sat at the core of her present troubles. She continued, 'If it had not been for him you'd not have come to know about the Kierneys. Nor their friends.'

In the ensuring silence she felt Morag's hostility envelop her like a clammy fog. Then: 'You'd better be careful, lady.' A cold, throaty delivery.

Annie began to move away, down the hill, but paused to throw a valedictory remark over her shoulder. 'If you see Maurice, tell him I won't be in tonight.'

'Problems at home, then?'

Annie did not answer but raised a hand in weary acknow-ledgement as she quickened her stride down the slope towards the bridge, hearing behind her an undercurrent of contemptuous laughter.

Colclough had almost finished his 'restorative' when Morag in-vaded the snug. Maeve Rafferty, comfortable in her old red shawl, had enjoyed sharing the latest gossip about the murder of the French woman over at Durrus (the main suspect being, gratifyingly, an Englishman) but rose lumberingly to her feet at the woman's en-trance, an exercise calling for considerable effort owing to her bulk, an exertion wasted when she realised that the intruder was not requiring paid service. She sank back into her armchair with a pained sigh, seeing no overwhelming need to vacate her comfortable space near the aromatic log fire merely to accommodate the American woman whom, she knew, was detested by Maurice who would not appreciate being left alone with her.

'I called in to let you know I'm leaving later this morning. You'll be shifting less of your vodka than of late.' Morag addressed Colclough exclusively, ignoring Maeve who pulled her warm Aran shawl more tightly around her less-than-supple knees with an audible sniff.

Colclough, in his customary armchair by the small, heavily-curtained window, raised an acknowledging hand, trying unsuccessfully to disguise his irritation. He had done what had been demanded of him and would prefer no further involvement with this disagreeable woman and her property, the restoration of which had, to his mind, been receiving a wholly unwarranted degree of supervision on her part.

Morag scanned the snug with a critical eye, taking in its faded green wallpaper, sagging armchairs, a carpet that had been laid when the Republic was a noisy infant, a much-scarred games table. Her plumage underscored the room's dowdiness. She said, 'Hell's bells, I can't believe that James wasted one whole night of his life staying in a place like this. Curiosity should have brought me here earlier. Nothing else would.' As there was no spoken response she continued, 'Still, he did well in discovering Bracken Point, so I guess this was the price he had to pay.' She fingered a smeared nineteenth century print of the Limerick Races before withdrawing her digit in distaste.

'I'm pleased everything has proved to be satisfactory in the end.' Colclough shifted his feet. 'After all the grand improvements you've made I expect Mr Tull will be keen to see it again.'

'I've absolutely no idea. I doubt whether he has much personal interest. You know very well that this was a corporate purchase.'

She gave him a sideways glance. 'By the way, I've just seen your lady friend. She said to tell you that she won't be working the bar today. Looked as though the poor woman has walked into the proverbial door.'

'What do you mean?'

'Exactly what I said. She won't be around today.'

'Annie?'

'Who the hell else? I just left her in the street and she looked a mess.' Morag moved closer. 'She probably spoke out of turn to someone who took offence. She has a bad habit that way.'

Maeve Rafferty stirred in her chair. ''Tis some help you'll be needing, Maurice, or so it seems. Should I be after giving Declan a ring to see if he can come in? He could use the extra cash from what I hear.'

Colclough did his best to appear untroubled. 'Thanks, Maeve, but I'll see to it. No great matter. Tuesday's normally quiet. I can probably manage on my own until I find out what's happening.'

Morag said, 'I should have thought that's pretty obvious.'

Maeve heaved herself to her feet. Formidable when roused, she imposed her bulk on the snug's confined space. 'That's quite enough. This is not your town and, sure to God, this is not your bloody hotel. You're no longer welcome here. You've said your piece, so you'd best be on your way.'

Morag pulled her coat protectively around her waist but otherwise stood her ground, keeping her eyes fixed on Colclough whose face dissolved into an embarrassed grin. She said, 'It's been instructive doing business with you and your associates. Not much fun, but instructive. Weird place, Ireland. Never known anywhere so pathetically dependent but pretending otherwise. You're a great people for self-delusion.'

'Dependent?' queried Colclough.

'On your well-off friends. Never seen so many signs telling you how Brussels has paid for this building, that new road, this docks scheme, that restored castle. You'd be fucked without it. Even the IRA couldn't function without bucks from the good old US of A.'

'Bugger off,' said Maeve. 'Now!'

'OK. I'm leaving.' Morag retreated before the advancing wall of flesh. 'Anyway, I'll be sure to give my baby brother your best when I see him next week.'

'Your brother?'

'James, of course. So don't go around bad-mouthing me, Colclough. He might not like it.'

They were silent as she swept out of the room, her right hand raised dismissively. Maeve turned to take Colclough by the arm. 'Jasus, Jasus, Jasus, Maurice. There goes one disagreeable bitch if ever I saw one.'

'D'you know, Maeve, I think I'll have another brandy.'

He was staring into the fire's embers when she returned with two generous measures of Hennesey's, still muttering, 'Jasus, she's a great one for spilling vinegar where it's bleeding. Have this one on yours truly, Maurice, and I'll be joining you, so I will. Were you just after hearing what she said about my hotel?' She handed over the brandy and prodded his chest with a pudgy finger. 'Mind you, it's wicked you've been. And careless with it. You'll be wise to keep well clear of Eamonn Fogharty for more than a wee while. And as for Annie ...' She left the advice unsaid.

He rubbed his chin thoughtfully, his brown eyes fixed on the last flickering flames of the logs in the grate. They made an odd couple: Maeve nearly into her sixties, lumpish, sloppy in her shawl and slippers, dwarfing Colclough in his smart suit and shining shoes, his features pointed, predatory, nervously aware; but they had long been comfortable with each other, companionable, especially since the death of Maeve's husband from testicular cancer four years earlier, a time when she had struggled to keep the hotel going, and when she had been grateful to Colclough who had stepped in to buy a 20% share of the business, a transaction known to very few. He had also, briefly, provided her with bodily comfort but neither of them had found it necessary to sustain that ill-suited activity, and it was no longer mentioned between them, nor was she resentful of his later misdemeanours.

He said, 'Nobody knew, not for certain, except you. And I know you're to be trusted. So it can be denied.'

'And don't you think Eamonn won't have beaten the truth out of her? Poor cow. But keep well away. Post her the wages due, and a bit besides.'

'Maeve, I'm fond of her.' He frowned angrily and she saw the stubborn streak in the man. 'This is the 1990s we're living in. Things like this happen every day.'

'Not in Ballydehob. And not to Annie.'

He downed his brandy. 'Well, I know who's to blame for spreading the muck. And so do you. She made it pretty plain, wouldn't you say? Pure malice.' He put on his overcoat. 'She's not the only one who can play that game. Rumour's a weapon with two edges. Did you hear her mention my "associates"? Not clever.'

'Be careful, Maurice. Best let things sort themselves out. They usually do, in the long run.' She put her arms around him affectionately. 'Anyways, you'll be coming here for your Christmas lunch, so. We'll get a little drunk together and gossip about happier times.'

'You're a good woman, Maeve.' He kissed her cheek.

Outside the wind had dropped. A cobalt sky stretched its unsullied canopy between mountain and sea. At his feet a pair of pigeons pecked keenly at some indistinguishable nourishment on the pavement. Normality appeared to reign. People he knew by name were about their business nodding to him with customary familiarity. He stared down the incline towards the river but there was no sign of Annie. A sensation of hollowness settled around his guts. Christmas with Maeve Rafferty. Was this all he had to look forward to?

He crossed the street slowly towards the bar he had until recently thought of his little 'rule and empiry', a phrase he had cherished since he'd first encountered it at school in Waterford. The words had echoed in his seventeen-year-old mind; his initial spur to ambition. Something to call one's own, however modest. Something on which one could build. Something more than Teresa, his mother, had managed to acquire: a rented terraced house, a miserable wage, nothing in the bank. Sure, she had her Republican politics and men friends who shared her passion in that direction, but that wasn't where his idea of rule and empiry might be found. He was shrewd enough to realise, however, that some of those men who hung around the house might be useful to him; and that if he did use them there might be a price to pay. But connections were all he needed. Given the right connections, he was confident he could do the rest. His mother had not fully approved but, when he asked, she had put a word in for him. And so his little empire had begun to be established.

Slowly, steadily, he had prospered. He'd moved away from Waterford, first to Dublin, then Kerry, now to Ballydehob; acquiring this, acquiring that. He did not pretend that he had shaken the earth, but that had never been his aim. A bit of rent here, a service rendered there; a few properties provided with decent bathrooms, primed by grants from sympathetic councilmen in pursuit of votes, and then sold on; and eventually his first wholly-unmortgaged bar on the outskirts of Kenmare. A decade ago he had installed his sister, Sian, as manager of the place which, by the time he had needed her assistance, he had expanded to achieve a modest hotel status, appropriately festooned with the Tourist Board's shamrock seals of approval. Sian's arrival had enabled him to move south to take advantage of the burgeoning market in residential properties along the Cork coast.

And the price expected of him had not proved to be exorbitant, not much more than keeping his ears open. Nothing too risky. Both he and they knew his limitations.

To everything a season, he thought somewhat mournfully as he unlocked Casey's front door. Perhaps it was time to move on again? Sian, although only in her late forties, was beginning to suffer badly from arthritis, and needed his support more than hitherto. He had also to consider his mother's situation. She was now over seventy and, although still robust, honoured among Fenians, couldn't be expected to look after herself for ever. Maybe consolidation in Kenmare was the answer? Maybe this difficulty over Annie provided the necessary impetus? But even as the thought occurred to him, he realised how badly he would miss Annie. Again he felt the inner hollowness. He had always taken pride in his self-sufficiency, and had been leery of exposing his peace of mind to possible interference by others, least of all a woman. Whenever any danger of that kind had shown its head in the past, he'd cut the relationship quickly, surgically, never a hesitation. But Annie had touched him. Walking away would no longer be the simple thing to do.

As he put his keys back in his trouser pocket he raised his eyes once more to the clear sky, his attention having been caught by the noise of the helicopter, a black, angry intrusion gyrating from the east towards Bracken Point. He slammed the door behind him.

Annie also saw the chopper. She had reached the plantain- and dandelion-infested patch that served as her front lawn when the reverberations throbbed from the estuary. She knew the concrete could barely have set on the re-positioned landing pad; they were wasting no time in trying it out. Standing by her ill-barbered privet hedge, breathing heavily from the haul up from the town, and gripping her shopping bag with unnecessary force, she recognised from the draining pressure in her belly that her period was due. She sucked her teeth and, placing her few purchases on the stained paving of the path, plucked a leaf from the protesting hedge, testing its waxiness, deliberately shredding green substance from its pallid spine as she listened to the rotor-blades vibrating through the thin winter air. She knew something indefinable was drawing to a close. Her body spoke to her, incontrovertibly. And a new something to which she was also incapable of ascribing a name was about to begin.

She became aware that her husband had emerged from the unquiet house and was standing behind her. He had always moved with a lithe athleticism. Although a heavy man with the first ripples of a beer gut, he propelled himself on strong thighs tapering down to narrow ankles and delicate feet improbably structured to support his matured weight, rather like, she though unflatteringly, an inverted version of one of those Russian dolls that somehow always manage to find their centre of gravity, however mishandled. She had once been in love with him, undoubtedly. The old story. Before the fat had started to coil around his abdomen; before he had taken the driving job that brought him home for no more than four or five days a month; before Colclough. Now only commitment remained.

But she still knew Eamonn's worth; knew that the manner in which she had treated him was not to be defended; knew that she dared not face Father Dominic, a sure measure of guilt.

He stood unspeaking at her shoulder, the late morning light standing out against his bristled chin. She shifted to face him.

'I know I've wronged you, Eamonn, and I'm truly sorry for it. But I need to know what you're really feeling. Is it just that something you hold to be your property has been tampered with? That your mates will think you a lesser man? Do you see what I'm saying? I must be sure about what's really going on inside you. Before I decide.'

'Decide what?'

'Whether to stay. Whatever you think, I do have a choice.'

He scuffed his boots on the gravel. 'You've bloody betrayed me. Worse, you've taken away something that has made me what I am. Or was.' His voice was clogged with pain. 'The whole sodding town must know.'

''Tis probably so, after what you've advertised on my face. But that's not the point. It's not the answer I was wanting.' She kept her eyes steadily on him. This was no time for flinching. What was it Marotti had said? Never apologise, never explain. Too late for that. And, anyway, such arrogance was beyond her. But now she had to stand her ground. 'If all that worries you is a need to show the world you're a hard man, then kicking me out might be an answer.'

'Why stop at a kicking?'

'Then you've thought about it?'

'I have so. And I've got that smarmy bastard in mind for some attention too.'

Despite her resolve she began to cry, wiping the wetness roughly off her bruised cheeks with her sleeve, but she still had more to say. If not now, when? 'If we stick together then I'll be after putting up with your hurt for the rest of my life. I know it so, but that's only proper, only to be expected, and borne. But I'll not pay that price if there's no love. What would be the point?'

'No love? Would I be in this fuckin' state other?'

'Could be. Self-pity's a powerful thing.'

His shaggy head dipped as if ducking from a blow. ''Tisn't self-pity. Not all of it. I thought we had a good marriage. I was happy in it. And I'd no doubt you were too, till now.' He held her by the shoulders, fiercely. 'You'll end it with Colclough?'

'Already have.'

'And it'll never happen again?'

'Not if I know you still love me, for what I am.'

He sucked in lungfuls of cold air, held it, then allowed a slow exhalation. She had a premonition of his next question, her stomach growing chill.

'And we'll make a baby?'

She held his gaze. 'If you still want one from me.'

'Then know that I do, woman. And know that I fuckin' love you.'

She could no longer hear the helicopter, its throbbings supplanted by the raucous jeering of gulls from the cove. She felt the world closing in around the anxious house.

CHAPTER TEN

As Christmas's prospective social engagements accumulated – office parties; invitations from networking literary agents; a dinner with Hugh Jennings and his editorial colleagues; the ritual Yuletide pilgrimage to her parents – Phyllis hit upon the idea of combining her traditional December outing with her brother with one of her regular weekly sessions with Emily Barton. The two had never met but Phyllis guessed they might prove to be compatible; besides she had news to impart and it amused her to speculate upon what their differing reactions might be.

They had agreed to gather for pre-prandial drinks at the King's Arms before moving on to Quaglino's, one of Emily's favourite restaurants, for lunch. As she approached Shepherd Market Phyllis felt more cheerful than she had been for weeks. At last, events appeared to be conspiring in her favour. As so often in mid-December, London's weather had turned mild and sunny. She had often observed how this regular benefaction was invariably greeted with dismay among her acquaintances who seemed to feel cheated by the absence of a climatic harshness which they deemed more appropriate to the season.

Phyllis arrived first and was well into her first glass of wine, speculating amiably with Marcus, behind the bar, about how they would spend £8 million should they be favoured by the newly-introduced Lottery (a professional hitman to dispose of Anne Robinson or other over-weening irritants of one's choice; a harem of catamites; taps in one's bath dispensing scotch and soda; a dedicated London taxi) when Emily waltzed in, her colour high, dressed to impress in emerald green trouser suit, shoulders swathed in a co-ordinated shawl. After being richly complimented by Marcus, she began to regale them with a graphic description of her recently-acquired 'fella' – unemployed but unabashed, divorced but domesticated in a charmingly disorganised way, mature but with the loins of a stallion on heat.

'Darlings, he's insatiable. Twice before lights out, with a repeat performance before breakfast.'

Marcus giggled. 'Great strike average. How's the deep receiver standing up to it?'

'That's for me to know and for you to fantasise about, dear boy. However, in your case, I know that such matters are of academic interest only.'

'For you, Mrs Barton, I'd make an honourable exception.'

Phyllis asked, 'How old is this satyr exactly?'

'A child of the Sixties, still sporting a pony-tail; pure Sergeant Pepper. Not the greatest of intellects but I like that in a man. I decided that it was high time I injected some vulgarity into my life. It won't last, of course. What does? But I'm pushing forty – you're not listening, Marcus – and the girls are largely off my hands. My job's going nowhere in particular: safe, undemanding and as dull as John Major's underpants. So what else has the world on offer to a girl in my situation except recreational sex?'

Phyllis smirked. 'Poor Emily. I do agree that you're a touch too young for the consolations of religion, or for gardening, the last refuges of the dried-up clitorati.'

Marcus slid along the bar to serve a trio of other early drinkers but, grinning, returned quickly to offer, 'I've always seen you as a politician-in-waiting, if I may say so, lady. All this energy, all this lippiness, all these crazy opinions.'

'D'you know, dear boy, you're very perceptive. The Lib Dems have indeed cast a fly over me, but it's all so dreadfully grubby these days, touting for the votes of Homo Tesco. "A common greyness silvers everything" as the poet said. Shelley, wasn't it?'

'Browning.' Phyllis shook her head reprovingly. 'Let's get back to this toy geriatric of yours. He seems to be rather a desperate throw. You're sure he's not simply into you for a free supply of fags and beer, or whatever other vices he enjoys?'

'Does it matter?'

'Not if you've money to burn.'

'My dear Phyl, if you have a fault it's your tendency to judge relationships exclusively in mercenary terms. What if he is using me? I'm certainly using him *con molte vivace*.'

'Just as long as you're happy.'

'Screw happiness. I'll settle for sensation. Whatever makes me feel alive in this sad, silvery, winding-down, old world of ours.'

Peter arrived, shrugging off his redundant raincoat, perspiration glistening on the rim of his unfashionable spectacles, apologising profusely for his lateness, shaking Emily's hand enthusiastically, kissing his sister on the lips and ordering a pint of Boddington. Emily appraised him with unapologetic frankness: a plump, Pickwickian chap with receding, nondescript, fair hair, prematurely-lined; but she warmed to his open smile, his friendly blue eyes. She also detected a sharp intelligence, a quality that Phyllis's prior accounts of her brother had not led her to expect.

'I understand,' she said, 'we share an interest in the law.'

'Oh, not really. Not in your sense. I've never practised. Although I do my modest bit on the enforcement front.'

Phyllis grimaced. 'Please don't encourage him to talk about his boring job. I've never really understood what it is he does in that ugly office in Liverpool Street, nor do I claim to have any curiosity about it. Indeed, I've never understood why he became a civil servant in the first place – and a tax collector to boot.'

'Sheer necessity, due to precipitate acquisition of a wife.'

They conversed amiably until the taxi arrived to convey them to Bury Street. Peter was obviously enjoying Emily's eccentricities and responded by relating a number of indiscreet stories about Ministerial foibles, past and present. Their laughter merged with and augmented the restaurant's genial cacophony as they claimed their table. They debated the menu's merits in high spirits, quaffing Chardonnay, soaking up the convivial atmosphere, the diners' mildly hysterical jollity echoing off chrome and crystal in contrast with the sobriety of uniformly youthful attendants clad in black and white moving with studied but swift formality between the tightly orchestrated tables. The newly-arrived trio scanned the menu, ordered wine and continued their chat, raising their voices to complement the general din.

Phyllis decided it was time to disclose her news. She addressed Peter. 'I don't think I've told you that I've decided to accept an invitation to spend New Year with James, in Ireland.'

'James Tull? So it's on again?'

'In a manner of speaking. Exploratory expedition. But I'm hopeful.'

'Why Ireland?'

'It seems that he's recently bought a house somewhere in West Cork. He wants to show me around that part of the world. Never having been to Ireland before, I'm excited by the prospect.'

Peter's expression was thoughtful. 'I suppose it will take your mind off Mum's problems.'

She bridled. 'I'm not exactly viewing the possibility of renewing my relationship with James as a mere diversion.' This was not the enthusiastic response she had been anticipating.

'Of course not. I'm very glad for you, if it will make you happy. But I can't understand the reason for your change of heart. I'd rather assumed things had petered out and that his sudden flight in the summer demonstrated – what shall we say – a terminal disinterest on his part.'

'It seemed that way at the time.'

'Oh, come on!' interjected Emily. 'I'd call three months of total silence more than a little discouraging. So what has changed?' She patted Peter on his arm. 'The man's a shit in my opinion. I know it's a problem for any man to match up to your sister's impossibly demanding requirements, and that Tull seemed to be the closest yet, but his sudden buggering-off was a complete bummer.'

Phyllis took a large mouthful of Chardonnay. 'You both ask what's changed. We find we have unfinished business.'

Emily snorted. 'And how exactly did you discover that? If you tell me that he made the first move, you must forgive me if I choke.'

'No, you're right. I contacted him. On Hugh Jennings's behalf and at his insistence. But I'm glad I did. Apart from the fact that I find I really miss him, I've learnt more about his background in the last few days than I was ever able to unearth when he was to hand, so to speak.'

'Such as?'

'For one thing, I've discovered that he's much wealthier than I'd imagined. Of course, I always knew that his lifestyle had to be sustained other than by his income from *The Mercury*, but Jennings now tells me that James's family is among the richest in Canada.'

'Now that,' commented Emily, 'does make a difference.'

Peter began to speak but checked himself, disguising his retracted observation with a dry cough. Phyllis noticed his worried expression but the arrival of their first course distracted her from probing his unease. Between mouthfuls of her gravadlax, however, Emily returned to the charge. 'So where does all this money come from?'

'There's some kind of private Trust owned by his family. Jennings gave me a brief account of it. I formed the impression that *The Mercury* is planning some kind of exposé of its activities, not all of which have been entirely honourable. Anyway, he was anxious to make contact with James and asked me to do my best to facilitate matters, which eventually led to my trip to Ireland.'

'Don't say that Jennings is travelling with you?'

'Certainly not. Although I do have another announcement concerning that fine fellow which I'll come to in a moment.' Phyllis, aware of Peter's continued pensiveness, said, 'I've a distinct feeling that you disapprove. Do you think I'm being too forgiving? You probably don't realise how low I've been these past few months.'

Emily spoke for him. 'He's probably uncomfortable at the thought of your visiting bandit country. I don't know that I'd be happy to allow my little sister to wander around those parts. This ceasefire is little more than a convenient fiction. Peter, tell us all. What do you think?

'Good grief, I've no more understanding of Irish politics than the next man. Not quite my field in Customs and Excise. For what it's worth I doubt if Phyl is likely to be blown up in County Cork. We're probably in greater danger here in London, not least from starvation. My stomach is desperate for the grilled duck to arrive.'

Emily refused to be diverted. 'Well for my part, I don't believe the IRA will ever voluntarily hand over its arsenal. A permanent peace is simply not in its interest.'

'So all the negotiations are a waste of time?'

'Pure posturing.' Emily was in the mood for debate and had identified Peter as a worthy adversary but one who needed to be goaded into adopting a defined position. She went on, 'It's a nonsense to treat the IRA as a bona fide political organisation, and even greater nonsense to swallow their pretension to be conducting warfare. In reality they are simply a criminal syndicate and should be dealt with as such. This isn't to say that the Catholics lacked genuine grievances about their treatment up to the 1960s. They were, of course, scandalously discriminated against. But now, the causes of those social disadvantages have been addressed by and large; yet perversely the IRA – for venal reasons of its own – is preventing the Catholic community which harbours it, like a malign virus in its system, from joining the human race.'

'So what would you do?'

'For starters I'd treat their spokesmen like bog-standard citizens rather than as privileged beings. Isn't it odd, for example, how the media seem wholly uninterested in the sex life of people like Adams and McGuinness? Let's shine the odd beacon of light into these corners. How come they escape such scrutiny? Your average Tory Minister, not to speak of American Presidents, would relish being treated with comparable delicacy. Then again, what about money?

All these newly-minted ethical standards being introduced in West-minster, under pressure of which the Tories are subsiding into oblivion, appear not to apply to Sinn Fein. Which intrepid journalist dares to poke a nose into all the sources of their funding? Our so-called free press is only too happy to be manacled when it comes to investigating touchy issues like these. A matter Phyllis might raise with Jennings, perhaps?'

Phyllis was beginning to allow her irritation to surface. She savaged a bread roll. 'I do realise that these questions outweigh the feeble news of my holiday with James, but is this quite the right time to be so damned serious? This is meant to be a festive lunch, for Christ's sake.'

'Literally,' Peter and Emily choroused, before together joining in impromptu applause at the arrival of their main course. Phyllis noted their cheerful empathy and, despite her having willed such an outcome, now found herself resenting their diminishment of her rapproachment with James. Emily had moved on to give her im-pressions of a much-lauded revival of *Guys and Dolls* which she had seen the previous week, prompting Peter to confess, in nerdish self-abasement, his inability these days to take advantage of the West End's offerings ('prior demands of the family, you know'). Phyllis squirmed as he attempted to compensate for his cultural impover-ishment by recalling every nuance of the Brando/Simmons/Sinatra film version. Emily's apparent mesmerism by his performance rein-forced her annoyance. She determined to impose upon them her rather more immediate concerns. She broke in, 'Apropos of abso-lutely nothing, I've more or less decided to accept Hugh Jennings's offer of a job. Assistant Literary Editor.'

They stared at her, impressed at last. 'Now that,' said Emily, 'is a development I believe I can unreservedly welcome.' She leant across to impart a kiss, but as she did so a doubt surfaced. 'Hang on, is this wholly compatible with the hoped-for outcome of your trip to Ballyawful?'

'I think it's possible to make it so.'

'And the money?' enquired Peter pragmatically.

'A signal improvement.' She grimaced. 'It would have to be to persuade me to work for Hugh. The point is, I can no longer take my allowance from Father for granted, no matter what he says to the contrary, so I've been obliged to face up the prospect of leaving Longstaff's, albeit with a heavy heart.'

'Doubtless Jennings will be expecting you to turn in some very special performances.' Emily turned to Peter. 'Are you aware that he has the hots for your sister?'

Peter smiled. 'A common, if inexplicable, condition. Incidentally does he know about your odyssey to Ireland?'

'No, why should he?'

'You said he was anxious to contact James.'

'So he was, but, I've done all I can on that front. I believe James, or his brother, has been in touch.'

'Ah. This brother. The mysterious Colin.'

Phyllis stared at Peter with a mixture of astonishment and curiosity. 'How on earth ...?'

'Presiding genius of the Tulliver Trust?'

'Amazing! Again, how ...?'

'My boring job. I'm paid to know about such things. I simply put together two or three of the titbits you've been dangling before us: the major Canadian company; *The Mercury*'s interest in its affairs; the Tull name. Actually, I'm ashamed that I failed to make the connection earlier.' Peter forked up a succulent portion of duck, waving it speculatively under his nose before despatching it. Full-mouthed he mumbled, 'Jennings was right to be concerned.'

'What do you mean by that?'

'Some other time. As you reminded us, this is a festive occasion. Emily, how's your lamb?'

'Devastatingly good. Pardon me, but I'm still stunned by your magisterial cross-examination. Poor Phyl. She came along today with her mouth full of news, like La Belle ...'

'Le Beau,' corrected Phyllis, unnecessarily she saw immediately as Emily broke into a teasing grin and continued, '... as you like it, and all we do is express one reservation after another. Most unfair. It seems to me that there hasn't been much gaiety in Phyl's life of late. I spend most of my time trying to cheer her up. So I say, hence vile melancholy and ring out wild bells. Let's assume a kindly corner has been turned.' And she raised her glass in a toast to her friend, her smile clear of all but the merest shade of doubt.

They lapsed into talk about the Booker novels, the laughable condition of the Windsors, the deathwish of Europhobes. Phyllis, warmed by wine, relaxed at last and melded into the collective geniality. Later, they strolled back towards Piccadilly along streets now damp and misty in a failing light, jostling past a party of youngsters spilling out of Jermyn Street armed with lager cans and burbling mobiles. Peter's bulk protected Emily as the group milled around them. Phyllis noticed without rancour that she herself was regarded as capable of coping unaided; but after Emily had twice repeated the ploy of crumpling gently into Peter's shoulder as they ambled in the direction of the King's Arms (each of them being unready to bring their carousing to a close) she was moved to murmur in his ear that he was being invited to teeter into indiscretion and that one adulterer in the family was perhaps sufficient. It proved to be a remark that spun the evening beyond recall.

Bridling, he asked, 'Have you spoken to either of the aged Ps recently?'

'To Mother, yesterday.'

'And?'

'She was composed. In my view, excessively. In denial, I expect. I suppose you've been demonstrating the usual male solidarity.'

'I met Dad two days ago, if that's what you mean. He's expecting to see you at home next weekend. We'll all be there, as usual. I'm to collect Sue at East Croydon.' He sucked in a deep breath. 'And Mum has invited Helen to join us for Christmas lunch.'

Phyllis halted. They had reached the far end of the arcade running greyly along the Ritz's frontage, a passage encumbered with people escaping from Green Park station. Unconscious of the temporary blockage she created, and of the curious looks she attracted, she raised her voice.'She said nothing of the sort to me. This is utterly outrageous!'

'Hang on, Sis. Calm yourself. Mum anticipated your reaction, which is why they left it to muggins to tell you.'

Ashen-faced, Phyllis turned to Emily who could almost smell her friend's distress. 'Sorry, but suddenly I don't feel in a celebratory mood. You must excuse me. I'll ring tomorrow.' She began to back away from them, her jaw rigid. Peter tried to take her arm but she shook him off. 'And don't imagine I'll be down next weekend.'

'Mother needs you there,' he said with quiet intensity.

Ignoring him, Phyllis walked silently away, retracing her steps towards St James's Street. Peter and Emily stared helplessly after her. He muttered, 'There are times when she's bloody impossible.'

'Never a dull moment.' Emily leant towards him. 'I, at least, am disinclined to shoot the messenger. And I'd still appreciate a vodka, now even more urgently.' She propelled him across the road, down the mean dimness of White Horse Street and into the ingratiating hubbub of the King's Arms where Marcus was still at his place of custom, his warm grin – cheeky Brixton out of lazy Barbados – as welcoming as the varieties of alcohol he dispensed with professional adroitness. They found a corner table and allowed the tension to ease out of their bodies.

'For myself,' said Emily, after a period of shared reflection, 'I judge life to be too short to waste emotional capital on situations one can do nothing about. And as the years pass fewer and fewer situations arise in which I feel it necessary to take anything other than an academic interest.'

Peter shrugged off his raincoat, his neck-tie askew, spectacles misted. She suppressed an urge to tidy him. He said, 'It's probably a father daughter thing, although they have never been particularly close. Phyllis isn't noted for displaying affection at the best of times and Father has always favoured my other sister.' He took out a handkerchief to wipe his glasses. 'I take it that you know what all this is about?'

'Phyllis has put me in the picture.'

'So, how do you explain her performance? Where does all this moral indignation come from? I've long been aware that Phyllis suffers from a serenity bypass, but this evening's exhibition is hard to take. It isn't as though her own behaviour has been impeccable. I know she's come close to wrecking a couple of marriages herself in the past. And was pretty cold-blooded about it.'

Emily sipped her vodka. 'If you want me to offer a character-reading I'll oblige. It may come across as harsh, but I want you to understand that I'm speaking as her true friend. Ours is very much a warts and all relationship. Our defects bind us together.'

'Proceed.'

'Phyllis is a woman of her age in many ways. She wants it all, on her terms. She values her independence, highly. She resents all forms of dependence, emotional or otherwise. The fact that she's financially supported by her father rankles a great deal. Why else would she bring it up so frequently? Every mention is a flick of self-laceration. That, and all other gestures of male generosity, are regarded with suspicion, if not hostility; and the more necessary the gift to sustain her life-style expectations, the greater her chagrin. It's a woman thing. I weep with debased fury every time I cash my alimony cheque.'

'Not all women. My wife empties my bank account with total equanimity.'

She smiled archly. 'Perhaps my theory should aim off to allow for relative perceptions of where true power resides.'

'Ouch!'

She patted his hand. 'Never mind, dear boy. Submissiveness, I'm sure, must have its own rewards.'

He grinned, before shaking his head. 'I can see some truth in your interpretation, but not enough to convince me. I can't see that mere financial indebtedness could generate all this truculence.'

'Well, that's only part of the problem. The trouble is that her obsession with securing independence comes at a high price. She has to clamp down, or has come to feel that she must clamp down, on anything, not least any emotions, that threaten her self-control. She is very wary of sensibility. Why else would she be so at home with 18th century literature? Why else would her affair with James Tull have progressed so slowly? She has been unable to tell him, at critical moments, how much she really wants him. Mention passion and she checks her wallet. Not a natural gambler, your sister. Then she suddenly finds passion and all the pain it brings in its wake banging about like crazy in her own family. Totally untidy parental behaviour, the one place she least expected to encounter it. I suspect that every time she thinks about her father it knocks back her readiness to commit to James. Added to which, Tull's not exactly strong on commitment either, which I guess has meant that she's had to act against her instincts when taking the initiative to contact him again; and has been persuaded to over-ride her inhibitions only because of some selfish prompting by Hugh Jennings, laced with an offer of a lucrative job. Am I speculating too wildly?'

'It sounds plausible.' He downed most of his beer in a single gulp. She pondered the wisdom of his having reverted to ale following so much wine but he seemed to be steady enough. 'You wouldn't try, I wonder, to persuade her, despite her objections, to come down to Kent next weekend? I doubt if she'll listen to me. I'd be most grateful.'

'I'll give it my best shot, but ...' with a shrug she left her pessimism unspoken.

Fifteen minutes later he began to make his excuses. The opportunity for flirtation had passed as had his inclination. Conversation had become sober, even grave. At one point he had asked whether she believed Phyllis to be genuinely in love and, on receiving her confirmation, had stared unhappily into his ale.

'Don't you like Tull?' she had asked.

'I wish she'd found someone else.'

'But all that wealth?'

'Precisely. I fear she'll be incapable of resisting it.' She noticed a delicate veil of mist reforming around the inner margins of his spectacles, and would have wished to gather it on a fingertip, thence to her lips. Instead she watched him reaching for his coat before shaking her hand. She was consoled by his holding it longer than required by mere politeness. 'It's been delightful to meet you at last, Emily. I can't imagine why it hasn't happened before.'

'Then we must make sure it happens again. I've actually found out alarmingly little about you. Phyllis has rather dominated the agenda. I still don't even know what precisely you do for your living.' She snorted apologetically. 'Terrible, isn't it? The English sin: defining people by their occupation.'

'The Much Malcock factor.'

She giggled. 'Apart from sounding like the story of my life, I'm afraid you've lost me.'

'A short story by Evelyn Waugh which captures the hierarchical subtleties of middle-class society quite beautifully. By the source of their revenue shall you know them.'

'Too obscure for me, dear boy. But I shall look it up, as a test of friendship.'

She watched his ample figure negotiate a path through the press of drinkers, his untidy head nodding a final genial acknowledgement before he stepped out into the darkness. Her glass was drained. She returned to the bar, attracting Marcus's attention.

'Left alone? That's bad.'

'Too married for me, I fear. But a cuddly creature, and clever with it.' She paid for another large vodka, and wondered whether she should telephone Phyllis. Loneliness descended around her shoulders like a shroud.

Phyllis, with a bitter taste in her throat, stamped across St James's Park, climbed Cockpit Steps, skirted the fascist exterior of Spence's Home Office, and crossed the ugly canyon of Victoria Street, thrusting past last-minute shoppers, bad-tempered commuters, the pathetic huddle of blank-eyed discards around Little Ben supping cider from brown paper bags; and finally reached Pimlico's approaches. The day which had begun with such promise – the prospect of good food, soothing wine, companionship, the smug imparting of her news – had degenerated into a series of frustrations.

Still seething, she decided more drink was required before imprisoning herself in her solitary apartment. She dropped into the Wine Vaults and ordered a bottle of Chablis. It was now four-thirty. The bleary remnants of lunchtime fraternities were knotted semi-coherently around the bar. She found a corner table and poured, swallowed and poured again, trying to fathom the reason for her anger. Nothing Peter had said had been sufficiently inflammatory to justify her reaction. Perhaps it was a flounce that had been predetermined, awaiting any pretext. Apologies would be expected; she would have to deliver them with as much grace as she could muster. But why had she loaded the embarrassment on her shoulders; why sentence herself to this miserable evening when she could still have been enjoying herself listening to Emily's salty conversation and teasing Peter? All that had been required to trigger her outburst had been an indirect reference to her father's sexuality.

David, the proprietor, came over as she was downing her second glass. 'You all right, Phyllis?'

'I've been better.'

'Life been treating you badly?'

'Not treating me at all.' She wanted him to go away. 'Actually, that's not true. I'll be fine. Just need a few quiet moments to reflect.'

He took the hint. 'I'm around if you need to chat. Or someone to get you home safely.'

'Thanks, David. Kind of you.'

Left alone, her thoughts returned to Arnold who, a few weeks earlier, had been entirely justified, she acknowledged, when pointing out that she was poorly placed to pass moral judgement on him. Only her mother had that right and, apparently, was opting not to exercise it. What was tougher to admit was the realisation that morality played no part in her condemnation of his adultery.

She remembered, not for the first time, her visit to her parents' home some five years ago. Having become habituated to solitary living in her London flat she had neglected to lock the bathroom door before showering. Having disrobed, she had felt a need to use the lavatory. She had been in full flow when Arnold had entered. Accident or design? Only he knew. Silently he had withdrawn but not as rapidly, nor with such confusion, as the occasion demanded. There had also been an involuntary twitch of his hand towards his groin. Neither of them had spoken of it since, but the recollection had remained with her, sharp and ineradicable. Worse, candour obliged her to admit to irregular fervid spasms when the inner eye of her imagination observed the rôles reversed. As now.

Leaving her bottle only half drained, she made her way the hundred yards home. The apartment closed protectively around her. Familiar objects – the geometric Turkish rug; two black leather chairs; the nineteenth century oil of Golden Cap in the lee of which her mother had been born; the neatly crowded bookshelves lining two complete walls; the shin-high table piled with scripts and magazines; the inactive word-processor in the corner – all conspiring to exude balm. Tull had told her how he envied the atmosphere she had created around her: its warmth and solidity, nothing of the poseur nor of the ephemeral. She pictured him sprawled in the chair nearest to her CD player, discussing whether it was the hour for Mahler or Marsalis and opting for the urban melancholy of the latter's midnight blues. He preferred to make love to the accompaniment of music. She remembered his story of the jazz drummer who could not achieve a climax unless prompted by Louis Armstrong's harmonies, a condition which had driven many women to madness in the days before the invention of long-playing records. Would they succeed in re-summoning that quality of intimacy in Ireland?

James had, at last, that morning, made telephonic contact to confirm details of her travel arrangements. She had to collect her air tickets from American Express. A car would pick her up to convey her to Stansted. Why had she neglected to parade these small luxuries in the faces of Emily and Peter? At least she might have elicited, on the tailcoat of such evidence, some expression of envy to balance their implied doubts. James had sounded warm, concerned, keen to embrace her, to talk 'open-heartedly' about their future. She was fearful lest her expectations were immodest but had responded as tenderly as she dared. Why couldn't she risk divulging how she truly felt? Why was there always this ultimate withholding of trust?

She slipped out of her town clothes and pulled on a track suit. The *Radio Times* informed her of an old Woody Allen film shortly due to be screened. Just what she needed. She extracted a wedge of brie and a handful of biscuits from the kitchen, and opened – with a self-absolving sigh – a bottle of Villa Corina. There was, she calculated, just enough time to telephone her mother before the film. She picked up the mouthpiece, composing her questions.

CHAPTER ELEVEN

Brendan Mulcahy occupied his usual seat in Casey's, near the corner door, his Guinness seven parts empty, rheumy eyes scanning the noisy celebrants marking the late afternoon of Christmas Eve. It being Sunday, Father Dominic was circulating among the past-Mass faithful, a glowing goblet of port in his plump fist, his colour high. He hailed the old man, laying an exculpatory palm on the latter's worn cap.

'Cheer up, Brendan. 'tis our Lord's birthday on the morrow. A time for rejoicing, not for long faces and sour thoughts.'

'If you say so, Father.'

'Indeed I do. I instruct you so. Sup up, man, and let me replenish your glass.'

When the priest returned with a fresh and creamy pint, Brendan obliged by raising a wan smile. revealing less-than-regular teeth. He said, ''Tis is my 75th Christmas. Not many more on the cards, wouldn't you say?'

'Well now, Brendan, Heaven's a wondrous retirement home. Something to look forward to. Best make sure that you're well-provided for the journey.' And Father Dominic moved on, smiling benignly.

The bar was already full, Colclough and his new girl busy at the pumps. There would soon be music: pipes, fiddle and bodhran were being warmed up, the heat rising amid a swell of voices, laughter from a group of women floating above a deeper male chorus. It should have been Brendan's kind of occasion but somehow it wasn't the same, not without Annie. The new lass – a thin, wispy thing with blonde hair out of a bottle – had no conversation. She knew fuck all about anything, and had no tits to brighten a man's eyes. Stare down the neck of her blouse and all you see is a crucifix. Not like Annie with her lustrous globes. Now there was a decent haven into which a fella might drop a proper anchor. Was it last Tuesday

that he'd bumped into her when she was waiting for the 'bus to
Schull? Someone had told him that she'd taken to shopping out of
town to avoid comment, poor cow! She'd more or less accused him
of gabbing to Eamonn about Colclough. Jesus, he knew better than
that! And he thought more of her than that. His protests, however,
hadn't cut much ice with Annie, that they hadn't. She'd stood there
defiant-like, pale as milk, skin with a look of bleached linen, flesh
sucked into the bone. And, bugger me, there's Colclough poncing
about behind the bar po-faced, chatting to the smug priest as though
nothing had happened, the sweat of avarice gleaming on his fore-
head as he pushes booze to the punters, counting the profit on every
measure. What does he care? Annie was unspoilt goods when she
started at Casey's, no more than twenty-one, newly-wed, the dew
still on her. It wasn't Eamonn that had removed the bloom, although
his travelling can't have helped. God help me, and hadn't it been
the same for me, all those years at sea and the other long times
among the English, the wife back home in Wexford with the bairns?
Although, unlike Annie, she hadn't been out of pregnancies long
enough in her prime to think about playing away from home.

He had known Colclough's father in Wexford during the '50s, not
well but enough to exchange the time of day: a thin-faced, hard-
drinking, sour bugger who was then holding down some kind of
paper-pushing job in the bus depot, having quit the ferry boats a
year or two earlier. And he remembered seeing the two children
around the town. Maurice had always been smartly turned out; no
ragged-arsed image for him, to be sure. Polished up beyond the
family's means. He and his younger sister had eventually moved
away with their mother – to Waterford, it was said – leaving George
Colclough to sort out the debts she'd saddled him with, a task which
had proved to be beyond him. He'd been found one January morning
face down in the river. It had been a ripe source of gossip that the
widow hadn't bothered to turn up for his funeral at Our Lady of
Nazareth's but then few had. Brendan had almost forgotten about
the Colcloughs until Maurice had surfaced, sleek as a seal, in
Ballydehob about nine years ago. They had never talked about the
old days. Never.

He wondered about Eamonn, a strong fella, an athlete – or had
been. Played Gaelic football for Kerry not so many winters ago. Why
hadn't he taken his boot to Colclough? Now there's a mystery.
Perhaps he's biding his time. He had speculated along those lines
the other day with the insurance man from Cork with whom he

enjoyed a grand *craic* from time to time. After all, Eamonn had raised a few bruises on Annie. Why not on bloody Colclough?

Perhaps, the insurance man had suggested, Annie had persuaded him to stay his hand? Or maybe the Americans, who'd done business recently with Colclough, had warned Eamonn off?

Not likely, Brendan had argued. It was sure as eggs was eggs that the Americans it was that had done the dirty on Annie. To be sure, that woman Morag – who, according to Maeve Rafferty, claimed to be James Tull's sister – had no love for Annie. He'd seen them with his own eyes having sharp words on the very day Annie had handed in her notice. That woman had taken against Annie from the first, and it had never been a fair contest. Annie was no pushover but the American bint had a mouth to strip the brass off a bar-rail.

The insurance man had suggested that perhaps it was Morag, not Tull himself, that had bought Bracken Point? Brendan had been obliged to consider the possibility carefully. To be sure, she it was that had been giving all the orders, putting herself about. For once, he had reserved judgement, but had commented scathingly on the fact that it had been she who'd been farting about in that bloody helicopter, and that – come to think of it – he'd neither seen or heard any sign of that devilish machine since she'd vanished from the scene a week or so ago. The insurance man had said, 'Now, there's a thing,' and had contemplated his whiskey for a quiet moment before moving their exchanges on to other topics.

Brendan would have welcomed the insurance man's company this afternoon but, on Christmas Eve, he was away in the bosom of his family, somewhere in Cork City, and Brendan was left alone, despite the crush around him, comfortless with his memories and apprehensions. He couldn't look at Colclough without bile rising in his gut.

Colclough too, despite appearances, was out of sorts. The music had begun to swell, a thigh-slapping jig for openers, but he took no pleasure in it. Playing mine host had become a penance. He longed for closing time when he could cease dissembling. He was unstringed, disconnected. Smiling affably at all, he felt related to none. He missed Annie. It was as though a chunk of his insides had been sliced away.

Yesterday he had driven past Brandon Point, cruising slowly by the secured gates, noting the newly-mounted video cameras. Four hundred yards beyond the house he had taken a sharp right turn up a narrow, climbing, weed-encrusted lane leading to O'Reilly's small-holding which spanned a rise overlooking the scattered residential properties lining the Rossbrin road. A wide grassy verge on one of the bends allowed him to park and afforded a clear view of the bay. He had used his binoculars, old British navy issue inherited from his father, to scan the coastline and slowly, deliberately, had focused upon the house that had become the source of all his discontent.

It stood snug against its tiny inlet, the repaired roof showing patches of brighter red tiles against the original ochre. A restored jetty protruded into grey waters, a tidy contract he had secured for the Flaherty brothers out at Goleen. Moored alongside snugged a powerful motor launch he had never seen before, a formidable craft that he judged, albeit no expert, would give the coastguards a lively run for their money.

He had spotted no movement around the house but guessed that such a vessel would not have been left wholly unprotected. It had been a cold, sparkling December morning, the sun blindingly low in the south-east. Twice he had been obliged to wipe his eyes as the light flared across his vision. On the second occasion he found himself remembering the Western movies of his youth in which the Apaches had unfailingly identified the approach of the doomed cavalry by the latter's use of such technology. He had tugged his overcoat more securely around his middle and leant inside the car to lift his mobile 'phone from the front seat. It had given him a brief surge of malicious pleasure to pass on news of the sighting of the launch to his contact in Bandon, but he soon relapsed into melancholy.

He had, a week earlier, caught sight of Annie in her garden as he had driven at deliberate speed past her house, not wanting to provide Eamonn with any further excuse for retribution. She had been sweeping the year's last dropping of leaves from her path, body swinging right to left, her burnished hair askew. She had not noticed him. A novel sensation of acute regret and nostalgia had assailed him. He had not welcomed the experience; it predicated a slow but inexorable descent into decay, irrecoverable loss; a closure behind him of doors to which the keys had been irretrievably mislaid.

He had once told her that he could contemplate no greater joy than to spend the rest of his life between her thighs. She had been pleasured by his words, but as he spoke them he had been lying, believing such passion to be no more than enslavement. He had often cited, with approval, the metaphor of the traditional Irish breakfast in which a hen was involved but to which a pig was committed. Colclough had always thought of himself as a natural hen. He secretly despised men devoted beyond reason to a relationship, a religion, or a cause. In his view newspapers depended for their sustained readership upon a continuous flow of miseries resulting from such irrational attachments. Zealotry was emphatically not his scene. His natural habitat lay on the semi-detached fringes of social activity: the golf club, the rotary, the church and one or two other less public fraternities; always in touch but never central to any. To proceed smoothly and comfortably through life and to leave it painlessly; a sensible man aimed for nothing more demanding.

His mother had taken a sterner view. A handsome woman of passionate convictions, her end-of-terrace house on the outskirts of Rosslare had, until she had moved to Wexford with her hurriedly-acquired husband, George, been a focal point for Republican activists.

His father had originally worked on the fishing boats out of Pembroke but had been serving in the British Merchant Navy towards the end of the War when he had bedded a lonely Teresa one wet Saturday night in Rosslare. What a mistake that had been! A man of zero aspirations, destined to succeed in that aim, and a woman desirous of shaking mountains, although doomed to fail.

Maurice had always known himself to be an accident of war, and that his sister, Sian, represented an unsuccessful attempt to turn that adversity into triumph.

After the War George had taken a job on the ferries plying out of Holyhead, Swansea or Fishguard, but had, shortly after his daughter's birth, decided to quit the sea. He didn't approve of the company Teresa was keeping. He believed that she would respond to a tighter rein, and that a move away from Rosslare would sever her troublesome political connections.

He soon discovered that his wife lost no time in her attempts to rekindle a subversive green flame centred upon their new home, a shabby bungalow near the gasworks, the hydro-sulphuric stench of which Maurice's nostrils could re-summon effortlessly despite the passage of some forty years. When Teresa ran into dour opposition from George she grew to despise his lack of spirit, his meagre horizons, his contentedness with his new sedentary job with the County bus company. She resented especially having been obliged to sacrifice her independent income on the altar of motherhood. Prior to Maurice having been deposited inconveniently in her womb she had been bringing in a decent wage as a doctor's secretary. Now she found herself reliant upon George's modest earnings, significant chunks of which she nevertheless had no compunction about donating to causes of which she knew he strongly disapproved.

When he discovered these disbursements, all hope of the Colcloughs' marriage achieving tranquillity vanished. She did not care. Serenity played no part in Teresa's attitude to the world. The two children found themselves struggling to find their way through a conjugal battlefield, sometimes literally. She did not shrink from backing her convictions with her fists on occasions when her husband's objections became too strident. And since she believed she had sacrificed excessively for the children, she saw no reason why she should not make sure that George's contribution was commensurately painful. He found that most of whatever portion of his wage packet was not being siphoned off to Republican causes was being lavished on Maurice and Sian. They were by far the best-dressed kids in the neighbourhood. She drove them remorselessly to set their sights above the run-of-the-mill, careless of the burden her ambitions imposed on George's ill-matched income. Shortly after Maurice's tenth birthday the marriage imploded. Teresa had simply packed their bags and, children in hand, taken one of her husband's buses, so to speak, to Waterford where she had a particular Sinn Fein friend who took care of her until she managed to establish herself as an hospital receptionist.

George had made no attempt to follow them. They had coped adequately, aided by the generosity of a succession of uncles, a period of calm barely ruffled by the news of their father's suicide some eighteen months after their exodus. A single trunk containing his belongings had been delivered to Teresa by a bus company van.

Maurice had learnt to regard marriage as an institution best avoided, a lesson he had never found occasion to doubt; nor had he developed any urge to procreate, progeny being only another category of commitment and irreversible at that.

He had taken a final look at Bracken Point before driving down the sharp incline back to the Rossbrin Road. It was when he had been swinging by the old schoolhouse on the outskirts of the town that he had passed Marotti travelling fast in the opposite direction. He had believed the Americans to have left the town a week earlier and had been slightly unnerved by that insolent grin as the dark red Mercedes flashed by. Someone had told him that the woman had definitely said that she was off to London, then New York; and he had assumed that Marotti would be accompanying her. For sure, they had not been sighted for the past several days. Although Colclough's remunerated involvement in Bracken Point had terminated some weeks earlier he had been asked to pass along any information he might unearth about goings-on at the property, its arrivals and departures, anything of interest. He was happy to do so, nurturing a deep resentment of Morag Ambrose and her spiteful works, and hopeful that her unlooked-for purchase of the house from Moira Kierney might in due course lead to some satisfactory measure of reprisal.

He was brought back from his dark ruminations by Father Dominic who was making his farewells before any risk might arise of his being an inadvertent witness to misdemeanours on the part of his inebriated parishioners.

'So how are you spending Christmas Day, Maurice?'

'Here, I suppose. And dinner with Maeve across the way. Nothing special.'

'You should get yourself a family, my son. A great hedge against loneliness.'

'You'll remember, Father, that I've a sister over in Kenmare. I've been thinking of visiting her for the New Year. She manages a hotel I own over there. A snug place, Father.'

'A grand notion.' The cleric fixed him with a cold stare. 'It'll do you good to spend a little while away from Ballydehob.' His pastoral smile returned as he shouldered his way to the exit.

At that same moment, had Colclough but known it, Maeve Rafferty across the road was, against her better judgement, being charmed by the young American who had settled himself comfortably in the snug and was sipping a mug of her best coffee, suppressing the protests of his taste buds. Dressed casually in a multi-hued sweater he was telling of the great time he had been having in Dublin, over the previous few days.

'Fantastic town! Magic people! Can't wait to visit again.' He leant forward to tap her arm. 'Sorry to confess, Mrs Rafferty, but being back here is not exactly the way I intended to spend my Christmas, know what I mean?'

'I can imagine, Mr Marty.'

'Marotti. Don't forget the zero. Make me the nothing man.' He grinned. 'But here I am, so we'd all better make the most of it.'

'Not I hope with that Ambrose woman?' she asked, arms folded.
'You don't care for Morag, I guess.'
''Tis trouble she is.'
'It has been known. But don't worry. She's in New York and is unlikely to be back for quite some time.'
'I can't say I'm sorry to hear it. I don't easily complain about people … anyone will tell you so … but she was truly nasty in this very room. I had to show her the door, so I did.' As he did not react, she continued, 'So what's brought you back here, then?'
'Something totally unscripted. Partly business, partly pleasure. Someone else's pleasure. The truth of the matter, Mrs Rafferty, is that I need a favour from you.'
'And what might that be?'
He drew his hands together in a prayerful gesture. She noticed first his beautifully manicured nails, then the power and length of his fingers. He said softly, 'Well now, would you remember Mr Tull? James Tull? He stayed here for one night in the summer.'
'Could I be after forgetting? He's that woman's brother, so he is. Which she took pleasure in telling us, Maurice and me.'
'Sounds, like her style. But I'd be surprised if James gave you any trouble.'
'True, he was a nice enough fella, as I remember.' She tried to summon up a memory of him: well-dressed, darkish, green eyes, not at all American. 'But he brought trouble at his back.' She hoisted her chins, hinting at resistance. 'And he might again. Some folk can't avoid it.'
Marotti shrugged. He examined his coffee cup speculatively. 'Say, it's not too early for a brandy, is it, Mrs Rafferty?'
'Not even for a nun.' She saw to his needs without hurrying, pondering the favour he was about to seek of her. He watched her large frame negotiate a familiar path between the shabby furniture as she returned with a generous measure in her pudgy hands; and registered the wariness in her eyes.
He said, 'It's really your advice I need. The problem is that James has decided to spend New Year at Bracken Point, and is inviting at least one guest to stay with him. We hadn't expected this, not so quickly. The work on the house is barely finished. The paint is still drying, so to speak. We haven't yet even begun to look for someone to run the place, you know, generally to look after it. A kind of housekeeper.'
'You're not after thinking of me, I hope.'

'Mrs Rafferty, you'd be ideal but I know you're a busy woman. No, what I'm after is someone to keep the place tidy and to cook breakfast for just a week or so, let's say for ten days, starting next Thursday. It's very short notice, I know, which is why I need you to point me in the right direction. James suggested that you might know someone suitable.' He switched on his most appealing expression. 'If you can't help I suppose I'll have to approach some agency in Cork, but surely there's someone local who would welcome the money? It's a question of knowing where to look.'

'Well now, it won't be easy at this time of year. Folk want to be with their families, so they do.'

'I'd hope we could arrange matters to avoid that kind of problem. The woman wouldn't have to stay around all day. Lunches and dinners will mainly be eaten out. I've already made reservations over at Blairs Cove and other good places. It's mainly breakfasts and snacks, that sort of thing. But James understandably wants to have the place kept in decent order.'

She pulled a face. 'Still, 'tis a bad time to be after looking for that kind of help at short notice. Would you be expecting the woman to say at the house?'

'Not if she was a local girl. We'd see to transport. And the pay would be generous.'

'T'would have to be, that's for sure.' Maeve who was planning shortly to be off to her sister's for a meal and hadn't yet bathed for the occasion, would have preferred to have avoided such a commission. But the man had asked very nicely and it was flattering to have been remembered kindly by Mr Tull. Marotti waited patiently whilst she turned over the possibilities semi-audibly, running through names which meant little to him and identifying disqualifying circumstances which meant even less. He sat, legs stretched before him, smiling encouragingly. When he judged the moment to be ripe, he offered, 'What about the young woman who works behind the bar at Casey's?'

'Who? Patsy? No, she wouldn't do at all. Maurice has only taken her on temporary-like. She's not very bright. I doubt she can boil an egg.'

'I don't know Patsy. I thought her name was Annie.'

Maeve produced a hard and thoughtful stare. Had he been leading her in that direction from the very beginning? Maybe he was more cunning than she had given him credit for, but his face remained open, enquiring, smiling innocently. She said, 'And did that suggestion come from Mr Tull too?'

'No, I've just thought of her. But I guess she may be too busy at Casey's.' He shrugged. 'I've got to come up with something. Maybe I'd better just telephone an agency.'

'Hold your whist a second.' She gave him another heavy look. 'Maybe Annie might be interested. I could give her a call. How much might you be paying?'

'I thought, being New Year, fifty dollars an hour. Say thirty pounds. Say four hours a day for ten days. Could be ...' he stared at the ceiling, calculating – 'something like twelve hundred pounds. No questions asked.'

'Jasus,' she breathed. 'For that money I'd ...'

'And,' he broke in quickly, heading off any ambitions she might have begun to nurture, 'if you can persuade her to take the job we'll make sure you get a finder's fee. Say a hundred pounds. This could be the start of a neat little arrangement. What d'you say?'

He lit a cigarette as she went into the next room to use the telephone. After a few minutes she returned, panting slightly from the exertion. 'I've to ask you, are you absolutely sure that other woman won't be around?'

'Morag? I can guarantee she'll be off the map.'

'And you? Are you planning to be there?'

He laughed knowingly. 'If that's a condition of Annie taking the job I'll make sure that I'm somewheres else. Anyway, I've been planning to leave for the States after I've welcomed James. If all works out, that is. But if she's gonna help out I'll need first to show her over the place, brief her on this and that, security arrangements, that kinda stuff.'

Maeve disappeared again, reappeared once more, now red-faced. 'She says OK provided she can be away no later than noon on New Year's Eve. She and Eamonn have made their arrangements. And you'd have to look to me to provide breakfast on New Year's Day. Same hourly rate.' She stood pregnant with expectation.

'You're a wonder, Mrs Rafferty,' he said, grinning. 'It's a deal. When do I get to meet her out at the house?'

She made a final expedition. He heard the receiver being replaced. He was looking at his watch as she bustled back into the snug. 'Tuesday morning at eleven. Eamonn will drop her off and wait for her. And she says she'd prefer it if he could drive her to and from the house the whole time.'

He shrugged. 'It's her call. I take it she'll fix things with Colclough?'

'That's not a problem,' she answered.

'Great! In that case ...' he took out a cheque book. 'Did we say a hundred? And more later, it seems.'

As she was clearing away his glass and cup, and he was shrugging into his heavy overcoat, he said casually, 'Hey, it's quite a coincidence, but I was chatting to some guys in Dublin and happened to mention Ballydehob and, guess what, they knew Maurice Colclough. Played golf with him or something. It's a small world.'

'That it is.'

'Yeah, I hadn't realised that he was so well-connected. Into politics and all that.'

Maeve straightened her back. 'I don't know ... we don't discuss such matters.'

'Well, there you are. Learn something every day. They mentioned something called the 32 County Sovereignty Committee. Have you heard of it?'

'I know nothing about such things, Anyway, why should it concern you what Maurice gets up to?'

He came closer, placing his hands on her shoulders, a gesture of familiarity she found suddenly worrying. She moved away towards the door, avoiding his stare. He said, 'Well, Mrs Rafferty, if Colclough is some kind of activist ... not that he fits the picture ... I'd like to be told about it. We both know that he and Annie are pretty close. I'd hate to find out that I'd exposed James to some kind of security risk, know what I mean? After all, it's my job to make sure things like that don't happen.' He was no longer smiling.

She forced a laugh. 'Maurice a security risk? 'Tis joking you are! He's no risk to anyone save himself. Gives himself airs, and tries to seem more important than he is. Loves a good *craic*, he does, which is why he joins all those clubs and societies and what have you. Jasus, the only risk with Maurice is that he's the last fella to keep a secret. Don't go telling him your business if you want to keep it close. And as for Annie, well ...' She left her incredulity unspoken.

Marotti buttoned his coat. 'That's very reassuring, Mrs Rafferty. Incidentally, may I call you Maeve now that we're working together, in a manner of speaking? Sorry to have raised the point, but these days you can't be too careful. I hope you don't mind my asking.'

She said, 'Don't you be after thinking Annie will be any trouble to you. If that's in your mind I'd sooner we dropped the whole thing this very instant. And you can have your cheque back.' She knew now for certain that he had had Annie in mind before he walked through the door, but for some reason had chosen not to approach her directly. Did he also know that Annie was no longer working for Maurice but was pretending ignorance? Maeve determined to volunteer no information on that score, that she wouldn't.

'No need for that,' he said. 'I'm sure everything will work out just fine.' And with an appropriate Yuletide valediction he went out into the darkening afternoon.

Maeve looked at her watch, poured herself a large port and telephoned her sister, asking her to put back dinner by an hour. Her bath would have to wait a while. There was only one guest due to check into his room that evening and he was a regular who knew where to find the key. Her absence for a little while would not matter. She downed her drink, dribbling a little amid the folds of her chin.

There was no sign of Marotti's red car in the street. Indeed, few souls were on the move in the quiet town. She shivered as she crossed the corner to Casey's. Two generations back Maeve's family had been travellers, and she oft times thought she had inherited certain of their reputed gifts. Sure it was that, as she sought out Maurice in the pub's inner haze, a queer feeling had taken hold of her, telling her that something momentous was about to grip the town. She caught Maurice's eye at the bar and waved, her throat full of soon-to-be spoken words.

CHAPTER TWELVE

Two evenings previous to that on which the conversation between Leo Marotti and Maeve Rafferty had taken place in the Ballydehob Arms, a dinner party hosted by Hugh Jennings in the private upper rooms of the Ivy had been intended, inter alia, to seal Phyllis's contract with *The Mercury*, but matters had failed to run smoothly.

She had sensed Jennings's discomfort as he greeted her with an attitude that combined over-the-top affection with awkwardness, his embrace displaying a glowing warmth but his eyes, behind fashionable spectacles, sliding away from hers.

In addition to Jennings and three of his senior colleagues, sixteen guests were in attendance. She had arrived among the last, narrowly within the bounds of punctuality, her timing dictated by careful preparation. A new Nicole Farhi dress had been bought for the occasion, deep fathoms blue with a full skirt slit on the left almost to the point of indecency to reveal legs of which she was unapologetically proud. She had been warned in advance that critical eyes would be upon her, and was resolved to impress. In his invitation, conveyed by telephone, Jennings had been anxious to make it clear that her appointment to the paper owed much to his patronage.

'There are those who question my judgement. They have little doubt about my motives.'

'How odd, given we both know the reverse to be true.'

He had demonstrated the grace to laugh but she knew it was prudent to change the subject. 'Have you heard from James's people yet on whatever it was that concerned you?'

'Indirectly, but I'm expecting more information imminently as it happens.'

'I'm pleased to have been of service.'

And she had been equally pleased to accept his invitation to dine, a pleasure reinforced initially as she scanned the room and quickly recognised a number of faces made familiar through media exposure.

She sipped an adroitly-delivered glass of champagne as Jennings steered her towards a group comprising his Arts Editor, the principal conductor of the London Philharmonic and a self-assured woman of around fifty whose status Phyllis did not at first detect but who it transpired was a Life Peeress and Junior Minister at the Department of Culture. To Phyllis's dismay the trio were locked in discussion of England's prospects in the forthcoming European soccer championship, a subject to which she had nothing to contribute save a forced smile which thinned by the minute as the informed debate ranged from the relative merits of Anderton or McManaman to Gascoigne's loss of acceleration over ten yards. But it was not in her nature to be intimidated. Although silent, she was resolved that her presence be registered; she waved airily across the Minister's shoulders to a publisher of her acquaintance to whom she would not normally have displayed such casual familiarity. It was, she acknowledged, immature to be so anxious to demonstrate social parity but she felt challenged, on her mettle, her colour high. Nevertheless she had still to utter a word when her group was joined by an effete, sallow-skinned gentleman from the Arts Council whose mission was to challenge the conductor's apparent desire to include a number of works by Edmund Rubbra in his orchestra's Spring programme, an intention apropos which the Arts bureaucrat entertained serious reservations.

'Of course there's a limit to the number of times one wishes to listen to Mahler or Mozart, but they are among the few tunesmiths guaranteed to put bums on seats. As I'm sure the Minister appreciates, one has never lost money by over-estimating the conservatism of an English audience.'

'We certainly have to reduce the tax-payer's subsidy to the London-based orchestras,' murmured the politician. 'I'm not sure that even I, who have fairly catholic tastes, could be persuaded to miss dinner in order to listen to some unpopular composer. One of these avant-garde chaps, is he?'

'Actually, Minister, he has been described as "the homeliest, the least difficult" of this century's English symphonists'. The conductor appeared somewhat peeved. He glared at the bureaucrat. 'Rubbra would not tax anyone's preference for splendid harmonies.'

Phyllis saw her opportunity. Arcane knowledge could, on occasions, yield dividends. She addressed the conductor. 'But is it not also the case that, in his later symphonies, Rubbra was greatly influenced by Teilhard de Chardin? Not exactly a homely chap.'

There was a momentary silence. The Arts Council man eventually ventured, 'Another unknown genius, perhaps?'

The conductor produced a wolfish smile, now having the bureaucrat at a temporary disadvantage. He addressed himself directly to Phyllis. 'His eighth was, indeed, dedicated to de Chardin. How extraordinary! I doubt if anyone else in this room would have known of the connection.'

The Minister sighed deeply. 'Certainly not me. I'm beginning to suspect this is a conspiracy to point up my ignorance.'

Phyllis said levelly, 'De Chardin was a subversive Jesuit, eventually excommunicated, who had a unique, ahead-of-his-time, view of cosmic inter-relationships. A close friend of mine has been much affected by his writings, which is how I came to know of him. He was also ... de Chardin that is, not my friend ... an eminent paleo-anthropologist whose ideas about the holistic, and incidentally holy, characteristics of matter have not yet been wholly ... with a "w" ... acknowledged, although their relevance is becoming daily more apparent.' She smiled benignly.

'Oh dear,' sighed the Arts Council man, fluttering his finger-tips. 'A little known English composer under the influence of a maverick religio-scientist unloved by the Pope. Doesn't sound like good box office to me.' With which he took the Minister's plump arm and drew her aside for some private negotiation.

The conductor touched Phyllis's elbow, shrugging in mock despair. 'Young lady, I don't know who you are ... perhaps I should ... and, despite the certainty that you may have cost my orchestra another 5% cut in budget ... I salute your erudition. Please, please, come to the Rubbra performances. And bring your friends. All of them. Dragoon them if necessary.' With which he departed, in search of more champagne.

The Arts Editor left alone with Phyllis examined her up-tilted, unrepentant face, her frank grey eyes. A handsome woman, he decided. Bold. Not pretty, but requiring – perhaps deserving – attention. He could see how Jennings might have been captivated. A pity about the complication with which he, himself, was struggling to come to terms. He wondered, with considerable uncertainty, how she would react to his news. Not serenely, he guessed. He said, 'Look, Phyllis ... may I call you Phyllis? ... I've been deputed to put something to you. These occasions invariably have a sub-text, although I could hardly have anticipated that a reference to de Chardin would have contrived to leave us so conveniently *à deux*, so to speak. Hugh would have dealt directly with you had you arrived earlier, as planned, but now he's busy playing the genial host, so the heavy responsibility falls upon me.'

Phyllis experienced a frisson. 'He's changed his mind.'

'Not exactly. But a certain, very recent, development means that a number of our plans have had to be shelved. Temporarily, we trust.'

'Why didn't the shit telephone me?'

'I did say the development was very recent. Within the last two or three hours, in fact. Things have moved, as these things do, with confusing rapidity.'

'Not, apparently, as far as I'm concerned.'

'Let me explain, please.' He drew her towards a quiet corner near the as-yet-unoccupied dining table sparkling with crystal. She stood, feet apart, balanced for conflict. He thought, what a formidable young woman.

'Well?'

'The thing is, have you already handed in your notice at Longstaff's?'

'Of course not. I wouldn't do that until I'd made absolutely certain of my appointment with *The Mercury*. Although I have given informal warning of my intentions.'

'That's a relief.'

She said, evenly, 'Please be more explicit.'

'Of course. But first I have to ask you to treat what I'm about to tell you as a matter of confidence. It's entirely to do with company business, you understand. It will all be public knowledge in a week or so, but until then we must keep the transaction under wraps, so to speak. Or rather, not so to speak.' He permitted himself a thin smile. 'It's all most unfortunate, but your intended appointment ... and it is still fully intended ... has become caught up in wider events.'

'Please get to the point.'

He glanced around to make sure he could not be overheard. Across the room he noted Jennings's bespectacled gaze upon him and responded with an eloquent shrug. 'OK. We've just learnt that a significant proportion, an influential proportion, of the paper's shareholding is being acquired by another group. You don't need to know the details, but the new shareholders will inevitably have a major say in the paper's policy and management. Not overall control, at least not yet, but enough to make a difference.' He steeled himself to confront her stare now assuming the quality of glacial ice. 'The bottom line is, we've been instructed to freeze all decisions on new editorial or operational appointments until further notice. Sorry and all that. I'm afraid you've been swept up in the ... what shall we call it? ... avalanche. Nothing personal.'

'That's an enormous comfort.'

He squirmed. 'Look, they're beginning to sit at table. I suggest you have a word with Hugh later this evening.' He attempted to take her arm to draw her towards her seat but she shrugged him off, careless of a possible future working relationship. Her initial sense of flat anticlimax was submerged by frustration and anger fuelled in part by an awareness that her substantial outlay on a new dress had proved to be such a poor investment. Infuriatingly, she doubted whether it would be suitable for the backwaters of Bally-dehob. She took her place at the heel of the dining table between the Arts Council epicene and the Director of the Tate Gallery, a duo already engaged in a discussion of the forthcoming exhibition of Francis Bacon's nudes. The Epicene nudged her elbow.

'Not, I judge, an artist much acquainted with Jesuitical niceties.'

Phyllis confined herself to a condescending smile, her thoughts elsewhere. She was halfway through her initial swallow of Meursault Clos de Cromin when enlightenment overwhelmed her. She could not believe her tardiness in making the mental connection. Diagonally across the table Jennings was dispensing bonhomie, his jowls quivering as he wiped his spectacles in response to some quip of the Minister to his right. Phyllis rose, ignoring the soup which had just been slipped before her, and walked with some emphasis to halt at Jennings's shoulder. She spoke directly into his left ear.

'It's the Tulliver Trust, isn't it? Your new partners? No wonder you were so anxious to contact James.'

He half-turned. 'I'm deeply embarrassed about this wretched complication. But don't be agitated, my dear. I'm sure it will all come out to our mutual advantage eventually.'

'But am I correct in my assumption?'

'Confidentially,' he was almost whispering, 'you are indeed right. Nothing to do with me, you understand. Not of my making. Out of the blue, really. The deal was done completely over my head.'

'Why doesn't that surprise me? I believe you, Hugh, I really do. But I hope you'll understand if, in the circumstances, I don't stay for dinner. Your colleagues' reptilian tears are rather overwhelming.'

She had actually stroked his ear. 'I'll remember you to James when I see him next week. No doubt we'll be talking over quite a number of related and consequential matters.'

She had not lingered to observe his reaction, or those of the other diners, but had departed, head high.

Her brother heard Phyllis's account of these events in the Dirty Duck on Christmas Eve. They had fled to the pub, mid-afternoon, to seek relief from parental tensions.

Peter had listened with a mixture of pride, amusement and concern, his beer cradled to his slack midriff, his eyes moistly affectionate. She thought: he deserves better than Sandra, whinging bitch, and that repressed weed of a son, prematurely calculating and self-absorbed. He had been immediately grateful when she had suggested a stroll to the watering-hole. They had walked, arm in arm, through the goose-greyness of late December, sky leaden, trees skeletal, grasses flattened and dusted with a frost that had not relaxed its hold since dawn. Behind them, in the unquiet house, they had left the three children squatting rancorously before the flickering images of an old James Bond movie, their father listening to a Brahms quartet in his study, mother coldly efficient and brittle in her kitchen, Sue behind the *Guardian* with a massive gin in her clawed hand, offering an occasional acerbic comment on the world's affairs to nobody in particular.

It had been decided, after much negotiation, that Helen and her son would spend Christmas Day only with the Nortons. Arnold had arranged, rail services on the morrow being non-existent, for them to stay in an hotel in Canterbury that evening and would be seeing them briefly for dinner. He would then return to collect them on Christmas morning before driving them back to London where he would remain over Boxing Day.

As brother and sister crunched their way up the hill, huddling close against the raw cold, he said, 'I am so glad that you changed your mind. It was such a relief to see your car in the drive when we arrived this morning. Sorry we were late, but Sue – as usual – kept us waiting at East Croydon. She'd missed her train from Brighton, hung-over again. I asked what she'd been up to last night but she seemed unclear about it. Said it was an impossibly technical question.'

'Bloody Sue. And those wretched kids.'

'So, what made you decide to come?'

Phyllis frowned. 'Basically, curiosity. I realised that I couldn't put

James fully in the picture about our little domestic comedy should I have failed to seize a chance to examine one of the farceurs in the flesh.' She paused. 'Added to which, I was emphatically told by Emily that I owed Mother my support, such as it is.'

'Ah, Emily,' he murmured.

They had found an unoccupied corner table in the busy pub made more crowded than usual by an eight-foot high Christmas tree glittering with silver tresses and crimson baubles. Everywhere there was laughter and the sparkle of conviviality. Peter had exchanged greetings with several of the celebrants, few of whom she recognised, as he ordered their drinks. He was, she noted, at ease and popular with them. One middle-aged woman with Chinese features had kissed him on the cheek, squeezing his comfortable waist. Phyllis began to realise there was much about her brother of which she had been unaware, and yet paradoxically she had never felt closer to him, never before so much cherished his solidity. He bore their beer – she too had requested a pint – to their cramped table, smiling but, she detected, concerned.

He said, 'So Ireland definitely remains on your agenda?'

'Of course. The more so, given the events at the Ivy. I'm determined to disjoint Jennings. I can't dislodge from my mind the image he was trying to project on the assembled company. El Supremo! The editor *sans pareil*. Do you know the Ingres painting of Bertin, the great 19th century Parisienne journo? I believe Hugh is trying to model himself on that Gallic mind-bender. What a prick!'

'Sis, Jennings is no fool. He didn't achieve his eminence by accident. And, anyway, his role vis-à-vis your career prospects would be the worst possible reason for – how shall I put it? – resuming your relationship with James.'

She froze. 'You don't approve? Is that it?'

Peter took a hefty throatful of beer. 'So when do you leave for Ireland?'

'On Wednesday. From Stansted. James is meeting me at Cork. Why are you so curious?'

'So, he's already in Ireland?'

'No. He'll be flying from Toronto a day ahead of me. He's spending Christmas with his brother. If he was already over here I doubt if I'd be sitting at this table, notwithstanding your charms.'

'Or Emily's persuasiveness?'

'Not even that. I've decided, finally, that I love the man.'

Peter shook his head. 'Not a matter, in my experience, open to decision.'

'You're an expert in these affairs, then?'

'More, I believe, than you Sis. Do you know these lines from de la Mare?' She sat, mute with astonishment, as he recited faultlessly and without hesitation:

'When love flies in

Make – make no sign;

Owl-soft his wings,

Sand-blind his eyne;

Sigh if thou must,

But seal him thine.'

He went on, 'The thing is, love chooses to fly in. He can't be summoned.'

'So, am I expected to be impressed by this wholly-unexpected lyricism?'

'Ah, you must await the final stanza –

'Nor make no sign' – a curious construction –

'If love flit out;

He'll tire of thee

Without a doubt.

Stifle thy pangs;

Thy heart resign;

And live without.'

'As I said, decision – yours or his – has bugger all to do with it.' He supped his bitter. 'Now or henceforth. What little I know of Emily suggests to me that she fully understands the force of it. I don't believe that you do. Consider our parents, as an object lesson.'

She pulled a sour face. 'To fall in love is one thing. How one reacts to it is quite another.'

'Agreed.'

They stared silently at each other across the table for several moments, the sounds of revelry around them fading into their unconsciousness. Eventually she said, 'Do you know what Mother told me this morning? That it seems wiser, at her age, to accept whatever attentions Father is able to give her with good grace. The world, she said, is bequeathed to us to share with others. She claimed, God help us, to be excited at the prospect of taking our half-brother into her arms.'

'Alex.'

'Whoever.'

Peter placed his hand over hers. 'Are you going to behave yourself tomorrow?'

'I intend to remain a wholly passive participant in the day's proceedings.'

'I suppose that will pass muster. As long as you don't behave like a silent, glowering, semi-dormant volcanic presence filling us all with dread at the prospect of imminent eruption.'

'Is that how people view me?'

He grinned. 'Those who love you know that, at heart, you're just a soft, cuddly kitten.'

'I wish I had Emily's capacity for meeting life head on, no holds barred. Or Mother's for bending gracefully, a deflective skill. I can do neither; or rather I attempt each, depending on circumstances, but invariably fail.'

He said, 'Well, it seems that, by whatever moral and emotional accommodations, our parents have arrived at some kind of acceptable relationship. The atmosphere this morning seemed relatively uncharged.'

'I saw little of Father last night. He didn't return from this place ...' she waved her hand at the Dirty Duck's cheery interior ...' until ten thirty or so, which limited my opportunity to engage in hostilities. We spoke briefly about James.'

Peter shuffled in his seat, suddenly uncomfortable. 'Now you've mentioned Ireland again, there's something I have been meaning to whisper in your shell-like ever since our lunch last week. Very delicate. For your information only.'

'You sound very official. The model civil servant.'

He said, dolefully, 'You've never taken much interest in my job. When Emily was pressing me about it over our Quaglino lunch I could see you switching off. But I do have my uses, even if they are not always welcome ones.'

'I'm all ears. But if we're about to speak about the Ministry I'd appreciate being fortified by another pint.'

As he rose to replenish their glasses he said, 'You may well need it.' His expression remained serious and on his return he came straight to the point. 'This place you're about to visit – the house in Ballydehob recently acquired by the Tulliver Trust? It's on our files. We've had it under discreet observation for some time, long before the Trust took an interest. I was completely taken aback when we learnt that James had been instrumental in negotiating its purchase.'

'It's on your files,' she repeated, uncomprehending. 'But it's in

Ireland, for Godsake. Is that what you do? Keep files on overseas properties?'

'Amongst other things. When the properties interest us. Or rather, what goes on in them. Like being used by the IRA to bring in stuff by boat. Weapons. Drugs. That sort of thing.'

'But you're in Customs and Excise.'

'We need intelligence too. More than most.' He saw anger around her tightening mouth but knew this was no time to retreat. 'And now we want to establish quite why the Tulliver Trust have acquired this house, given its history. Our eyes – and those of our colleagues in Dublin – are still on it. I thought you should know. Improper of me, quite improper; but you're my dear sister and I don't want you to walk into trouble unwarned. And you should also know that I've reported the circumstances of your intended visit, for your own protection. And for mine.' He removed his spectacles to wipe them carefully, a gesture which she recognised from past experience as indicative of an inner turmoil. She had no intention of giving him an easy passage.

'And this is what you describe as intelligence? Some would use another term.'

'Probably, but at least you now know what you may be getting into. I stress "may". I've absolutely no idea whether the Trust in general, still less James in particular, is involved in anything unto-ward. From what I know of James I'd say it was most unlikely that he's anything other than an innocent party.'

'That's most generous of you.'

'I'm simply asking you to be careful.'

'Are you sure you're not asking me to report on what I find at Ballydehob?' Her face was drained of colour, unglazed porcelain, close to fracturing.

'Not at all, but I'd be much happier if you were, even at this late hour, to arrange to meet James in Cork, or Dublin, or anywhere other than at ... what's its name? ... Bracken Point.'

She shook her head in dumb fury. For several minutes they sat in silence, scarcely aware of the arrival of carol singers who gathered around the decorated tree to launch into God Rest Ye Merry Gentlemen. She began to laugh, close to tears. 'Christ, can nothing in my life be simple and uncomplicated?'

'I'm sorry, but I still think it right to have told you. It's not easy for me either.'

She saw through the inn's low window that the December evening had now drawn in upon them. The frieze of elms across the road stood desolate and black against the descending greyness. There would be a frost.

CHAPTER THIRTEEN

Joan Norton, early on Christmas morning, stared through her kitchen window across her cherished rear garden which rose gently to face a line of hills lying eastwards. She liked to think of it as hidden Kent: a tangle of quiet, secluded valleys dotted with villages of which few had heard and even fewer visited with touristic intent: Bodsham Green, Wingmore, Bladbean, Rhodes Minnis, Derringstone; symbols of quintessential Englishness, or what once had been considered such. Now she was less certain.

Her family, having breakfasted, was scattered throughout the house and elsewhere, the children demolishing their various presents under Peter's lax supervision, Phyllis reading the latest Rushdie novel, Sue taking a late bath. Her husband had left to collect the woman from her hotel. Sandra had felt the need to take a walk through the frost-etched woods. Alone with a pile of brussels sprouts the outer shards of which she had ferociously stripped into her tidy, Joan was holding the sharp kitchen knife in her clenched hand as she looked across the grey-stoned patio towards her heavy accumulation of planting, half a lifetime's devotion: hebe; fuchsia (its stems pinkly stark in winter nakedness); glossy laurel; a low bank of sturdy yew; the dull green foliage of viburnum; the sleeping exoticism of camellias and azaleas; syringa in need of a heavy pruning which in present circumstances, she coldly considered, she might neglect to administer. Her lawn, eschewing symmetry, wound around the bushes caressingly, its greyed year-end surface shaded with mosses whose darker softnesses promised a complaisant receptivity to exploring feet. Beyond a line of limes marking her boundary rose a proud squadron of sycamores, regal weeds of the forest, their powerful limbs in sombre outline against a pewter sky. The previous night's clear air had persisted until first light, spangling the Weald with delicate ice, but around ten of the morning a milder breeze had pushed in a belt of dismal cloud from the west. There would be no festive snow. Her instincts predicted that rain would arrive before the sprouts, defenceless in her hands, were consigned to hot water.

She had long hated Christmas. Both her parents had died – two years apart – within days of the Annunciation and the sight of tinsel-clad firs in domestic corners always aroused desolate memories. Terrible events had also haunted many of her friends around the baleful winter solstice, almost as though abundant sacrifices had to be offered before sap was allowed to flow once more. It was, she felt, appropriate to have inflicted upon herself the pain of inviting the woman to lunch: surely a generous oblation.

Arnold had been shaken when she suggested it; shaken and, she was pleased to observe, embarrassed.

'I'll need to see how Helen feels about it.'

'Naturally. She may have other plans. But if she wants to spend Christmas Day with you it will have to be here. I'm entitled to impose that condition.'

He had not demurred. She had asked him for a photograph of the woman on the grounds that she would be more capable of greeting her without the requirement of too withering an initial scrutiny, but Arnold claimed not to possess one. It had been then that he told her of Helen's African provenance. He had described her: tall, well-rounded, black. This she had not expected but swiftly saw the funny side. Arnold would probably have the intriguing task of introducing her to his daughters. She knew that Peter had already met the woman, but would he have mentioned her colour to the others? Either way, she concluded it was – in a manner of speaking – no skin off her nose or, at any rate, no more skin than had already been gouged.

At the time she had seen her suggestion as brave, open-hearted, very Nineties, non-judgmental. But the moment it became a reality her emotions scattered uncontrollably. And now the hour was almost upon her. She gripped the kitchen knife more tightly and decided to ward off panic by attending to the carrots, something substantial, scraping their coloured surface and watching it degenerate into an indeterminate thin sludge as the blade deprived the vegetables of their outer bloom.

'I am,' she told herself, 'a good woman. I've not deserved this.' But her sense of righteousness did nothing to ease her awareness of betrayal, of having been demeaned, devalued, corrupted. Could she survive the day with something left of value to which she might cling?

Phyllis entered the kitchen. 'May I help?'

'No dear, everything's under control.'

'You sure? Not that I'm a genius in the culinary department, as you know.'

'Perhaps later you could keep an eye on the turkey? It should be carvable by two-thirty, and I may not be entirely reliable by then, things being as they are.'

Phyllis glowered. 'I really don't understand how you can put up with this farce. Even less how Father had the gall to create the situation. It's intolerable!'

'Today ... if that's what you mean by the situation ... wasn't Arnold's idea. My initiative entirely. I'm sure that he's uncomfortable with the whole thing. Which pleases me.'

'I can't believe that this is your notion of a malicious joke.'

'No, it certainly isn't a joke.' Joan's knife moved steadily across the last of the carrots. 'I suppose I decided that one has to confront the mind's monsters. I'm sure that, like most things in life, it will become easier with practice.'

'So you're not going to kick him out?'

'What would that solve? I certainly don't fancy loneliness. I want him around. But I will expect him to be more forgiving of my occasional misdemeanours. And I shall indulge my selfish pleasures more hungrily. In a curious way it's been a liberating experience. I'm belatedly becoming a modern feminist. Really, very liberating.' She began to cry. A spasm shook her. The knife sliced along her left thumb. A thin line of blood appeared. The women held each other, silently.

They looked up to see Peter and his son, Tom, standing awkwardly at the door. Tom fumbled with the manual to his Auntie's gift: a complicated computer game, access to which he had just cracked. He wanted to share his triumph but was stymied by the tears.

Peter said, 'It's OK, Tom. Grown-ups usually cry at Christmas.'

'But Nan's bleeding.'

'Good Lord, so she is. I'll get a bandage.' He rushed upstairs to the bathroom. Phyllis, never comfortable with children, steeled herself to put an arm around Tom who, by the look he threw her, unerringly divined the effort she was demanding of herself.

She said, 'Just a teeny accident. Nothing to worry about.'

The boy shrugged himself free of her embrace. 'I once cut myself on Dad's razor. On my ear. He was really angry.'

'Did it hurt, Tom?'

'You bet! I couldn't stop the bleeding for hours.'

Joan pulled herself together. 'I don't think this finger will take so long to recover. But we'll have to be brave, won't we? I think a nice cup of tea is called for; a Coke in your case, Tom.'

'Oh please! Before Mum gets back. She doesn't let me drink Coke. Rots the brain, she says.'

Joan smiled. 'You've plenty of brain to rot, Tom, before it becomes a problem.'

'And by then,' interjected Peter, returning with medical supplies, 'you'll be coping with stronger stuff than Coke, like me.'

They were all sitting around the kitchen, Sue having been prompted to join them by the rattle of crockery, when they heard the sound of wheels on gravel.

'Now children,' said Joan firmly. 'Everyone on their best behaviour, please.' She moved with sturdy grace to the hall and opened the door to the front garden in a stance that managed to combine a show of welcome with proprietorial dignity. Phyllis, proud of her, came to her elbow.

The woman, waist encircled protectively by Arnold's right arm, advanced tentatively, cradling a coffee-hued child. Dressed in a peacock-blue sweater and white slacks, she stood – Joan judged – not much under six feet. She was marginally taller than Arnold, large-breasted, wide-hipped, with powerful but not pretty features. Lacking a free hand to be shaken, she offered a nervous smile.

'I'm Helen.'

Her mouth was full-lipped and wide; her eyes brown pools of a lustre in which, Phyllis had to admit, most men would have little difficulty in drowning.

'Well,' said Arnold neutrally. 'Here we are.'

Joan was conscious of the curiosity of her grandchildren milling around her skirts. Severely tempted to invite them to meet their great-aunt, she managed instead to say, 'You've made good time, and beaten the rain. You didn't see Sandra in the lane, by any chance? I fear she may be less lucky.'

They were still poised in the raw air as though waiting for some external force to extricate them from their predicament. Arnold made another attempt. 'And here is baby Alex. And ...' gesturing rather helplessly to Helen he added, 'this is, of course, my wife. Letting in the cold.'

'How thoughtless of me. Please come in.'

Arnold stood back. 'We'll need the carry-cot.' He retreated to the car leaving the three women standing in the hall amid assorted children. Phyllis felt as though her skin had stiffened around her bones. She knew she must be projecting an attitude of raw hostility but the shock of the latter's blackness had unnerved her. And her size. She belatedly constructed a thin smile but remained silent as Arnold returned, ushering them ahead of him as he shouldered into the house with his burden, using his heel to slam the door behind him.

'Why are you all cluttering up the hall? Go into the drawing room, please. Meet the others.'

Peter emerged from the kitchen, smiling. 'Helen, good to see you again.' He took her hand, hooking his other arm around his mother's waist, drawing her closer to the newcomers. 'Just look at Alex. Hey, he's bigger than I expected. What is he? Six months?'

'Seven.'

'That could explain it. Let me hold him while you take your coat off.' Ignoring Phyllis's baleful stare, he gentled the boy in his arms, raising him high. 'Tom, come and look at your, er, well I suppose ...' He broke off, grinning in confusion.

Tom said, 'It's the same colour as Alice. But this lady isn't like Auntie Sue.'

Very much like in some ways, thought Phyllis, but did not voice the sentiment as they all moved gingerly into the drawing room's warm confusion.

Three hours later lunch was about to be served. Arnold carved while Joan distributed, the children's animation mingling with more subdued adult voices. Liberal consumption of alcohol had failed to disperse an atmosphere of polite neutrality. On her return from a long walk Sandra had elected to stay in the kitchen with Joan. Whereas Susan had taken Helen's unexpectedly sable appearance in her stride, Sandra had not even attempted to conceal her surge of outrage, had uttered no greeting and had made it very clear that Philip's failure to alert her to this added dimension of her father-in-law's unacceptable behaviour would, at the earliest possible opportunity, be held severely to account. Arnold and Peter sat by Helen as she fed the baby, discussing trivia; Sue watched TV glumly; Phyllis, irritated by all of them – especially by Peter whom she had not forgiven for his unwelcome revelations of the previous evening – had remained taciturn, largely ignoring Helen who was clearly uncomfortable in her presence. For most of the time Phyllis had buried herself in her book, curled up in a corner chair, stirring herself only, when sated with the extravagance of Rushdie's over-cooked prose, to lecture her younger sister on the necessity of putting her shambolic life in better order.

Susan, who had abandoned her job as primary school teacher two years earlier, was currently working as part-time barmaid, part-time shop assistant, activities which didn't strike Phyllis as being entirely consistent with responsibilities associated with caring motherhood of two small kids. She had only once visited Sue's housing association flat near Brighton Station across the road from the gay bar at which she earned the larger part of her income. Her sister remained unmoved by Phyllis's entreaties.

'I do all right. Better than most. The kids are fine. And life's never dull. But if it makes you any happier I started a course in fabric design last September. Two mornings a week. I'm really enjoying it. They say I have a good eye. So who knows, it could lead somewhere. Astbury's – the store at which I work weekends – are encouraging me. There could be an opening as a buyer. Anyway, it beats acting as an under-paid minder of a bunch of no-hope kids. I'll never go back to teaching. Not ever.'

'It's just that I think you've been wasting your talents. You could do so much better for yourself.'

Sue snorted. 'Pots and kettles; kettles and pots. You're no different. Like me, you'd find life hard without Dad's allowance. From what I hear you're never going to have a glittering career at boring, old Longstaff's, but you're far too cautious to go looking for something more challenging. And your love-life is non-existent. If you're not careful you'll end up as a dried-out, desiccated blue-stocking.'

'That could change. I'm off to meet James in Ireland on Thursday. I think I may be ready to make a commitment.'

'Bloody hell! Is this Phyllis Norton I'm listening to? Dreadnought Phil, repelling all boarders? This guy must be something special.'

'James Tull. I've known him for some time. Surely we've spoken of him?'

'Oh, that one. I thought it was all off months ago.'

'Merely suspended. A yellow card.'

Peter, whose attention had been caught by mention of Tull's name, commented, 'A yellow card is a caution, not a suspension. And caution would be very appropriate, wouldn't you say?'

Phyllis had flushed angrily, but catching Helen's eyes upon her, full of curiosity, had bitten her tongue and returned to her novel. But over lunch, at the pudding stage, a slightly drunk Sue brought the subject up again.

'Remind me. This bloke James. A journalist, isn't he?'

'Was. Currently of no fixed occupation.'

'That doesn't sound promising. Can you afford to keep him?'

'No worry on that score,' said Peter, well into his second bottle of burgundy. 'Loaded. Mega-loaded.'

Sue looked up sharply. 'What counts as mega?'

'Millions. Billions probably.' Peter blinked around the now stilled table. 'I joke not.'

Phyllis pushed away her plate. 'I don't wish to discuss this. It's pure speculation. Peter, I had enough of you last night. You're being bloody unfair. Shut up about it, everybody. Please. Or I'll have to leave. There's not much keeping me here as it is.'

Helen said, 'I think it was a mistake for me to come down. You've obviously got family things to talk over. I'm in the way.'

'I won't have my family indulging in gossip about my relationship with James, whether you're here or not. You're an irrelevance. At least to me.' Phyllis rose. 'Do I leave or not?'

Arnold murmured, 'From what you've contributed to this festive occasion I doubt if anyone would notice, or regret, your absence.'

'Oh, that's too cruel!' Joan slapped the table. 'Please sit down, Phyllis. I appreciate, if nobody else does, that you're only here to support me. Why is everyone being so beastly? Think of the children. They don't understand what is happening. Just look at their little faces. Look especially at Alex. Babies sense bad feeling. Poor mite. He's upset. Nothing is his fault. Oh, the whole day is a disaster. Why did I bother?' She began, again, to weep, then sob.

Only Helen of the adults moved. She placed her disturbed child on Arnold's lap and came to Joan's chair where she knelt, her head against the older woman's thigh, silently, until the sobbing ceased. Then, taking her hand, she led Joan from the room.

'Bloody hell,' breathed Susan.

Sandra turned on her husband. 'You started all this. We were just about managing to get through the day until you provoked Phyllis with your talk about Tull's millions. You're fucking useless.'

Peter threw up his arms. 'You may be right. Or maybe I merely speeded up a crisis that was about to happen anyway. But I knew I could rely on you to lay the blame on me, come what may.'

'Bloody hell,' repeated Susan, less softly.

Phyllis sat down. 'We can always trust Sue to offer an intelligent observation.

Tom said, 'Can I please leave the table?'

'May,' said Sandra. 'Not can. May.' But her correction was drowned by a cry of 'Yes, yes!' from Alice, while Michael, anticipating approval, was already heading for his electric racing car.

'Should I see what's happening?' asked Arnold, still clutching the mewling Alex, gesturing towards the door through which Joan and Helen had departed.

'Don't dare move,' hissed Phyllis. 'Leave them alone.'

'I'll get the coffee,' volunteered Peter, and retreated to the kitchen.

Sue said, 'You wanted an intelligent comment, Phyl. Here's one. Ultimately, does anything matter? Answers on two sheets of A4.'

'Being able to get a good night's sleep matters to me,' replied Sandra. 'And paying the bills, which amounts to much the same thing. And not getting pregnant again, to spite Peter.'

'But ultimately? In the long run? Post-millennium? Or when the sun explodes which, one fine day … so to speak … it must? What price our little Christmas drama then?'

Phyllis said, 'You're implying that to take up any moral position is a waste of time, that we shall all go equally into oblivion regardless of how we've chosen to spend our lives, selfishly or otherwise.'

'Perhaps I am. Maybe the hedonists have been right all along. Let's grasp one's temporal pleasures, for nothing else counts.' Sue paused to administer a light slap to Michael's wrist, detaching his imploring fingers from her skirt. 'I read something recently. Some scientist. Don't smirk, Phyl. Even barmaids read occasionally. He said – I paraphrase – deep down, at base, there is only corruption, decay and chaos. Bleakness at the heart of the Universe. Something like that. The one phrase I clearly recall is, "Gone is purpose; all that is left is direction." I remember that because I'm not clear what he means by direction.'

'Gravity, I suppose,' supplied Peter, returning with a loaded tray. 'Aimless movement of matter, pulled hither and thither by mere lumpiness.'

'That way insanity lies,' said Phyllis. 'If one denies the possibility of perfectibility or, less ambitiously, of some prospect of a living continuity … even if in a form inconceivable to us now … we might as well cut our throats.'

'Painful,' replied Susan. 'One can at least maximise such pleasures as corruption allows us.'

Arnold was disturbed. 'I can't accept that, Sue. You don't really mean it. One must have faith.' His three children stared at him. He had the grace to blush.

'I suspect, Father, that your instincts tell you that sin is no fun unless it entails the risk of damnation. Take away the possibility of a fiery furnace and all excitement evaporates.' Phyllis was beginning, at last, to enjoy herself. 'That sprog on your knee is the equivalent of a highly speculative investment. Once a broker, always a broker, gambling with your soul.'

'This is beyond me,' said Sandra. 'I'll get on with the washing-up. Come on, Tom and Alice, you both can help. No, shut up, Alice. Michael's too young. You're not. I don't care what your Mum says. Out! Now!'

'Formidable woman,' breathed Peter.

Arnold stirred uncomfortably in his chair. 'Alex will need feeding soon. I'd better find Helen.'

'Stay where you are. He's perfectly quiet for the moment.' Phyllis, revelling in her imperiousness, was keen to sustain the debate. 'It's not often we indulge in philosophical dialogue.'

'Actually,' said Arnold,' I consider your last contribution to have been unnecessarily personal.'

'Which, if we adopt Sue's hypothesis, is of zero consequence, like everything else.'

Peter, having distributed coffee, sank back into his seat, smiling benignly. Outside the light had faded. Rain spattered against the windows. Within, a scented candlelight cast a mellow glow over the remains of their feast. Half-empty bottles of Gavi di Gavi and Chambertin – Napoleon's tipple, he recalled – invited his further exploration. He adjusted his spectacles and peered affectionately at Michael, his godson, who, having abandoned his racing car, was now energetically defacing a story-book with crimson crayon. Whilst in the kitchen, he had observed his mother and Helen in the adjacent drawing room conversing peaceably, knees touching, eyes locked. Awed, stunned, delighted, he had busied himself quietly among coffee cups, not daring to intrude on their secular epiphany. Perhaps all could still prove to be well in their small world; perhaps the Nortons could, if only for a short space, insulate themselves from strife, find a point of balance.

But Phyllis would not allow tranquillity to intrude. Her insistent voice disturbed him, dragging him back into dispute.

'How does one cope with Sue's vision of an unpurposed life? It's a fair question. Science speaks of a universe slowly unwinding, suns dying inexorably, time expiring, unrelieved darkness once again upon the face of the deep. But will there, in the end as in the beginning, be the Word?'

'And if so,' asked Sue, 'What exactly is the Word saying to us? It's a rather fuzzy concept onto which to hang one's chance of eternity.'

'Hold on a minute,' interjected Peter. 'It seems to me that we're in danger of confusing several concepts here.'

'Oh hell, up speaks the tidy-minded bureaucrat, just when things were getting interesting.' Susan dug her brother in the ribs.

'Not to me, they weren't,' commented Arnold. 'I don't hold with discussions about religion, especially at Christmas. Wholly inappropriate.' He heaved himself to his feet. 'Besides which, Alex's nappy needs changing. Much more pressing than bloody metaphysics. And this time, Phyllis, I'll take no further orders from you.' He departed with a snort, the child over his shoulder, his left hand clutching a consolatory scotch.

Phyllis stared pityingly after him. 'There goes a fine example of appropriateness. Carry on, Peter. Remove our confusion.'

He said, 'I'd sooner watch James Bond. Isn't the movie just about to begin?'

'You've seen it before. And will again. I won't be denied. You've already done much to ruin this weekend for me, so I believe you owe me an indulgence or two. Besides, this isn't idle speculation on my part. Isn't there a Shakespearean phrase, "Hot for certainty"? Well, that's where I'm at.' She frowned. 'Not a comfortable situation.'

'I'm no ethical guide. No certainties in my pocket. Only problems.' He took Phyllis's hand. 'Look here, Sis, I'm truly sorry to have upset you yesterday. I was only trying to be a caring brother, believe me.'

'Then, help me to unpick Susan's mystery. That's what I need at this very moment. In the bosom of my family. The Word.'

He recognised that she was serious. 'I'll try, for what it's worth. But don't expect miracles. Or Pauline revelations. The modern pathway to truth consists of providing options, most of which are unpalatable, certainly not blinding.'

Susan knelt to cuddle Michael. She too had divined that her sister was a point of crisis, not least since it was wholly untypical of Phyllis to expose her deeper concerns to review by others. She looked up at Peter lovingly, admiringly. Not an intentionally hurtful bone in his soft body.

He said, 'One notion … which we might define as Sue Mark One … is of a wholly mechanistic and finite cosmos. It begins with a Big Bang which eventually runs out of steam, at which point all activity, sentient or otherwise, comes to a halt. This concept appears to exclude any possibility of infinity, whether spiritual or material. It reduces morality to nothing more than a set of convenient rules, established by custom and practice, to enable the majority of mankind to get through their earthly span with minimum discomfort. The only intellectual problem I have with this approach is that it is silent as to what caused the Big Bang in the first instance.'

'You mean that there must have been some antecedent condition which caused the Bang to Bang?' offered Phyllis. 'A primal cause? The Logos?'

'That seems logical to me. Which leads on to a second concept: Sue Mark Two. Here we can posit a system which is just as mechanistic as Mark One, but which is agreeably renewable. This notion not only accommodates the pre-Bang phenomenon but also opens up the prospect of some unimaginable cosmic state beyond the point at which our universe terminates. You might envisage this as a series of academic experiments conducted by some unknowable energy source, let's again nominate the Logos. This could also be reconciled with a Buddhist vision of perfectibility, if not of an eternal soul. It offers the possibility, however remote, of some sense of moral progression playing a tiny part in this rolling experiment.'

'Not very reassuring,' commented Susan. ' I doubt if my contribution, for better or worse, will make any difference to the outcome.'

'And the third concept?' asked Phyllis.

Peter shrugged. 'Simple faith, I suppose. If you have it. And with all due hesitation, I suspect that I do have it. On my better days.' He poured himself more burgundy. 'And this is a good day, on balance. Goodness has been on trial, and has prevailed. I offer Mother in evidence.' He grinned and departed to watch television.

The two sisters, left alone with Michael amid the detritus of their meal and the scattered toys, stared contemplatively at the fire glowing behind its protective grille. Phyllis murmured, 'I doubt if Father would agree with Peter.'

'I wish you wouldn't take so much pleasure in his embarrassment. OK, so he's proved to be more of a randy bastard than we suspected, but should we be surprised to discover that he's a man with all the characteristic defects of that gender? Normally we wouldn't want them any other way, so why should we make an exception of Father?

Actually, I think he's shown rather good taste. I like Helen, from what I've seen of her today. A gutsy lady. I wouldn't have had the front to turn up and face us all. And I salute Mum's courage for inviting her. I suspect they are both better women than us, Sis. Better and stronger.'

Phyllis snorted. 'I've always had doubts about your values, and your judgement isn't up to much either. I can't believe that, as we speak, Mother is in the next room communing with that woman. That doesn't resonate to me of strength. Capitulation and humiliation are words that spring to mind.' Even as she spoke, she was beginning to despise herself.

'If Mum has come to terms with her situation, why the hell can't you? No skin off your nose.' Susan gulped her wine. 'Or am I witnessing the first signs of advancing spinsterdom? Your retarded biological clock striking back? Come on, Phyl, get a life. What about James Megabucks? Go for it, for Chrissakes.'

Phyllis closed her eyes. She was suddenly drained. Almost in a whisper, she breathed, 'I suspect I might. If he still wants me.'

'Make him want you. Make him!'

'I could end up very hurt. And broke.'

'Fuck the broke bit! The hurt bit might make you a nicer woman.' Susan, uncharacteristically, leant across the cluttered table and took her sister's hand. 'Try Sue Mark Three. Have faith. Don't waste your life. Surprise yourself. Look at Mother. Learn from her.'

'I'm not sure Mother regards her life as wholly unwasted at this moment.'

'Don't be so judgmental, Phyllis.'

They looked up to see Joan standing in the doorway, pale but smiling. She had obviously overheard the last few exchanges. The sisters came to their feet. She raised her hand. 'No more talk. Be good. Sandra is alone in the kitchen. It's not fair. The poor woman is coping with the children and with all that mess. And the table uncleared.'

Left alone with Michael, Joan knelt by the child who, now bored with his crayons, was intent upon dismantling the picture book, page by page. Shreds of paper littered the carpet. She ruffled his dark hair, feeling its crinkly strength. The rain had intensified with the onset of dusk; she heard it spattering violently against the windows. A hostile wind rattled the sash frames, resenting resistance.

She said, 'I hope Father Christmas has managed to get home quickly or he'll be getting a soaking.'

The child pondered that possibility briefly, screwing up his eyes, before firmly dismissing it. He said, 'Silly old Nanna,' before reapplying himself to his demolition duties.

She thought, Arnold will have to leave soon. It will not be pleasant driving around the M25 in this weather. But he doesn't deserve pleasant, and my little trial of resolve will be over. Glad I risked it. Proved something to myself. Family behaved not badly, even Phyllis, despite being out of humour with Peter. Something about Ireland. Better not probe. Sleeping dogs. Smoking guns. Peter will tell me when he's ready. Always does. Arnold also quiet. Guilty or sullen? The latter probably. Guilt and Arnold not easy bedfellows. Anyway, soon be gone. And her. For the time being. Wise not to peer down the long and winding road. What if he doesn't? But he will. Be back. Proved I can cope, but if he doesn't, would I still? Cope? Probably. Would miss the sex desperately. Funny how it's assumed people of my age, women of my age, don't. Easier if we didn't, though. What did George Melly say when passion died: like being unshackled from a lunatic? But seem to get randier by the month, especially of late when he hasn't often obliged. Could always look elsewhere. Plenty of options. But can't compete with her in that department. Nice woman, though. Have to admit. Not what I expected. Genuinely warm. And intelligent. Can't get used to the idea that blacks can … a generational thing, I suppose. Expected mangled English. Down to Colonial heritage. Father all those years in Nigeria. But didn't put my foot in it. Far from it. Could genuinely come to like … or at any rate to sympathise. Not easy. Single mother. Has to work. Peter says she's very competent. But needs someone to look after Alex. I suppose I might …? Not a brilliant idea. Arnold would hate it. But comes down to money. Where I've the whip hand. Mostly in my name. Will curtail his self-indulgence. But not mine, no by God! Go for it, girl! Gather ye belated rosebuds. Citizen Kane, wasn't it? Supposed to refer to mistress's vagina. Did Herrick have the same notion? As short a spring, as quick a growth to meet decay. Well, mine's still springing. Not conceding defeat yet. Carpe diem. So no more self-sacrifice. Happy days are here again. Except that my thumb still hurts. Stupid business with that knife. Pull yourself together, old girl. One diem at a time. One happy, happy diem.

CHAPTER FOURTEEN

As Brendan Mulcahy recalled it had been a fuckin' miserable Christmas. Wet as a duck's bum, dampness taking the sparkle from the Holy Day. His sons, or, more accurately, their bloody wives, had insisted that he be imprisoned in the family's clutches until early evening when he'd fled, mildly worse for cheap wine, to sink a few pints at Casey's. The bar was, in the eyes of the law, not open for the selling of booze on the Holy Day, but following local custom, he'd slipped in by the rear door, only to find the place half empty, the new lass serving with a face on her like she was smelling armpits. Colclough was said to be over the way with Maeve Rafferty, shovelling her turkey into his belly. Them as had been in earlier had been treated to a buckshee Guinness, so Brendan had been grasping onto the hope that he might benefit similarly if he was able to hang around long enough to witness Colclough's return.

He had, however, taken little pleasure in the company, the *craic* flat, no music other than that seeping from an over-familiar tape. Around nine, there being no sign of Colclough and feeling unseasonably depressed, he had thought bugger it and had made his lonely way back up the hill, his feet making uncertain contact with pavements slick with rain. A nothing day. Not one on which Christ should have elected to be born.

Boxing Day, Tuesday, had been more memorable. It had brought a change in the weather, a sharp wind from the north-east clearing the skies till they shone like blue ice but giving no trouble to the idle fishing craft at safe anchor below the town bridge. Brendan, in his warmest coat, had pottered along the shoreline to clear his head. Sure, he'd had a drop or two more than usual, and that brandy had done him no good at all, but it was the television that had fucked his brain. So, he'd needed a walk to blow away the ache. He'd taken his grandson along, young Mikey, and he it had been that had first spotted the coastguard's launch nosing around the bay's mouth, and they'd joked about what a grand thing it was that the sods had to work when the rest of the world had their bums in easy chairs. Otherwise the town had been as quiet as a cemetery. After a while Mikey had gone off to kick a ball around with some pals who'd called to him from the old school grounds and Brendan had stumped back up through the main street, getting to Casey's at eleven thirty or thereabouts.

Colclough had let him in by the side door. The smarmy bastard had commented on missing him the morning previous and had remembered to pull him a pint on the house, so he'd borrowed an old newspaper and taken his usual place, waiting until others arrived. What bugger else had he to do? When the place began to fill he'd been gabbing, as he recalled, to Sean O'Leary who'd kept them creased with stories about that woman, Morag Ambrose, and her doings out at Bracken Point. She'd taken against the squirrels who kept scratching holes in her new-laid lawn and kept on complaining to Sean as though he was to blame for not teaching the poor creatures better manners. Eventually she'd turned up with some stuff, imported from France, which she'd had them paint around the trunks of all the trees on her property, and on some along the road. It was a kind of special glue. The poor squirrels were caught up by it, stuck like brown blisters against the bark. Then the woman would wander around with a hand gun, cool as a daisy, and shoot the buggers, leaving their bits hanging around as a furry warning, she said. Crazy bitch.

Anyways, it had been around one thirty when Eamonn Fogharty had turned up with Annie in tow. Colclough had turned pale but had held his whist, for a while. His new girl had served them and they'd taken a table next to Brendan, passing the time of day civil-like, although Annie looked as though she'd been locked up inside her skin. Eamonn kept his eyes on Colclough, not glaring, but cold. He'd joined in some talk about the football, Cork not doing too well of late, but mainly he'd been clammed up. Then the musicians had arrived, and it was the very moment that Tom, the fiddler, had stepped up to the table for a crack or two that Colclough, bloody fool, had taken it into his head to bring over free drinks to Eamonn and Annie. Eamonn had come to his feet, jolting all round him. I'll not be after taking any bloody thing from a thieving bastard like you, he'd said. The whole bar heard him. And I'll make damn sure you won't be taking anything again from me, or from any other bugger.

Annie just sat there, like a stone washed grey by heavy seas, Brendan remembered: it's funny the things that stick in your mind. Allus been the world's greatest admirer of Annie's tits, wondrous mounds of mammary tissue (a quote from my insurance friend, fellow lecher). I'd dreamt of sinking my nose into them many a night, but while this kerfuffle was going on around us the only thing I noticed was how they'd seemed to shrink into her ribs. Shrivelled is the word. Not scared she was, or upset. Just shrivelled. Diminished.

Eamonn could easily have landed one on Colclough. They were within arms length. Colclough was the colour of a wilting lily but – Brendan had to admit – the little shit stood his ground. He was expecting a pasting but he just propped himself, his arse against a chair, glass in each hand, holding them out sacrificially to any taker even though they'd already been rejected. And Brendan could see that his eyes, soft as butter, were fixed on Annie, lovely poor cow. But Eamonn didn't touch him, just leant forwards, eye-balling, a good twelve inches the taller, and you could smell the anger on him. Then Annie had hauled herself to her feet and made to leave. Brendan had felt her hand on his arm as she squeezed past him, had taken in the rigid line of her jaw and the broken fingernail as she clawed her anorak over her shoulders. Nothing more was said. Eamonn moved after her, heavily, glaring like a gargoyle at Colclough who hadn't shifted an inch, whose extended hands still gripped his snubbed offerings.

Every bugger there knew what it was all about, recalled Brendan, but nobody spoke up, not even me although I wasn't one to waste a pint of Guinness so I relieved Colclough of the jug he'd brought over for Eamonn. I don't know what happened to Annie's gin. Anyways, we all just got on with our drinking, and the band began to play.

And the next day? Wednesday? That, reflected Brendan, was when he'd called in at Pearse's store to buy some fags. There'd been talk of the coastguards being busy along towards Rossbrin and out as far as Mizen Head. It hadn't surprised Brendan because he and Mikey had seen their launch the previous day. Then he'd bumped into that American, Marotti, in the street. Looking for Maurice Colclough, he was. Said that no-one was answering the door at Caseys. Told him, at that hour of the morning, he might have better luck trying the Ballydehob Arms, where Colclough seemed to be spending more and more time of late. Seeking consolation, doubtless.

Told him, too, of the row with Eamonn, which might explain why Colclough was lying low; and that he'd let it be known that he was planning to visit his sister in Kenmare for New Year. Maybe he'd already gone, keeping out of Eamonn's way? 'Twas more than likely.

The Yank had been not best pleased. Said he had a few questions he needed to put to Colclough, the sooner the better. But he'd been civil enough. Brendan had commented that he was surprised to see Marotti still in the town, and was told that he'd had to stay on to make sure Bracken Point was ready for that fellow Tull who was expected later that very day. And then he'd told Brendan that he'd been with Annie at the house on the morning of Boxing Day, that she'd be working there for a spell, and that he'd also met Eamonn for the first time when he'd driven Annie to Bracken Point in his old van. Marotti had laughed to see how he'd not been trusted by Eamonn to pick up Annie himself, nor drive her home, and now he knew why. Eamonn had hung around for nearly an hour so as to collect Annie but had sat outside in the drive until she'd finished with her – what did he call it? – familiarisation or some such fuckin' nonsense. Anyways Marotti had laughed again because Annie had told him that, as from Thursday, Eamonn wouldn't be able to ferry her about because he'd been told, unexpected-like, to get back on the road with some urgent load. Eamonn was unhappy about this unlooked-for job, she said, and we all knew the reason for his sourness.

Brendan had told Marotti that he'd met Tull the once. The Yank had pulled a face, said that his visit was a damned nuisance, had ruined his Christmas, but that he'd be on his way back to New York once Tull and his guest had been settled in. Said Tull was already in Limerick and that the helicopter they used would be picking him that afternoon, but he'd really hoped to have a word with Colclough before meeting Tull.

Marotti had then headed off towards the hotel. Last time Brendan had seen him. Said he'd be over to buy him a drink later, grinning in that knowing way of his, but never showed. Probably too busy, he was. Looking for Colclough.

Maeve Rafferty remembered events somewhat differently. Christmas Day had been a grand occasion. She'd invited her sister and brother-in-law to lunch along with Maurice and they'd had a fine time feasting, lashings of turkey with all the fixings, the cooking having gone well, and no stinting on the booze. Maurice had brought over the champagne and a bottle of Paddy, and had been in sparkling good humour. Gossip about the town's goings-on (all bar one obvious complication) had been rich and salty. Her in-law, a Kerryman, had amused them with an account of an old fisherman from the Dingle, Robbie, a true Catholic, who'd been truly shocked when the Dail had voted to allow the use of contraceptives, and who'd been even more appalled when his friends at O'Shea's bar told him that it was now a legal requirement that every man who called upon his doctor had to submit to being measured for size. Poor old Robbie had suffered a heart attack when, having at last been obliged to summon his medic because his lumbago was so bad, he found Dr Callaghan entering his cottage with a tape measure around his neck.

And Maurice had then described some of his passages of arms with that woman at Bracken Point; but they hadn't been so funny because Maeve knew the grief she had caused: Morag's speciality.

The party hadn't broken up until around ten when Maurice, the worse for drink, had become a bit too maudlin and she'd seen him across the road before embarrassment could set in.

The next day Maeve had heard about the incident with Eamonn. She wasn't surprised. It had been long coming. But Maurice had been shaken. He'd called on Maeve around five of the evening in very low spirits, but by then she'd already been told about the affair and was prepared to give what comfort she could. She'd told him that Annie and Eamonn would have been over at Bracken Point earlier that day, before they fetched up at Casey's, and if it had been those people who had first poisoned Eamonn's ear, then seeing them again could well have put him in a black humour. She'd advised him not to brood on the threat, but he'd already decided to advance his trip to Kenmare and planned to be away the next day, staying with his sister for longer than he'd originally intended. He'd squared it with Declan and had agreed that the bar would remain shut all New Year's Day. He'd had two or three of her brandies, and was seriously worried, not just about himself but for Annie too. Said how miserable he'd seemed that morning, had seemed to have aged. He was missing her for sure and, thought Maeve, 'twas not beyond question that he might be bold enough to risk asking Annie to come away with him. She remembered that he'd said something about it not being too late.

She hadn't told him that Annie had 'phoned her that very morning from Bracken Point to let Maeve know that her services wouldn't be needed after all over New Year because Eamonn had received a summons from his bosses in Cork City telling him to return to work no later than Thursday. They'd asked him to take a particular load to Vienna and he'd be getting special rates for the job. Eamonn was tighter than a violin string about it, but they badly needed the money. Annie had said that Eamonn had been building up to confront Maurice all over Christmas; and the prospect of leaving her alone had brought matters to a head. She'd asked Maeve to warn Maurice to keep out of harm's way but she hadn't found a spare minute in which to get across the way before the Foghartys had themselves fetched up at Casey's. Bloody sod's law! Anyway, she'd decided not to put temptation in Maurice's path by telling him that Annie would be free of Eamonn from Thursday. It would have been entirely beyond the poor man to resist, and she couldn't be after conspiring to make a bad situation worse. So she'd kept quiet. Left it in God's hands.

Then on Wednesday morning, Leo Marotti had come looking for Maurice. She hadn't seen him that day, and her first thought had been that he was already away to his sister's place in Kenmare, but Marotti said that his Range Rover was parked behind Casey's, so he must be around somewhere but wasn't after answering the door. Maeve told him that Maurice sometimes didn't want to be disturbed, which was his right to be sure, at which point Marotti took one of those mobile phones from his pocket and tried Maurice's number but still got no answer. He wasn't at all happy at that. He said something about guessing why Maurice was keeping under cover, and a few minutes later had asked Maeve if she'd heard about the coastguards boarding the Tulls' boat on Boxing Day, which she hadn't although she knew they'd been busy along the coast and had told him she'd expected the Guards to have been concerned with those characters of ill-repute down at Crosshaven who were thought to be bringing in stuff they shouldn't. He'd asked what sort of stuff, and she'd told him that only a couple of years earlier a parcel of guns had been seized in those parts destined for the wild boys in Derry. That had made him thoughtful, but he said he was still pissed off because his launch had been pulled about more than somewhat, which was a great shame because he'd hoped James Tull might have been taking his houseguest for a trip up towards Bantry but now that seemed unlikely. 'Twas then Maeve had recalled, with a chill, that Maurice had once spoken to her of rumour-spreading being a game two could play, and she thought she might know what Marotti wanted of Maurice. But she'd said nothing of these matters to the American.

Anyways, Marotti had looked at his watch and said that as it was getting on for eleven he'd best prepare for collecting Mr Tull from Limerick but that he'd call in again at Casey's before leaving, that would be around noon, in the hope of catching Maurice, and could Maeve kindly let Colclough know – if she happened to see him meanwhile – how keen he was to have a word. Marotti hadn't said anything about Maeve not needing to help out at Bracken Point, nor compensating her for the loss of the extra money she would have earned, but she didn't think it prudent to bring the subject up.

When he'd left she'd tried to ring Maurice to warn him that someone else was on his case but she'd had no more luck than Marotti. She didn't know whether the two ever met up but had noticed, when she made a trip to the foodstore at around three that afternoon, that Maurice's Range Rover was no longer in its usual spot.

Annie Fogharty's remembrance was of Eamonn driving her to the Tull house on Boxing Day. The weather was sharp, a frigid wind attacking her ears and eyes, bringing tears which she had to keep wiping angrily from her stinging cheeks with her gloved hand. She'd had enough of tears. As they crossed the bridge before turning west towards Rossbrin she noticed black-headed gulls, swept from the skies, riding the waves' grey ridges around the old staithes. Not a day to be aloft.

They were late for her appointment with Marotti, delayed by a telephone call from Eamonn's employers, a haulage firm in Cork, insisting that he report to the depot by Thursday afternoon. It meant he'd be away for the New Year, their intended reconciliation dinner in Schull aborted. He'd protested vehemently, cursing, but they'd promised him a substantial wedge and Eamonn needed the extra money now that she had no regular wage coming in, and him newly determined to move away from Ballydehob to a bigger house nearer the city, a large place of their own with room for children. Nevertheless he was sick to the stomach at the notion of leaving her unattended. Sure now, he'd said, sure now I do trust you to keep your word, woman, but I've had no such word from Colclough, and the time has come to have a talk with the fuckin' bastard. She knew better than to suggest otherwise. Even thinking about it had put him in so foul a mood that he'd come close to thumping her again; she'd seen the wish in his dark face, and kept her gob shut. She'd watched the muscles working along his jawline as he drove the draughty van, and wondered what he'd make of Marotti and his unnerving smoothness.

They'd been made to wait at the dolphin and seaweed patterned gates, grace concealing resolution, until she'd spoken into the intercom. Once admitted, they'd been met by Marotti at the freshly-painted door. Although he'd put on his usual crooked smile she could see that something had irked him. She'd introduced Eamonn and hurriedly explained why they were unpunctual. It was well past eleven. He had barely acknowledged her husband, allowing his Malkovich eyes to appraise her body with frank appreciation. She could sense Eamonn's anger building. She'd thought: best get on with the business before he makes a bloody fool of himself. Felt herself shrinking.

Eamonn declined an invitation to make himself at ease in the house. He'd seen the motor launch at the new jetty and asked if he might take a closer look. Marotti had first frowned, then shrugged, muttering something about why not, since everyone else had seen fit to crawl over it.

So, she'd entered the house, marvelling at the money that been lavished. Sharp-angled furniture, not to her taste, and lots of oriental rugs on the freshly-laid hardwood flooring; a kitchen to dream about. Marotti hadn't offered to show her upstairs, and she didn't ask, although he'd made it clear she'd be expected to clean the bathroom. She'd heard someone moving around above her head but nobody put in an appearance. Probably whoever crewed the boat. She'd asked how many people she should expect; he said three at most. He'd been vaguer than usual, his mind elsewhere. Kept looking at his watch, even when demonstrating how the bloody space-age cooker worked. Something peeving him. There'd been none of his usual cheek. Could be, he was mindful of Eamonn. Whatever 'twas, the entire tour didn't take more than thirty minutes or so. Didn't have much to say even when she'd told him that she was available over New Year's Day after all, and had asked permission to stand Maeve Rafferty down. He'd lounged in a chair while she'd used the house's 'phone to tell Maeve, smoking, not looking at her, an impatient foot tapping. Arrogant bastard.

Eamonn was back in the van when she'd quit the house. Marotti had stayed inside, barely a goodbye, but he'd handed over a cheque, in advance, a quarter of what she'd eventually earn. For some reason she hadn't shown Eamonn the money. Should have done so. Might have put him in a better mood. Might have avoided trouble. Anyways, he drove to Rossbrin, not asking her for an opinion, to the bar he favoured where he sank a couple of whiskeys in the company of a couple of his cronies. She'd been ignored, pretended to watch TV, kept quiet, hoped he'd soon take her home. Instead, he'd grown more morose. After an hour he'd dragged her off to Casey's where he made of himself the idiot he'd been after making all that long morning.

'Twas the first time she'd clapped eyes on Maurice since Eamonn had returned from his last trip, had been poisoned in his mind and had given her the beating. Maurice was thinner, she thought. Looked unwell. White as milk, but that wasn't surprising in the circumstances. Still, she'd been impressed by the way he'd fronted Eamonn. More guts than she'd credited him with. She'd tried not to look at him, though. Whole bloody thing made her sick to her stomach. Had concentrated on some nonsense chatter between old Brendan, Sean O'Leary and Tom Reilly until Maurice had come over with those drinks. Suppose he felt he had to. Glad to get out of there, she was, without blows being struck. Although she couldn't shake out of her head the look on Maurice's face, stricken behind the steady eyes. She could read the goodbye in it. She knew then, finally, how much he wanted her, would always want her, written in those soft brown eyes, melting away, ending it, unspoken.

CHAPTER FIFTEEN

'So, you're away tomorrow.' Emily brushed the crumbs off the
tablecloth. 'Destiny summons you. Lucky bitch.'

Phyllis stared out of the window towards the outline of Charing
Cross station. They were lunching in the Festival Hall restaurant,
not far below the spot on which she and Hugh Jennings had debated
Wagner some three months earlier. Well, all that was over, history,
burnt boats. That very morning she had posted her letter to Hugh
advising him that she was withdrawing all interest in the post he
had offered her. Her wording had been polite but implacable. She
had also submitted her resignation to Longstaff's, an act requiring
considerably more valour.

It was, she explained to Emily, the combined influence of her
mother and Peter which had forced her to a point of decision. 'I
can't claim to understand Mother's acceptance of her situation but
her forthright refusal to behave in any way expected of her is truly
heroic. She's astonished us all. On the other hand, Peter – lovely
man though he is – has been utterly, depressingly predictable.
Perhaps I shouldn't tell you this, but he confessed to me late on
Christmas evening that he had been seriously tempted to make an
improper advance to you, Emily. His words: improper advance. But
much as he lusts after you, he's resolved to be faithful to his
appalling Sandra.'

'Darling Peter,' chortled Emily. 'Captain Sensible. I wonder if he
really means it.'

'Anyway, I told him that you were already in a hot relationship.'

'Oh, that's all over. Finished with the last of the festive turkey,
and ... come to think of it ... tasting much the same. The first few
helpings were ravishing but it's not much cop as a steady diet, and
can be heated up only so many times, you know.'

'Where are the snows of yesteryear?'

'Quite.' Emily paused as her main course arrived: monkfish,

spinach, sauté potatoes. Salivating, she inspected the waiter's haunches with indiscreet attentiveness as he laid the platter before her, nodding her approval. 'But what has my rejection by Peter – temporary I'm sure – to do with your deciding to abandon dear old, safe old, Longstaff's?'

Phyllis had opted for pasta. She stabbed it with her fork, rolling it expertly. 'I have decided for the first – and probably the last – time in my life to place myself wholly in the hands of fate. Since childhood, or at least since I moved away from parental control, I've striven to achieve total independence but I've learned that, taken too far, such striving leaves one pretty lonely. And, it doesn't work anyway; it's unattainable. Other people have an unfortunate knack of battering your independence into submission whether you like it or not. And I suppose, if I'm honest, whatever self-sufficiency I've claimed for myself has always been fraudulent because, although I hate to admit it, I wouldn't have been able to live in the manner I've been enjoying without my father's bloody allowance.' She broke off to point at Hungerford Bridge. 'Did you know that Charles Dickens worked in a shoe-blacking warehouse by the stairs to the Bridge? Just over there. He was twelve. No convenient allowance for him.'

Emily was serious for once. 'I'm not sure that you're in an appropriate frame of mind to tackle James. It would be a mistake to treat him as a port in your mental storm. I'm convinced that the shock of your father's behaviour, your belated discovery that he's capable of acting like any other lecherous male, has destabilised you. Please don't be precipitate.'

'Are you saying I shouldn't go to Ireland? As it happens, Peter's been warning me off but for different reasons.'

'Such as?'

Phyllis shrugged. 'He's changed his mind and decided that Ireland is not a safe place to be at present.'

'He is a super-cautious creature, isn't he? Dear Peter. But I don't agree with him. I think you should certainly go. An opportunity not to be missed. But please try to exercise a little of your old clear-sighted objectivity. No flying into his embrace regardless.'

Later they stood together, arms locked, on Westminster Bridge. A chill wind from the Thames assaulted their exposed faces as they looked eastwards at the russet façade of Old Scotland Yard and, beyond, to the last exhausted gasp of the neo-classicism occupied by the Ministry of Defence, its green copper roof confronting a brilliant, cold sun.

Emily said, 'I suppose James will be welcoming you in Cork.'

'I spoke to him this morning. He 'phoned from Limerick and will be travelling south as we speak.'

'With what degree of enthusiasm?'

'For James, what passes as high excitement. At least, that was my impression.'

Emily stared down at the slick-running river coloured like gun-metal, its unreflective surface concealing an infinity of discarded dreams, abandoned tokens of human presence flushing slowly in a sub-aqueous slime towards some final dark resting place. 'They say that dolphins have been sighted at Teddington Lock. Unlikely, wouldn't you say?'

'Anything is possible. Truly.'

Emily turned, her face pinched. 'It may be quite a while before I see you again.'

'Not so long. I'll telephone over New Year. Promise.' Phyllis touched her friend's waxen cheek. 'But in case I'm away for longer than expected, I'd like you to keep an eye on Peter for me. I wasn't kind to him over Christmas, and he needs someone in whom he can confide.'

They parted at Westminster tube station, silently. Phyllis walked slowly through a crowded Parliament Square, and, homewards, along the Embankment. There was packing to be done. Frontiers to cross.

Peter telephoned at around seven that evening. 'I'm on a public line without much change. This will have to be swift. Are you listening carefully?'

'Always.'

'*Vis-à-vis* Ireland. There was an exercise on Boxing Day. A motor launch was intercepted. Nothing found. But feathers were rustled. Cages rattled. I thought you should know.'

'What was expected to be found?'

There followed, for Peter, an expensive silence. Then, 'You know perfectly well which commodities we believe to be associated with that house. Don't make me spell it out.'

'But nothing was found.'

'This time. But please be careful, Sis. And this conversation didn't occur. Are you listening? No hints to Tull, or to anyone. Please.'

'I'm listening. Carefully. But Peter, doesn't the result of the so-called exercise suggest to you that perhaps, just perhaps, your prior assumptions might have been ill-founded?'

'My mind remains open. Does yours?'

'Possibly. But I'm at a disadvantage. I can't judge the reliability of your sources.'

Peter sighed heavily. 'Just be careful. OK?

She said, 'I lunched with Emily today. She sends her love.'

Another pause. 'That's very kind of her.'

'I asked her to take care of you in my absence.'

'That was considerate of you; but unnecessary. I doubt if I'll be seeing her again.' His voice had become icy. 'I, at least, know how to avoid trouble.'

'Happy New Year, Peter.'

'And Happy New Year to you. Truly. But please be careful.'

'Peter, I'm sorry about my ill-humour over Christmas. I know you had my interests at heart. You're still my favourite brother.'

'I'm your *only* brother.'

'That too.'

The line went dead, its demise announced by a derisive whine. His coins had run their course. There was more she could have said, wanted to say. But time, these days, was allocated in pre-paid units, and not everyone had the price in their pockets.

He was waiting by the reception barrier. Their lips brushed. Taking her luggage trolley he led her to an awaiting red BMW. They did not exchange words other than conventional generalities until he had driven away from the airport and had pointed the car southwards towards Kinsale.

'I thought we might lunch before driving to Ballydehob. It will also give Marotti a little more time to get the house in order. Plans for our arrival have been somewhat knocked back by one or two unforeseen complications. Only to be expected, I suppose, when the house has been fitted out in such short order.'

'Not *the* Marotti?'

'Son of. Leo, not Joseph. But he's leaving this evening. You won't see much of him. We'll have the place to ourselves except for Annie. She's a local girl who'll be looking after us, but won't be staying overnight. Otherwise, peace and quiet.'

'Sounds wonderful, James.' She adjusted the car seat the better to examine his profile. He seemed thinner, more finely drawn; but the green eyes with their restless flickerings, the pale shadow between mouth and chin, were reassuringly familiar, as was her sensual response to them. She said, 'Is this the house you bought when you visited Ireland in August?'

He glanced at her, his eyes narrowing. 'How did you know that?'

'An assumption from your letters which I've re-read many times. You spoke of having carried out some family business here, and then, later, of a house having been acquired. Am I right?' As she replied, she was thinking that they had been together five minutes and already she was dissembling. Would he?

'A not-unreasonable deduction,' he said.

'And are you pleased with it, now you've seen it again? First impressions and all that.'

'It will serve its purpose.' She detected a slight grimace. 'I was acting on behalf of the Trust. It's not a place I'd choose to live, although I hope you'll find it's an excellent base for exploring West Cork and beyond. Anyway, we needn't stay there the whole time. I can show you other wonderful stretches of this much-maligned country.' He placed his left hand on her knee, squeezing gently. 'We're not time-limited, are we?'

She recalled her thoughts about rationed time, only yesterday, when Peter's pay-phone had run out of it. What price was she prepared to meet in order to spend hours, days, a life-time, with this complicated man? And was, in reality, such a prospect being held out to her? She said, 'We certainly have much to talk about. Isn't that why I'm here?'

'In part. I hope only in part.'

Soon she saw the sea glistening ahead, herring-hungry boats along its salt margins, and, there, beyond the huddled town, Old Kinsale Head, its southern flanks pointing to Portugal. She was conscious of the unexpected foreigners, the strangeness of a landscape which, although in outline little different from the marsh and pebbled extremities of Kent, yet had lingering over it some indefinable sense of unsatisfied longing that she found unsettling. It was her first time in Ireland and already, without a single encounter with its natives, she sensed a disjunction, a people whose lives stood at a tangent to the rest of humanity, belonging but not belonging.

They ate handsomely: smoked salmon with dill sauce, shank of lamb, cheese and coffee. She had not breakfasted before leaving for

Stansted, and had been taken unawares by hunger. He watched her eat, happy in the confirmation that he had not been misled by false memories. He began to speak, without restraint, of his family: especially of his father with whom, he had come to believe, he had much in common.

'He wasn't greatly interested in accumulating wealth, the only Tull, until me, of which that could be said. He should really have been born four hundred years earlier. I could imagine him as a Carthusian or Jesuit carrying his other-worldly attitudes into the empty wilderness, communing more happily with the beasts than with his fellow humans. He resented everything that the Company demanded of him, which included the necessity to produce children. I was twenty-five when he died but can't remember his offering an affectionate word or gesture towards any of us.'

'And you've inherited his nature? Not very promising!'

He smiled sadly. 'Elements of it. I find it hard to express emotion, as you've noticed. I'm not unreservedly fond of the human race. Nor was he. And I'm not a committed Company man. I've tried, like him, to break away, but I've never been strong enough to succeed. So I remain caught in resentful semi-allegiance. But, unlike my father, I've certainly found myself capable of loving. Much to my surprise.'

They sat quietly for a while. She took his hand. 'Tell me about your mother.'

'I believe you already know that my natural mother, Francine, died when I was barely two years old. I have no memory of her. My stepmother, Constanza, is caring and warm but – and I don't mean this unkindly – knows her place. She provides comfort but no support.'

'But she's a Marotti, isn't she?'

He shrugged. 'I suppose so.' He did not elaborate.

'And your brother and sister?'

'Deeply dysfunctional.'

'Then we have something in common.' They laughed, and the warmth between them grew. Phyllis leant back in her seat and stared out at the surging waves. Spume floated above a grey-green tide swelling against charcoal rocks. She watched a cormorant, black flash against the creamy spray, dive, vanish, re-emerge unrewarded; then looked back at her brooding companion. He divined her unspoken question.

'The Trust has consumed them. They are my grandfather's true heirs. The virus of acquisition is endemic in their systems; acquisition without purpose other than that of feeding their appetite.' He allowed himself a thin smile. 'An appetite currently devouring Hugh Jennings.'

She quoted La Rochefoucauld. "We are all strong enough to bear the misfortune of others." Will Hugh survive?'

'Unlikely. Marotti is unsympathetic, and I haven't pleaded his cause. Should I?'

She pondered, stirring her coffee. Then, 'No. An unprecedented reversal might improve his character.'

'My sentiment entirely.' They laughed again, savouring their malice. And, as they laughed, both experienced an erotic charge. Eyes locked, they leant closer to each other, fingers touching.

Phyllis said, 'I've been celibate for nearly six months. I want you inside me, James. Action this day, please. Can we get to the house, quickly?'

It was as though they had never parted. Warmth flowed across the table, spontaneously, gently, naturally. Both sensed the restraints which had lain between them since their encounter at the airport dissolving; but not wholly. Both knew there were understandings yet to be reached.

When they were motoring westwards, a few miles beyond Bandon, he returned to the subject of his family.

'We agreed, did we not, to be honest with each other?'

'Honest and open-hearted.'

'Then, there's one thing I have to say. Now, at the outset, even though it could prove uncomfortable. At any rate what I have to say will, I hope, make my feelings for you transparent.'

'James, don't you think it might be better to wait until we're at the house? Is this exactly the right moment for us to confront what may turn out to be a crisis, bouncing along a far-from-sympathetic road?'

'I have to seize the moment.' But he pulled over and halted the car midway along a straight stretch. 'I want these next few days to be brilliant, unclouded, memorable. So we have to begin them clear-eyed, or not at all.'

She tensed and, for a moment, dared not look at him. He wound down his window, despite the cold air which seeped in, causing her to shiver. He turned to examine her, attempting to see her as though for the first time; as though she might appear when exposed to, say, Leo Marotti's candid scrutiny, as soon she would be. Reports would be made, judgements expressed. She sat, head slightly inclined away from him but there was no lack of resolution in her powerful mouth, her chin set at its characteristic confrontational angle. Her sensuality could rarely be deciphered on the surface of her skin; and she kept any vulnerability to either charm or intimidation well concealed. Eventually her grey eyes locked onto his. She smiled. She was ready.

'I want you to understand more about my brother and sister. Whereas I know we could largely insulate ourselves from your family, it can't, won't be allowed, to work the other way round. I want to share the rest of my life with you but you'd have to cope with Colin and Morag. I'd like to build a wall around us but they'd tear it down.'

'You make them sound like ogres.'

'Unfortunately, they are. What is worse, they are childless ogres.' He saw that she didn't understand. 'The Tulliver Trust is a private concern. There are only four shareholders. Colin owns 60 per cent. Basically, he runs the show. My share is 15 per cent, as is Morag's. Joseph Marotti has the remaining 10 per cent. I've taken no really effective part in the business for the last three years. There are aspects of it that I find distasteful, if not worse. Handling the charitable foundation – the Glendale Trust – is much more to my taste, and I think you'll enjoy helping me with the work, if that's what you choose to do.'

She leant back in her seat, a combative glint in her eyes. 'I'm not sure whether I've just received an offer of marriage or of a job.'

I'm afraid the two are inseparable.' He remained serious. 'Hence the need for clear eyes.'

'And the reference to childlessness?'

He sighed. 'There has always been a strong dynastic tendency in the Tullivers, going back to Hamish of blessed memory. My father was an exception but even he was prevailed upon to do his duty and produce heirs. I'm mentioning this now so that you're under no illusion about the pressure you'll be put under to have a child.'

'I would have thought Colin has the greater responsibility.' Her voice hardened. 'This conversation is taking a bizarre mediaeval turn. Do I take it you've decided that I'm acceptable breeding stock? Funny, but I've never viewed myself in quite that light.'

They fell silent, staring through the windscreen at the road ahead, lined with rock-strewn fields edged by wintering brambles and withered fuchsia. Eventually he said, 'I suppose, in a way, that's exactly what I've decided. May I take you back for a moment to last summer? When I left London I was in a state of confusion. Colin was pressurising me to return to Canada and to become more involved in the company. I wasn't strong enough to resist him and Morag who also weighed in. And I was unclear then about how powerful were my feelings for you, or vice-versa. The last thing I wanted to do was to expose you to Colin's influence and then discover we'd both made an horrendous miscalculation, especially when I didn't know how my own future would be mapped out. So although I went through the motions of inviting you to accompany me to Ireland we both recognised that it was an invitation you were expected to decline. But now things are different. I've discovered how much I miss you, want you. And to judge by your letters, you've been making the same discovery. That's a reality we must now deal with, isn't it?

She remained cold. 'You used the words, mapped out. Do I take it Colin has now completed your mapping, and that it includes a reproductive obligation? How convenient that I happened to be available. Am I scheduled to be another Constanza, knowing her place?'

He turned the ignition key. 'We may as well get on to the house now. We can talk more later, when you've had time reflect. We both know your last remark was unfair. Honest and open-hearted, re-member?'

The house was more modest than she had expected. It was smaller than her parents' although she guessed – in the darkness it was difficult to be certain – that the grounds in which it stood were more extensive. Her bedroom overlooked a stretch of grass running down to the rock-fringed bay into which, illuminated by floodlights, extended a neat L-shaped jetty harbouring a gleaming motor launch. She knew nothing about boats but imagined that its cost was fear-some. The house's contents were tasteful but boringly new. Her eyes sought in vain any object suggestive of affection having guided its acquisition. She found no books, only a scattering of magazines. The walls carried three or four over-bright reproductions of Irish land-scapes, obviously bought as a job lot. The furniture, mainly pine and leather, was comfortable enough, albeit characterless. An odour of fresh paint lingered in a couple of the rooms whilst a competing virginal smell arose from the sandy-hued carpeting.

They had been met, once admitted through the security gates, by Leo Marotti. She had been prepared to dislike him on sight but had been disarmed by his show of warm welcome, his impertinent grin. A light rain had been falling by the time they reached Ballydehob. Marotti had been standing by the front door, a waterproof around his shoulders. He had greeted James familiarly, and had politely squeezed her hand before carrying her suitcase to her room, preceding her up the staircase but pausing on the bend to subject her to a frank appraisal, noting – she was certain – her air of abstraction, her lack of any overt display of affection towards James who followed on her heels. There had been no assumption that she and James would be sharing a room, a consideration she found strangely touching. Marotti had placed her case on the bed, an amused lightness in his strange, slightly off-centred eyes. He said, 'If you don't mind, we'll leave you alone to sort out your things. There's some small matters I have to talk over with James. Won't take long; then we'll have a drink together downstairs. Real good to meet you, Phyllis. Hope you'll enjoy visiting with us.'

James, leaning on the doorframe, had emitted a small groan of annoyance. 'I haven't come all this way to work, Leo.'

'Not work. Just something you should know.'

'Then let's make it quick.'

Left alone, she had peered from her window across the floodlit approach to the sea before hanging up her clothes in the large pine wardrobe facing her bed. Flowers had been arranged on a side-table: delicately-veined freesias overwhelmed by the scarlet bracts of a vibrant festive poinsettia, both competing in turn with the fragmented ruby and emerald reflections of a Tiffany globe. She sat on the bed, staring at these bizarre combinations. Only a man, she decided; only a man.

The final hour of their drive along darkening roads had been spent in a bruised silence. The earlier excited mingling of expectations had cooled into frozen resentment. Now she stared down at her stiff knees, close to tears. She had been, again, too swift in taking offence, had not allowed him time to explain, had permitted her harshness of judgement untrammelled expression. Where did these demons spring from? She had even, for a moment, thought of directing him to return her to Cork, unreason boiling in her guts. Would he have acquiesced? Probably. But that extremity had been avoided. Now, somehow, they would have to find a path back to a point of understanding; and the first step would have to be hers.

'Do you feel like another meal? For myself, I'd be content with a morsel of cheese. The kitchen is adequately stocked.' Tull stood, his back to the log fire, cradling a glass of Meursault. They were alone. Marotti had kept them company for an hour but had then excused himself. He was leaving for the States on the morrow and explained that one or two tasks had to be completed before his departure. Phyllis had sensed his restlessness. Towards James he had shown a degree of deference laced with occasional flashes of impudence. Their talk had focused initially on Marotti's recommendations on how best they might spend their time together, places to visit, places to avoid, people worth meeting, restaurants that had already been reserved. His briefing had been amusing and well-informed. It was clear that he had taken trouble thoroughly to absorb the local flavours. She had asked whether he would be sorry to leave.

'I won't be in a sweat to return, that's for sure. Not everything has worked out as planned, and it's best I leave it to someone else to smooth matters out. But it's sure been interesting.'

'What's been the problem?'

Marotti had glanced at James. 'Let's put it this way. When James identified this location it looked as though it would be a great spot from which to expand our interests. We haven't done much in Ireland up till now, and wanted to find a quiet corner from which we could begin to build without attracting attention. Avoiding attention is the Tulliver way. You'll come to see what I mean, Phyllis, the better you get to know us.'

'Well, they've certainly noticed you in London.'

Marotti had given her his full attention. 'What d'you mean by that, exactly?'

Observing the sudden coiled tension in his shoulders she found herself, at that moment, beginning to believe that Peter's apprehensions might have been well-founded. 'Your buying into the The Mercury. Possibly James hasn't told you that we both know its Editor, Jennings, who is most definitely, and uncomfortably, aware of the Trust and its depredations. I'm afraid, Leo, he has a low opinion of your father.'

There had been laughter which grew less whole-hearted as she went on to describe the energy with which Jennings had been researching the Trust's activities.

'Well, I guess you already know more about the Tullivers than I'd imagined.'

'I'm sure there's still much to be uncovered. I'm finding it fascinating enough peeling the layers off James, so God know what surprises the rest of you have in store for me.'

When Marotti had left them, they had sat quietly before the fire, sipping their wine, pondering James's suggestion about food. They were both trying to use normality as a way of re-establishing their earlier, albeit short-lived, warmth.

'I'm not hungry either. And we need to avoid being distracted by others, don't we?'

He joined her on the brown leather sofa, taking her hand. 'May we start again? Explaining my family? Our peculiarities?'

'Why don't we begin with Leo? I make him, as Constanza's brother, your step-uncle. But he can't be much older than you?'

'About ten years.'

'So Constanza …?'

'Is thirteen years my senior. I've always thought of her more as an elder sister.'

'But only Joseph is a partner in the Trust?'

'I expect Leo will inherit his father's share, if he keeps his nose clean. But Joe is still a vigorous man. It could be a long wait for Leo.'

'Is Leo married?'

'Yes. And he has a young son.'

'Whereas the Tulls are not exactly prolific in that department.' They were once again stepping into debatable territory, but she now felt sufficiently calm to proceed. 'I'm sorry I snarled at you earlier, but the manner in which you raised the subject was disagreeably cold-blooded.'

'It's difficult to discuss my family in any other fashion. Will you allow me another chance to explain?'

'Of course. I'll try to contain myself.'

He rose to his feet, taking up a position with his back to the fire, arms folded, as though about to address a public audience, clearly uncomfortable. She had never before seen him lacking such composure.

He began, 'I tried earlier to explain how obsessively Colin seeks to maintain the family's control of the Trust. It's all at one with his driving ambition to amass wealth, to exercise dominion over others while himself being beholden to no man. What we have we hold

and, by your leave, a little more besides. For example, Colin increasingly resents, with a cold fury that frightens me on occasions,
grandfather's decision to hand over part of our empire to Joseph
Marotti. He can't understand the debt we owe to Joseph and his
father, Salvatore. So, he does his best to keep them in what he regards
as their proper place, especially Leo whom he sees as a threat to the
exclusive maintenance of the Tull hegemony beyond this generation.
And behind all this lies an even darker story.'

He poured himself more wine. It seemed to Phyllis that he was
no longer speaking for her benefit alone but was attempting to drag
into words some torment that had long been suppressed in a grey
area of his psyche, a bitterness which only now, and to her, he had
brought himself to articulate.

'Colin adored his grandfather, Gordon, who was in his eyes, the
rock on which everything we have was built. Gordon tutored him
in the ways of business, indoctrinated him into the usages of guile,
subtlety, remoteness of access, concealment of purpose. I, on the
other hand, was always known to lack the necessary resolve, or
commitment, to become Gordon's true successor. Like my father, I
was not sufficiently rapacious. I never resented the fact that Colin
was his favourite grandson. Indeed it still seems inevitable and right
that Gordon should have gifted Colin control of his Trust. The price
to be paid, which neither donor nor recipient anticipated, emerged
much later.' He came back to sit by her side, collecting his thoughts.

She asked, 'So your father never ran the business?'

'No. Nor wished to. Father was always, through no fault of his
own, a problem.'

He began to recount the failed, acrimonious and short-lived marriages of both Colin and Morag, dissolutions triggered by the
discovery in each instance of their sterility, followed by long and
painful researches into possible causes and the eventual emergence
of the probability that a genetic defect might have been passed down
as a result of Gordon's fateful coupling with his niece.

'I learnt of this sordid story only weeks before I came to Europe
in 1990, not long before I met you. Colin had unearthed a clue in
some of our grandfather's papers, exchanges of correspondence with
a banking family in Toronto to whom, it appeared, we are distantly
related through one respectable marriage and one improper liaison.
The irony is that Colin only discovered these connections as a result
of a proposal he was considering to acquire the Leplange bank. They
were appalled at the prospect of the Tulls re-entering their family

history. The Leplanges are an even older Canadian family than us, and well-connected in political circles.'

She said, 'I begin to understand why you've been, until now, reticent about your background. This genetic disorder: I don't suppose …?'

'I'm clear of it, apparently. Colin insisted I should be subjected to exhaustive tests once he'd established the probable cause of his own, and Morag's, infertility.' He frowned. 'Incidentally, I'm still reticent about this whole business. I'm trusting you to keep my confidence.'

'Of course.'

'So now you know pretty well everything. The rest, I think you can work out for yourself. The reason for their imposing pressure on me to carry forward the Tull name becomes clear, as does – I hope – my reluctance to yield to that pressure until I was certain that I'd found a woman strong enough to sustain the burden of it.'

She said, heavily, 'I doubt if you'll find I make a natural mother. Nor am I ready to assume that responsibility just yet. Eventually, but not tomorrow. Certainly not at anyone's command. And it's obvious that any relationship I may have to develop with Colin would be turbulent.'

'You're marrying me, not Colin. I hope.'

'It's your prerogative to hope, and mine to prevaricate. You've given me a great deal to think about, James. I won't be rushed. I still haven't come to terms with the obscene scale of your wealth which is enough in itself to cause a girl to tremble at the knees.' She threw back her dark head, challengingly, before leaning into him and kissing him, fully, slow, open-mouthed. 'Marriage is one thing, calling for sober reflection. On the other hand, making love to you is an instinctive matter which gives me no trouble at all.'

He smiled and led her up the stairs.

CHAPTER SIXTEEN

She was awakened by a sound of hoovering. She looked at her wristwatch, struggling to focus in the gloom: eight o'clock. James slept still, his left arm across her midriff. She had forgotten the allure of his musky smell; for a few minutes she lay inertly, savouring their intimacy, but a momentary spasm of her constricted blood vessels obliged her to stir. Moving stealthily she slid into bra, panties, dressing gown, slippers, before easing open the door and making her way down the dimly-lit stairs.

A young woman in a heavy sweater and jeans was tidying away the evidence of last night's drinks. She paused warily as Phyllis greeted her, then nodded non-commitally. 'Is it breakfast you're after?'

'I'm ravenous. Bacon and scrambled eggs would be marvellous. Is that possible?'

'Surely.' The woman raised her pale unsmiling face. ''Tis what I'm being paid for. And would Mr Tull be after joining you then?'

'He's still asleep. Perhaps later.' A pause ensued during which consideration was given as to how an appropriate relationship might be established.

'I'm Phyllis,' was the modest outcome.

'Annie.' The woman was gathering up her scourings when foot-falls, approaching from the hall, caused her to hesitate, her cheeks tightening over her bones like dried parchment. Marotti appeared at Phyllis's elbow, smiling.

'Great. You've met. Annie's a wonder. Ballydehob's best. If she hadn't agreed to help us out you'd have been starving over New Year.' He threw himself into a chair, legs outstretched. 'Sleep well, Phyllis? You look as though you had a swell night.'

'Most satisfactory, thanks.'

Annie had lingered, uncertain of what was required of her. Marotti waved a hand in her direction. 'Why not take a cup of coffee up to

189

James? The chopper's due to pick me up in thirty minutes, but I need a word with him before I go.'

Phyllis said, 'I'll take the coffee up, Annie. And perhaps we'd better delay my breakfast until he joins us. No point in your cooking twice.'

Annie nodded impassively. Marotti closed the door behind her and shrugged. 'She's going through a bad time. You'll have to make allowances. But she won't let you down.'

'What's her problem?'

'Take longer than thirty minutes, Phyllis. But perhaps it's enough that you should know that the guy she's been working for, in the local pub, was killed in a car accident a couple of days ago. Very nasty.'

'How awful!'

'Yeah, but best not to mention anything to her. Leave all the sympathetic noises to James. He's met the guy. I brought James up to speed last night. Sorry. Wrong metaphor.'

'I'm surprised he didn't tell me something about it.'

'Why should he? Wouldn't want to put a damper on your first evening together, would he? Careful. Zip up! Here comes the coffee.'

Phyllis took the tray from Annie and attempted a smile. 'We'll try not to keep you hanging around in the kitchen any longer than is strictly necessary.'

'I'm not going anywheres. But thanks.'

James did not stir until Phyllis nibbled his ear. An initial moment of vagueness was followed by a warm rush of mutual delight. They lay silently in each other's arms, the coffee disregarded. It was several minutes before she remembered.

'Marotti wants an urgent word. He said something about a helicopter.' When his groan of mock anguish subsided she added, 'I also met Annie. Not a happy lady.'

James swung his legs out of bed. She was always aroused by the dark, silk hairs creaming his upper thighs, reminiscent of a faun; he pulled on a pair of slacks and woollen sweater. He said, 'Leo will soon be away. Then we can really relax.'

'He mentioned the car crash. Dreadful.'

'He shouldn't have told you. There was no need. I'll have a word with Annie.'

They descended the stairs hand in hand. Marotti was waiting in the hall, muffled in a heavy-duty fleece. James said, 'All ready, then?'

'Yeah, pretty well. Ten minutes to ETD. Will you walk me to the pad?' Phyllis's intuition that she was not invited to join them was confirmed when he offered her his hand. 'Nice to have met you, Phyllis. See you soon in New York or somewhere, I'm sure.'

'Possibly.' She suppressed a shiver at the prehensile touch of his fingers. 'Very impressive. The helicopter. Beats a Number 24 bus.'

He grinned but she was beginning to recognise the manipulative nature of his affability. She turned away, heading for the kitchen. 'I'll tell Annie we'll be ready for a full breakfast by nine. No later, James, please. I really have developed an appetite. Must be the sea air.'

Annie was seated by the window staring at the scudding clouds. She said, 'I heard.' Jerking a thumb at the outside, she added, 'Bloody wind. Driving me mad, it is. Not stopped for a week. Sometimes wet, sometimes dry like now, but always bloody blowing out of the north. 'tis after sweeping everything away altogether.' The kitchen looked out upon the southerly aspect of the house, towards a circular target of concrete which Phyllis now recognised to be a helipad beyond which a hedge of straggling brambles marked the property's limit. The two men were standing on the concrete, hunched against the cold, Marotti shaking his head in emphatic denial of some observation made by James.

'So it's finally away, he is,' said Annie. 'Good riddance.'

'You don't care for him?'

'Makes my flesh crawl if you want the honest truth.' Noticing Phyllis's questioning expression, she added, 'Sorry to be speaking out of turn. What's it to me, anyways?'

Phyllis said, 'I've just been told about the car accident. It must be very distressing for you.'

Annie stiffened momentarily. 'Marotti's been after feeding you the local gossip. 'Twould be his style.'

'I don't know about gossip, only that your employer has just been ... well ... involved in a fatal crash. It must be a shock.'

'Former employer. I stopped working at Casey's some three weeks ago.'

'So you weren't all that close? I'm sorry, Annie, but I was given the impression that ... well, perhaps I simply misunderstood.'

Annie stood dumbly, arms folded as though gripping some memory to her breast lest it escape, and Phyllis saw that the woman was close to tears. She changed tack. 'May I have some more coffee? What on earth can those men be talking about out there in the chill?'

They heard the approaching helicopter only seconds before it appeared, skimming the bay's margins. Marotti began the final assembly of his baggage. He saw them watching and waved, the pale sunlight catching his alert features. Phyllis raised a dismissive hand but Annie turned her back on the departing American as he ducked under the rotating blades. She said, 'Help yourself to coffee. I'll be after starting breakfast,' and rattled the frying pan with scarcely-concealed resentment.

Phyllis was now convinced that James's attempted dissuasion of her speaking to Annie about the car crash must have something to do with Marotti. The helicopter rose, banked, drummed out of her line of vision. She watched James, hands in pockets, scuffing the newly-laid gravel path with moccasined feet. He didn't appear to feel the cold, dark head bowed in contemplation. She thought, now we're alone. Now we can restore what was almost lost, almost gained.

After they had eaten an excellent breakfast, they showered together, warm streams of forgiving water cascading over their intertwining flanks and knees, laughter echoing off the tiles. They had decided to motor out to Mizen Head, followed by a lunchtime drink at Crookhaven, a stroll along the strand at Barleycove, and a leisurely drive to the calmer northern side of the peninsula, skirting Dunmanus Bay to Blair's Cove for a dinner already booked on their behalf.

James was keen to show her the lighthouse. He said, 'With the sea as rough as it is today the views should be spectacular. But you'll need to dress warmly. Stout shoes. We can take a change of clothing with us for the evening.' He was excited, boyish.

They had forgotten Annie until, on their descent to the hall, they met her waiting by the main door, glowering. She was wearing a red anorak, red wellingtons.

'You'll have to drive me home. Didn't Marotti tell you?'

'So he did, Annie. No problem.'

'Tomorrow I'll cycle, but you'll have to let me through the gates.'

'We'll take a chance and leave them open overnight.'

They drove towards the town, Annie directing them to her terraced house but otherwise silent. In her presence their recent gaiety was supplanted by sober reflection. Phyllis was further dismayed by the drabness of the 1960s estate in the centre of which they deposited their passenger: grey prefabrication, dirty-green paintwork and unkempt privet. She could have been in one of the communes of Lewisham or Lambeth were it not for the clarity of the sky speckled with swooping gulls. James eased himself from the BMW, incongruous in its glossiness, to escort Annie to her shabby door. They stood well beyond Phyllis's hearing.

He said, 'Dreadful news about Maurice.'

'You did us an evil turn when you took a fancy to Bracken Point, so you did. I don't think we deserve what your people have brought to this town.'

'My people?'

'Marotti. And your bloody sister. If I had my way ...' She left the sentence unfinished, but her next remark indicated something of her train of thought. 'I noticed that the motor launch was gone this morning. I guessed that there must have been some other bugger around to crew it. Kept himself well hidden, didn't he so?'

'A hired navigator. The launch was chartered by Leo, I believe. I let it go because we won't be needing it.' He saw no need to elaborate, but as she inserted her key in the lock, he asked, 'Is it true they're waiting to question your husband?'

'So they tell me.'

'Do you think it possible?'

'No way. Eamonn may have had good cause to be vengeful but he's not that stupid. He thought Maurice worth a beating but not this. Jesus, not this.' She stared up at him defiantly.

'Just an accident, then.'

She summoned a bleak smile. ''Twould be comforting to think so, comforting all round.'

'See you tomorrow, then.'

'I've no other plans, Mr James Tull, no plans at all.'

She closed the door.

As they drove back through the heart of Ballydehob Phyllis noticed the sign for Casey's Bar, its green paintwork challenging the eye. She thrust a finger in its direction and commented, 'Marotti tells me you learnt of the landlord's death yesterday.'

'That's what Leo took me aside to talk to me about last night. Apparently the Gardai had been round to question him.'

'The police? Why on earth?'

'Maurice Colclough ... that's his name ... besides running his pub was the agent who handled the local end of our purchase of Bracken Point. He'd been acting for us until quite recently, that is until Morag paid him off. Overseeing repairs and improvements, that sort of thing.'

Phyllis, noting with some unease that his explanation had not, in any way that made sense to her, addressed the puzzle of police involvement, persisted, 'Did you know him well?'

'Met him once only, last August. In all honesty I found him a somewhat slippery and bumptious little man.'

'But Annie obviously cared for him.'

'Too obviously.'

She absorbed the implications of this last remark. They were now climbing beyond the town, driving towards the south-west extremity of Ireland, further west than any other part of Europe except Iceland which, she told herself, didn't really count, being a late volcanic intruder. They had momentarily lost sight of the sea as the road wound up through a rock-embedded wilderness. She could not, however, abandon the local mystery into which she had stumbled. She asked, 'Don't you want to talk about this?'

'Actually, it would be massively reassuring if, once I've put you fully in the picture, you could take the whole thing in your stride. It would tell you almost everything you need to know about what life with the Tulls would entail.'

Phyllis began to feel irritated. 'How bad can it be, for heaven's sake? This air of mystery is becoming rather tiresome.'

He glanced at her flushed face, weighing his options. After a heavy protracted deliberation he said, 'OK, you win. I'll tell you all there is to know about Bracken Point. But later. For the moment I want you to enjoy the scenery.'

On they drove, through Schull, past the restaurant where Colclough had sought out Tull five months earlier; out beyond quiet Golleen, the point where they observed a sweet curve of invading breakers exhausting their strength in a sweeping amphitheatre of receptive dunes. He had pointed out the miniature harbour of Crosshaven nestling to their left behind its neat breakwater, indicating – as he deployed his binoculars – the inn to which he intended they should later retreat to enjoy a light sardine-rich lunch. And finally they emerged under a pale, translucent sky on the spine of the majestic headland fronting a grey, seething Atlantic. They walked, hand in hand, to the narrow iron bridge spanning a gothic gorge through which, a hundred feet below them, the sea boiled, coiling and recoiling like an angry beast. They stood on the leeward side of the lighthouse watching cormorants arrowing over the spume.

'Now tell me,' she demanded.

He described how his brother, last summer, had asked him to keep his eyes open for a property on the west coast of Ireland with certain specific characteristics: secluded but with direct access to navigable water; within easy reach of a national motor route; and, preferably, a house whose restoration might arouse some local comment. James had no need to be advised of the purpose behind the search. He knew Colin wished to establish a base for importing illegal substances; but had initially been puzzled by the requirement that neighbourly interest in the acquisition be titillated. The explanation emerged only when Colin, who could not believe his luck, discovered that the previous occupants of Bracken Point had been active members of an IRA unit.

'Marotti, father and son, were extremely dubious about proceeding with the purchase once the IRA connection became known but Colin was adamant. He's well aware that the IRA are themselves heavily involved in drug dealing, indeed that for many of its so-called combatants, it's their principal activity. He encouraged Leo who was to become, together with Morag, joint leader of our set-up team here, to make contact with the local commanders and negotiate some kind of joint venture.'

He paused to gauge her reaction. She attempted to register an appropriate degree of astonishment. To a large extent, this was not feigned: the coolness with which he admitted to an involvement in criminal conspiracy was breathtaking. Playing for time, she probed him further. 'How did Leo manage to make contact with the IRA? Was this another aspect of Colclough's involvement?'

'No, Leo made no use of him for that purpose, but your guess is nevertheless inspired. It transpired that Colclough had Republican connections but we didn't discover this until well after we'd bought the property. As it happens, Leo was never happy about Colclough's role in this whole enterprise, fearing his involvement would complicate matters unnecessarily. But then, Leo was never aware of the complete game plan, and still isn't. To answer your question, we were provided with the necessary contacts by one of the previous occupants, a lady of uncertain virtue called Moira Kearney whose husband has a few dismembered bodies on his conscience. Is this whole affair shocking you, Phyl?'

'I'm still trying to make sense of it. Are you telling me that the Tulliver Trust is, in essence, some kind of criminal organisation?'

'Not at all. Most of its endeavours are wholly legal, and always have been. But like most complex organisms we have errant genes. There has always been a darker element in our dealings. Colin is captivated, entranced, by the possibility of living in a condition untrammelled by conventional restraints.' James stared out at the grey sea, choosing his words. 'Colin, of course, rationalises his attitude. Just as war is diplomacy by other means, so stands criminality in relation to business. What, he would argue, is the difference between making a profit by selling cocaine to the delinquent masses and polluting the Danube with cyanide as a result of a legitimate mining operation? Nothing except that the former, whilst probably less harmful, carries the risk of a criminal sentence.'

'So he regards business as a morality-free zone?

'Entirely. The market is a wholly neutral mechanism in terms of social values. Ethical considerations need not apply. Not wanted. It's simply a matter of recognising that certain activities carry more risk than others, and planning accordingly.' He grinned. 'Colin wouldn't have much time for Teilhard de Chardin. D'you remember our arguments about his ideas on the expansion of human consciousness?'

'I remember. But you're sliding away from the point again.'

'Not really. It strikes me that there is a parallel between the difficulty in trying to match the concept of evolutionary consciousness with that of a selfish gene, and the problem of reconciling morality with commerce. Colin, however, wouldn't even admit that the problem exists.' He moved a little away from her, the wind catching his dark hair. She saw that he was troubled. He continued, hesitatingly. 'I've been trying to work my way through this maze ever since I left London. And simultaneously I began to realise how much you've come to mean to me. I spent some weeks incommunicado, up in the wilder parts of British Columbia that appealed so much to my father, attempting to convince myself that I could walk away from the whole Tulliver thing, make a new life for myself. But I discovered that I wasn't able to do it. The corruption's gone too deep. A lifetime's exposure to privilege, real money and the power that flows from it has sucked something out of me, if it was ever there. Maybe I've never had that strength. I began to understand what my father must have been experiencing, but I don't want to batten down my emotional hatches the way he did.' He paused, trying but failing to gauge her reactions. 'Anyway, I doubt whether I'd manage to avoid being found, and dragooned again, by Colin, however hard I tried. And I also found that I couldn't bear the thought of not seeing you again. So, in the end there was nothing for it but to knuckle down to my allotted role in the scheme of things, yet at the same time to try to re-configure the landscape a little, to nudge the company in a different direction, to seek a better path. But I've also come to realise that I can't do it alone. I absolutely can't. I really need you, Phyllis.'

She came to his side, stroking his cheek. 'I can see at least how important it is that I'm made to understand. And I'm still listening.'

Kissing her, he murmured, 'Before leaving Toronto I had a lengthy talk with Colin. We came to an accommodation. He had to take me seriously. I warned him that I'd already drawn up a will leaving my share in the company to a third party not of his acquaintance and that I wouldn't alter this provision unless he met my demands. That concentrated his mind wonderfully. I've made it clear to Colin that, henceforth, I'll play no part in any of his more exotic ventures. Even in this business in Ireland I've been little more than an informed spectator.'

'Nevertheless ...'

'Oh, I know. And now I've implicated you.' He stared back at the approach to the lighthouse. A group of four were on the path; soon they would no longer be alone. 'Shall we move on?' They strolled back to their car, exchanging convivial greetings as they encountered the newcomers, acting as though nothing abnormal had passed between them. He sat behind the wheel, his green eyes scanning her face for signs of disapproval, ignition untouched. She would not yet, however, betray any reaction; would not make it easy for him.

He said, 'You must at least recognise that I've placed myself in your hands; that I've gambled on your willingness to accept me despite my questionable baggage.'

'Yes, I see that. But I still need to know more about what precisely is, or has been, going on around here.' She drew a deep breath. 'Let me, too, breach confidence. Something you may not know. Something that demonstrates how I too was taking a risk in coming here to meet you.'

He said, 'There is no risk.'

'Really? Did you know that Bracken Point has been under continuous scrutiny by the security people for months, if not years, before you lit upon it, and still is as we speak? Did you know that anyone associated with it will inevitably find their name on an Intelligence file, including both of us? Do you find this a comfortable thought?'

His tone of voice hardened. 'How do you know all this?'

'As all good journalists say, I'm not prepared to divulge my source, but I assure you it's utterly reliable. The spooks are on to the Tulls.

Colin had better clean up his act. The Marottis were right to be nervous.'

He stared thoughtfully at the gun-metal ocean. 'That would explain why the motor launch was intercepted by the coastguard earlier this week and thoroughly taken apart. They found nothing. There was nothing to be found. Nevertheless, in Leo's view, the whole operation is terminally compromised. He's convinced someone has been feeding information to the authorities. His IRA friends, of course, are totally pissed off.' He took her hand, frowning. 'Incidentally, London and Manchester ... according to Leo ... are cities one would be wise to avoid in the next couple of months. Class A drugs aren't the only commodities his acquaintances have been importing.'

'So, the ceasefire ...?'

'A smokescreen. Always has been, always will be. Only sentimental fools think otherwise. But Semtex is expensive. Street collections by Noraid don't go anywhere near covering the invoices. That's why the drug trade is so crucial and why they aren't exactly ecstatic about having seen their prospect of lucrative earnings from Ballydehob blown out of the water. You might inform your reliable sources that they've formed their own implacable ideas about who might have spoken out of turn, and what had to be done about it.'

She shivered. 'We're back to Colclough again aren't we? Which explains why Leo had a visit from the police.'

'I wouldn't jump to conclusions, Phyl. For one thing Colclough was seriously threatened a few days ago by Annie's husband because he'd learnt they'd been having an affair. The police want to question her husband about his movements. And then again it could still prove to be nothing more than an unfortunate accident. Colclough was known to have been drinking heavily and the bend his car failed to negotiate is, I'm told, notorious for punishing anyone not fully alert.' He paused. 'I think that's the most likely verdict to be reached. Much as I disliked the man, even after a single encounter, I wouldn't want his death on my conscience.'

Phyllis shook her head. 'But you can't be certain. All you know ... or believe ... is that Leo is not directly responsible.' She bit her lip, remembering Annie's hostility. 'You are sure about that, aren't you?'

'Utterly, if you're asking whether I believe Leo forced him down that ravine. But I suppose it's possible that Leo's suspicions might have been voiced rather too emphatically, and could have prompted others to act. We shall never know the truth of that. The real trouble is, Leo didn't know the complete game plan.'

She now experienced a surge of intuition but internalised it behind a stony expression. She said, 'You've lost me this time.'

'It's the way Colin operates. I was told the whole story only hours before flying over here. Previously only Colin and Morag were fully aware of the plot, and I gather she acted out her part splendidly, far too well in Leo's sour opinion. Here he was, trying to keep everything low profile whilst Morag was steaming around the place, triggering gossip, sounding off as only she can, making enemies. The whole point, you see, was to attract attention to Bracken Point. Colin was doubtless delighted when Leo e-mailed news of the coastguard interception. Another notch on his belt. And the undoubted genuineness of Leo's anger kept the whole deception rolling merrily along.'

She said, 'I suppose it would be considered far-fetched to suggest that Colclough's death was also calculated to add verisimilitude.'

His face darkened. 'Poor Maurice. At least, one might argue that, if true, it invested his death with rather more purpose than would otherwise have been the case.'

She stared through the car window at the lighthouse, solid and squat against a pale sky laced with thin skeins of cloud. 'I think I've worked it out. You spend thousands on a house, ostentatiously, and allow people to speculate that it's to be used for criminal purposes, when all the time it's no more than a decoy.'

'Speculation would have been insufficient. Leo and the rest had genuinely to believe.'

'And meanwhile …?'

'A lucrative transaction has been completed elsewhere in Ireland. Don't ask me where. I neither know nor wish to know. A massive return, however, on an outlay of some half a million, mostly recoverable when we sell Bracken Point. Or would you like the house as a wedding present?'

'I don't come so cheaply.'

'But do you come at all?'

She thought of many things. Of Emily and their dismissive discourses on men and marriage. Of Peter and his conventional, rectitudinal, albeit heartfelt, concerns. Of her mother and her fortitude. Of Sue and her fecklessness. Of Annie and her pain. It was when she thought of her father that she experienced the chill of vulnerability, of powerlessness, of an ancient anger.

'I demand,' she said, 'to be valued above rubies. I wonder if Colin is prepared to pay my price.'

'It's not Colin's choice.'

They both knew she was prevaricating. He drove them to Barley-cove. They walked out onto the beach, beyond the low dunes, and watched the tide recede. Wet sand ephemerated their progress, now several feet distant, now close met.

'Tell me about your house in Canada.'

'It doesn't yet exist. I've been camping out in a series of company apartments in New York, Toronto and Vancouver. I've been considering buying a place in Ottawa where Glendale's head office is located, a fairly civilised city, but' – a sideways glance – 'I wouldn't want to take that decision unaided. Of course, we still have the old family place in Sault St Marie. Only Constanza uses it these days.'

She asked, 'Would Ottawa be a sensible place from which to run your charitable operation?'

'Very sensible. Canada's bureaucratic heart. But it could be run from anywhere these days. Even London. Given that I want to internationalise Glendale's activities, especially in terms of medical research, it wouldn't be a bad idea to have a base on both sides of the Atlantic.'

She commented dryly, 'And it would make it much easier for you to keep an eye on *The Mercury*'s affairs. Rub salt in Hugh's gashes.'

'That thought had occurred to me.' He took her hand. 'You could play your part there too.'

'Outrageously tempting.' She scuffed her shoe in the sand, watching the ochreous particles as they fell; unpatterned yet unquestionably part of some larger design into which they melded, indistinguishable within seconds. To see a world in a grain of sand; visionary Bill Blake anticipating quantum physics. She remembered last week's exchanges with her siblings: moral or amoral logos, or blind belief: tough choice. But choice was inescapable. Humankind's lot. The penalty of consciousness.

She said, 'Did I tell you that I've resigned from Longstaff's? Last week.'

'Time for a change?'

'Yes.'

They reached the water's retreating edge, daring the ripples to surprise them, to invade their laughter.